Caught in a pincer movement between the sudden death of Evelyn (her favourite aunt) and the Corona virus, Ascher Lieb finds herself unexpectedly locked down in her aunt's retirement community with only Evelyn's grief-stricken dog Freddie for company.

As the world tumbles down into a pandemic shaped rabbit-hole Ascher is wracked with guilt that her aunt was buried without the Jewish burial rights of purification.

In order to atone for this dereliction of familial duty, Ascher – in her own words 'a profane, unobservant, atheist Jew, frequent liar and grieving loser' –volunteers to become the newest member of Valley Haverim Chevra Kadisha, a Jewish burial society on-call twenty-four-seven during lockdown and performing Mitzvot at no cost to the bereaved.

What follows is a journey through the insanity of lockdown in Los Angeles as Ascher attempts to bring peace to a troubled soul, and perhaps in the end redemption for herself.

In the hands of a lesser-writer a novel set in the time of covid could lead to a cliché ridden trope-fest, but instead with the skill and grace we've come to expect from Jo Perry she has delivered a book that is wise and beautiful and uplifting.

This edition first published 2021 by Fahrenheit Press.

ISBN: 978-1-914475-11-5

10 9 8 7 6 5 4 3 2 1

www.Fahrenheit-Press.com

F 4 E

Pure

By

Jo Perry

Fahrenheit Press

Also by Jo Perry and available from Fahrenheit Press

- *Dead Is Better*
- *Dead is Best*
- *Dead Is Good*
- *Dead Is Beautiful*

In memory of my parents—whose voices I always hear and whose faces I always see.

"You are a little soul carrying about a corpse..."
—Marcus Aurelius

"Once I am dead, there will be no lack of pious hands to throw me over the railing; my grave will be the fathomless air; my body will sink endlessly and decay and dissolve in the wind generated by the fall, which is infinite."
—Jorge Luis Borges

"…the soul which Thou didst place in me is pure. Thou hast created it, formed it, breathed it into me. Thou preservest it in me. Thou will take it from me and wilt give it back to me in the world to come…"
—Elohai Neshama (Traditional Jewish morning prayer.)

"What men call the shadow of the body is not the shadow of the body, but is the body of the soul."
—Oscar Wilde

1.

It happened during my third corpse. The old, olive-skinned female under a wet sheet had already been cleaned. The Betadine-stains had been rubbed off her discolored skin with rubbing alcohol and the bandages, toe tag and the hospital I.D. bracelet had been cut away. Soon we would slide freshly scrubbed boards beneath her body to raise it off the metal surface.

The newbie in the group, I'd filled the painters' buckets with lukewarm water, placed them under the head of the table, and had slipped off and baggie-d the red polyester, no-slip socks. The others had handled the bruised purple and black eyes' and mouth closings, the hair combing, the careful to-avoid-the-nostrils back-handed face rinsing, the washings and swift re-coverings of the bruised greenish black breastbone, right side, then then left—arm, deflated breast, armpit, shrunken abdomen, navel, and sparse white pubic hair. I'd helped tilt the body for the bathing of the speckled widow's hump and the plugging of the rectum with cotton.

The only noises are the rhythmic sloshings of poured water hastening from the raised head of the steel table to the drain at the foot-end. The woman across from me uses a wooden stick to clean the fingernails of the right hand and foot. Another takes care of the rinsings.

It is my turn. I silently address the corpse in English. Her name—Rachel—there are no parents' names—is written in Hebrew on the board. I tell Rachel I am sorry and lift the white sheet just enough to disclose the right forearm, wrist and hand. A purplish, grayish wing-like bruise spans the gray, ropey veins and bracelets the wrist.

Cold shocks my gloved palm where the dead hand touches it. I push a wooden stick's tip under the left thumbnail to scrape away a brown fleck, scrape the other nails, and return the hand—clay-cold and heavy¬—to the table. One of my mute, masked colleagues empties her stainless steel bowl of water backhanded across the hand and the room spins.

The water meets the hand and the bruise coagulates into a drenched and startled dove, wings vibrating into panicked flight, the water droplets rolling off its wings ricocheting like BBs off the metal table into tiled walls and floor, the porcelain sink and my apron.

I hold the table edge to steady myself as table, body and the soul lingering above it rise from the floor to meet the panicked bird and the fluorescent lights crackle and flicker.

Then the world goes black.

Is this death?

2.

I arrived in the parking lot behind the four-story Sunny Morning Elder Living Center the assisted-living, memory/dementia/Alzheimer's care, skilled nursing and hospice provider on the Burbank/Glendale border where my aunt Evelyn and her dog, Freddie, had recently moved. The sun was a hot white splotch baking dust and bird shit into the surface of Hans's dusty, once-black, now graying BERNIE bumper-stickered Prius.

I walked to the front of the sand-colored Italianate building and read the notice taped to the doors: "Due To Covid-19 Virus, No Visitors. Sorry!" I tested the door, and it was locked. I tapped the glass and tried to see inside the salmon and olive-green lobby, but the reflection of the sun rising ominously behind my shoulder blinded me. Then I called the number that had awakened me three hours earlier.

After five rings, a woman's voice said, "Sunny Morning. hospice three."

"I'm the niece of Evelyn Mendel," I said. "You or someone called me earlier and said to come. I'm here outside the lobby."

Whooshing and buzzing, then, "Please wait, Miss. Someone is coming to get you."

As I waited, I read the notices taped to the lobby doors. They were illustrated with clip art suns and also musical notes, playing cards, hot dogs, walking shoes, an open book and an orange silhouette of a female figure in the downward dog pose—"Summer Barbecue and Sing-A-Long!" "Blackjack!" "Walking Club!" "Armchair Yoga with Heidi!" "Trivia!" "Scrapbooking!"

A man in Sunny Morning Elder Care peach-colored scrubs appeared from the back of the building, plugged an electric leaf blower into an outlet and forced a blanket of Jacaranda blossoms over the curb and into the grilles of approaching cars.

The lobby door opened a crack. A woman wearing a puffy blue surgical hat, a stethoscope and the same peach scrubs spoke from behind her white mask, "Miss Mendel? Come on in."

I stepped inside, waited for my eyes to adjust to the cool dimness, and put on the paper mask the woman handed me. "I'm Ms. Lieb," I explained. "Miss Mendel's niece. What happened? Can I see her?"

The woman—plump, short, and with beautiful dark eyes and expressively penciled eyebrows above her mask—motioned me to follow her through the lobby— where a few residents sat in green and orange floral-print armchairs and read newspapers or watched CNN with the sound off and the subtitles switched on. We were not going toward the independent living wing where my aunt's apartment/condo was.

The woman led me past the community room, the dining room, the activities/crafts room, past closed administrative offices through a series of corridors which required a keycode to enter. She hurried me down a hallway in Skilled Nursing/Rehabilitation, along a curving hallway in Memory/Dementia/Alzheimer's Care to Acute Hospice Care Area 3 and a closed door that had a red and white vinyl sign taped to it:

"Restricted! Do Not Enter. DROPLET/CONTACT PRECAUTIONS: Clean hands when entering/leaving room. Wear face mask. Wear eye protection. Gown and glove at door. When doing aerosolizing procedures fit-tested N-95 mask or higher required. KEEP DOOR CLOSED. Use patient-dedicated or disposable equipment. Clean and disinfect shared equipment."

Jesus Christ.

"Please wait here," the woman said.

I tried not to faint, to not to wonder what an aerosolizing procedure might be and if my aunt had been subjected to one. I worried about my aunt's dog—how long had he been alone in the apartment? Could I ask the nurse to check on him? I looked at the gray linoleum floor flecked with an incongruous lime green. I tried not to deeply inhale the air-conditioned, disinfected, Ensure-sweetened and soured-by-something I couldn't identify air penetrating my thin, blue paper mask.

3.

A tall, slim, perfect-postured man in a blue surgical cap with a blue neck-to-ankle paper robe over his scrubs and a plastic shield over his mask asked me my name and checked the chart he held in his gloved hand. "You're the patient's agent, correct? Her niece?"

"Yes," I said. When my aunt had completed her advance directive for healthcare, she'd asked if I'd be her agent—the person to make sure her wishes were honored if she couldn't—and I'd agreed.

"One moment." The man stepped around the corner of the hallway toward the nurses' station. Shit. I forgot to ask about the dog. I faced the door with the warning sign and told myself that if my aunt were dead, the man would have told me. The tap of clogs announced the arrival of a new female nurse in the same get-up. She carried a face shield, a yellow paper gown and a pair of nitrile gloves for me to put on. When I had everything on and rubbed my gloved hands with a dollop of hand sanitizer from the dispenser next to the door she said, "Please don't touch anything, Ms. Lieb. And I'm sorry but we can only give you ten minutes." She pushed the door open for me with her elbow.

The narrow, windowless mint green room was quiet except for the ventilator's rhythmic hisses—and dark except for the fluorescent light bar behind the bed and the thin radiance of wavering monitors and machines.

The nurse nodded toward the bed which I interpreted to be permission for me to step between two white machines to the bed's safety rail. One machine had a white tube snaking up, into and down a forced-open human mouth to the lungs. The other machine's hose bifurcated into tubes that entered the nostrils. Some sort of strap thing on either side of the mouth kept the tubes in place and went behind the back of the head elevated on a huge pillow.

The head that belonged to the nose and intubated mouth was the size of my aunt's head—small. The wispy silver curls against the white, egg-crate pillow looked like poodle hair. The body connected to the head was three mounds—chest, knees, feet—under a thin cotton basket-weave blanket. The eyes were closed. The face had been carved out of a slab of pinkish gray marble.

"What happened?" I spoke to the head on the pillow and, despite being cautioned against touching anything, I held the bed rail to keep from sinking into the floor, then through it. "What the fuck happened?"

The nurse lengthened her neck, to indicate that the "fuck" had offended her. "Your aunt complained of fatigue and muscle aches three days ago, then developed a cough and a fever." The nurse retreated to the door—as far away from my aunt and me as possible. "The doctor prescribed antibiotics, steroids and supplemental oxygen, but very early this morning her fever spiked, she had trouble breathing, and despite being given high-dose oxygen, she rapidly progressed into acute respiratory failure and respiratory arrest."

"Three days?" Why didn't someone call me? I'm her emergency contact."

"When your aunt became unwell and the social worker suggested calling you, your aunt refused to let us, Ms. Lieb."

That chunk of information hit me like a fist.

Oh, and the fact that when they finally did call me well before midnight, the Valium I'd taken at eleven had deadened me to the phone's buzz and until 6 A.M.—too late to do my aunt any good.

The blanket rose. Then it settled onto the place where my aunt's small chest must be.

"Is she going to—improve?" I was going to say, "get better," but I had eyes. Still I couldn't help desperately wanting my aunt to recover no matter what it might take to save her. Was a heart transplant possible? Or maybe lung transplant? And I couldn't stop myself from silently praying to a deity I didn't believe in to give my aunt more time and to give me the chance to tell her how much I loved her. "Isn't there some way to save her?"

"She's eighty-two," the nurse said.

I knew how old my aunt was. But the being in the bed seemed ancient. Unreal, like the life-sized plastic "doll" they called Resuscitation Annie in the CPR class I took in college.

"Is she dead?" The sobs rising from my solar plexus that I choked down into my throat made my voice sound strange.

The nurse looked at the clock on the wall, then at her patent leather clogs as if they were black mirror-portals to an alternate universe. "Your aunt has pneumonia. And hypoxia."

"What does hypoxia mean?"

"It means her lungs are filled with fluid. There's no room for air. Not enough oxygen is getting to her organs. They're shutting down."

"Her brain, too?"

"Hypoxia affects the brain first. And because the patient's advance directive was clear about not prolonging life—"

"Then why is she on a ventilator?" I recognized the machine from the Covid 19 reports on CNN and I resented this hostile takeover of my aunt's body.

"Dr. Christiansen wanted to wait until the patient's family arrived, which we assumed would have been earlier."

I accepted the blow, felt its sting, then kept going. "Will she regain consciousness?"

"I'm sorry. No." The nurse's beeper beeped. She fished it out of a pocket in her long surgical gown and looked at it.

"So, is she dead right now?"

"That's Dr. Christiansen. He's on his way."

I looked at the blanketed-to-the-neck figure in the bed and imagined my aunt's soggy lungs being force-inflated and deflated like wheezing cartoon bellows.

I needed to hold my aunt's hand.

I pulled the blanket down to her waist. Wide blue restraints with white Velcro straps lashed my aunt's wrists to the bed rails. An oximeter pinched one of her bluish fingers.

"Why is she tied up like this? Why would you do that to her?"

"Patients can become combative when ventilated. They can feel as if they are choking or drowning until the sedative takes effect." The nurse looked at the floor. "I'm sorry."

"Unhook her from the machines," I said as I loosened the straps on my aunt's wrist with trembling fingers, then moved around the bed to free her other hand. "Then get the fuck out of here."

4.

My parents' sudden departure gave me the idea that death was a speedy transition. A light switched off at end of day. The brief confusion and shock before the blackout and collision. A sunset bleeding into night. Snow disappearing a world inside a snow globe. A slide into a longed-for, dreamless sleep. The fade to black after a lightning flash. Or as in my parents' case, the few seconds it took for a frantic bird—don't ask me why but I always imagine the bird to be a snow-white dove—to fly through my mother's open passenger-side window and to distract my father long enough to swerve out of his lane and into an oncoming semi-truck.

But I was wrong about death. I could tell from the way my aunt's arms—bruised by injections and IV's—jerked, from the way her cool, bony, mottled hand—the IV port still stuck on with tape—twitched in mine.

My aunt died cell by cell—that's thirty trillion suffocations in a few more minutes than the ten the nurse had allotted.

My aunt's death took forever. Hers was the ultra-slow-motion drowning of a butterfly in a cocoon-coffin. An ice age passed before my aunt relinquished her hostage ghost ,before the big-ass, white death light at the end of the tunnel I've heard so much about extinguished her and forced that long wet rattle up and out of her chest—a noise that Dr. Christiansen—his plastic shield shiny with light fixture's fluorescence—explained was not a cry of pain or terror, was nothing at all to worry about—merely a to-be-expected, reflexive, post-life exhalation—.

Jesus Christ. That death had just bludgeoned the life out of my aunt and that I just heard her anguished last gasp were exactly what I should fucking worry about.

Doctor Christiansen waited a moment after the final shudder and wheeze. "She's gone," he said and to make sure I understood, and added, "I and everyone here at Sunny Morning Elder Care Living are deeply sorry for your loss."

Well, my aunt wasn't "gone." She was still right there, her small, cold hand in mine.

5.

I unlocked the avocado green door to my now late aunt's Sunny Morning Elder Living apartment/condo with the extra key my aunt thoughtfully had made for me to keep on my key ring, switched on the light and stepped inside. Her little dog blinked and growled from his purple, arthritic dog bed next to my aunt's chair.

The still air held the honeysuckle and orange blossom sweetness of her Arpège perfume, the deep chocolate of the cocoa butter my aunt used on her hands and the cinnamon of her favorite tea.

Nothing indicated the catastrophe. The pleasant, compact single apartment was as it had been. My aunt's walker was folded closed against the closet door. The framed autographed movie posters and headshots hung perfectly straight and dust-free on the wall behind the yellow velour sofa. The moss-green quilted bedspread's seams were exactly aligned, my aunt's white cotton sweater folded into a perfect rectangle at the bed's foot, the needlepoint floral pillows just so against the headboard. My aunt had been a neat freak, a pretty freak and an organization freak—but never a control freak. At least, she never tried to control me.

"It's only me, Freddie." I approached the black, brown and white-chinned dog. "It's Ascher. Don't be scared." I didn't want to upset Freddie. Before my aunt adopted him from the Mini-Pinscher rescue, Freddie cowered and starved behind a Van Nuys supermarket. Vacuum cleaners, leaf blowers, brooms, fireworks, door slams, garbage trucks, thunder, the sound of heavy footsteps, hair dryers and the tick-tick-tick of the "Sixty-Minutes" theme induced panic, panic-shits and or panic fits in poor Freddie.

"Are you hungry, Fredster?" I tried not to cry and to keep my voice singsong and cheerful. Freddie's reedy growl dropped an octave and he looked at me with shiny, questioning black eyes.

"Is it time for dinner?"

Nothing from Freddie.

"Or is it time for your meds?"

Freddie tilted his head then gazed at the green door. Of course. He was waiting for my aunt.

I went into the too-clean and too-orderly galley kitchen and saw the two five by seven notecards held to the side of the refrigerator with the flag magnets I'd brought my aunt after my twelfth-grade trip to Washington D.C.

The top one—in red ink in my aunt's curly but very legible printing––said,

"Freddie-important! 7.5mg phenobarb 2 x day 9am/9pm in 1 tsp cream cheese rolled in a ball for seizures. 1/2cup dry food morning 1 cesar cut in chunks evening. Treats after walks. Vet dr. Sochi sweet paws animal center 818 555-4553."

My aunt had taped a card that said "Treats" to a Tupperware container on the counter and another that said "Dry Food" to a yellow canister. She'd stacked three one-dozen towers of Cesar Chicken Flavor and Cheese Souffle dog food trays, and had lined up prescription bottles for "Freddie Canine" next to the treats and dry food. I opened the refrigerator. Six silver boxes of Philadelphia cream cheese sat on the front of the top shelf. The cream cheese was for coating Freddie's phenobarbital.

The second notecard,with my aunt's signature neatly unfurling under the words said,

"No CPR, no ventilator, no feeding tube"

A faded color photo of my parents and me on the Jungle Ride in Disneyland—my parents squinting toward the camera from behind very black-lensed sunglasses—held against the freezer door by a yellow Sunny Morning "Frequently Called Numbers" magnet shaped like blazing sun.

Were my parents and aunt going to be dead together or dead apart? Were my parents welcoming my aunt into the place where the dead congregate, or where my parents had been hanging out for the last fifteen years? Or was my mother—faded to an almost-transparent version of her opaque, alive self—the one guiding my aunt, her exhausted-from-dying older sister into the Big Where Ever?

Why did I even think such bullshit?

Because I was freaking the fuck out. Because I was afraid.

I read the cards again. My aunt had specifically demanded that she not be intubated or attached to a ventilator. She'd asked that no invasive measures nor any of the things they did to her be done to her.

Why didn't they listen?

I knew why.

Freddie whined from his bed and I pushed the answer away. It was too early for Freddie's meds. I checked his water bowl. Full. Above the bowl, Freddie's purple leash hung on a hook attached to the side of the counter.

I couldn't silence the noise of my aunt's ventilator inside my head. I needed air.

"Let's take a walk, Fred. What do you say?"

6.

Freddie tugged me down the tomato-soup colored hall of the Summer Morning Elder Living independent living section to an unmarked exit he knew about and I didn't, then pulled me outside, around the corner and past the still-locked, "No Visitors" lobby doors. I didn't know it then, but Freddie was taking me on a tour of his favorite pissing and shitting spots and demonstrating his need to urine-mark every discolored patch of grass and to nasally-investigate all gum gobs, turds, crumbs, food wrappers, discarded tissues and sidewalk stains. Freddie snarled and bark-screamed at vans and trucks and at every dog that happened to be white, then—energized by all the barking—concluded our journey out by taking a massive shit beneath a rose-entwined white picket fence and wagging his undocked tail.

I'd forgotten to grab a poop bag from the box my aunt had placed with the dog treats and food on the kitchen counter, then noticed a purple bag tied to the purple leash right below my hand.

God, I was out of it. But my aunt had thought of everything. I wouldn't have been surprised if she'd left a dinner she'd cooked ready for me to microwave for my first post-Aunt Evelyn's-Death supper—the lamb chops she'd always make for me with dilled new potatoes and asparagus—neatly double-wrapped in foil with a five by seven card taped on that read,

"Ascher's dinner for after I'm dead. There's also haagen das ice cream in the back of the freezer for dessert."

Haagen Das white chocolate raspberry truffle was our favorite.

I knotted the poop bag as the swollen sun dropped behind an ugly new condo building. When did my aunt write out her end-of-life wishes on that card? Had she planned her death long ago, written the card and kept it ready in a drawer? Or did she have a premonition of what was coming? A prophetic dream, maybe? Or did the pandemic remind her of how old, vulnerable and alone she was?

Not alone, I told myself as the neurotic dog she loved so much led me back to my aunt's empty apartment.

When my aunt wrote those cards, my aunt had me.

7.

A big black gurney and a group of blue-uniformed, masked LAFD paramedics stood in the hall by the wide-open door to the apartment/condo across from my aunt's. Every light was on and paramedics in surgical masks and blue gloves moved like giants in the small living room. A female paramedic knelt to apply chest compressions to the collapsed barefoot man in gray, plaid pajamas on the floor—the widower my aunt called Golfing Gary. As I lifted Freddie and squeezed my way to my aunt's door, I had brief, clear view of a paramedic adjusting the oxygen mask covering Gary's face.

Freddie trembled, then stiffened in my arms and his legs begin to twitch.

8.

Was it the paramedics' deep voices, the sizzle and crackle of their radios, the rattle of the gurney and the slamming doors that triggered Freddie's seizure, or was it the alarm that buzzed and the voice of the Activities Director broadcast through the Sunny Morning Elder Living public address system?

While Freddie twitched on the blue, waterproof pad I'd taken from the package my aunt had left next to Freddie's bed, the Activities Director announced to the "Sunny Morning community" that one, perhaps two Sunny Living residents had presented with symptoms consistent with the novel Coronavirus, that an ambulance was transporting one of them to Sisters of Endless Penitence Health Center, and that the other had tragically "passed" that afternoon.

Sunny Morning Elder Care Living was on lockdown.

Special handwashing, masking, distancing and other protocols were now in place. The dining room, lobby and other communal spaces were now off-limits to residents, meals would be delivered to residences, and all residents would receive twice daily wellness checks. One section of the independent living wing had been declared a highly restricted "Red Zone" whose residents—like those in the Roach Motel—would not be checking out except the way my aunt and Golfing Gary had—for the next twenty-one days at least.

The intercom sputtered. Freddie drooled, his legs paddled and his unseeing, unblinking eyes remained fixed on something definitely not here. The future? The past? The abyss?

Freddie's neurological electrical short-circuit felt like the appropriate response to my aunt's fatal, maybe Covid-pneumonia death, to Golfing Gary's collapse, and to the life-eating shadow over everyone now locked inside No-Longer-Sunny Morning Elder Care Living.

I pressed my ear to the door to listen for more doors being flung open and for the thunderous arrival of more first responders, but all I could hear was the air conditioning's otherworldly hum. Not a creature was stirring except Freddie who blinked and resumed eye contact with reality, lapped water from his purple bowl, snarfed up the reeking gelatinous dog food "pate" I gave him and swallowed the half-tablet of phenobarbital I'd tucked into a ball of cream cheese.

Then Freddie scratched his bed with his toenails, curled up white chin on black paw, set his sleepy eyes the door and waited for my aunt to return.

My aunt.

My aunt.

Why did I think that my aunt had me?

She didn't.

Disorienting grief consumed me after my parents died. When I decided that finishing school in Santa Barbara would be the way to manage it, I never considered my aunt's sorrow. Then I was busy with community college and busy writing papers for friends and then for their friends for money I didn't need. But I liked the distraction and feeling that I was smart and getting away with something it gave me.

Then I was busy writing for a bullshit magazine so I could tell my aunt that I wasn't doing what I was really doing. When Covid hit, I was too busy worrying about my "future"—whatever that was—to think about my always self-sufficient, reliable–as–an–atomic- clock, old, increasingly frail and only living relative's future.

I drove to L.A. to visit my aunt maybe every eight or ten weeks—which is why I have no idea when my aunt began to prepare for her death. During our breezy, twice-weekly—Sundays from 6:30 until just before "Sixty Minutes—and Wednesday 7 P.M. phone chats—I never asked my aunt if she was lonely or worried or depressed after breaking her hip and having to sell her home. I never bothered to teach her to use to Zoom, so I didn't see how she looked or check if she'd lost weight. At the end of each call when I'd always ask if she needed anything, I knew that my aunt would reply the way she always did—by saying she had everything she needed—me.

9.

Twenty minutes or two centuries after Dr. Christiansen had pronounced my aunt deceased, two men dressed in head-to-shoe blue protective clothing rolled a narrow gurney into the hospice room. It took about three minutes for them to lower the bed rails, remove my great grandmother's diamond engagement ring from my aunt's stiffening ring finger, give the ring to me, wrap her in a fresh sheet, slip her into a long white plastic bag with a long white zipper, slide her onto the gurney and wheel her into the hall. I followed them through the exit to a white Eternal Home Of Peace truck in the double-long spot next to a plastic sign that said "Van Parking Only."

I wasn't the one who called them. I never thought to ask the Sunny Morning Elder Living social worker who'd come in after Dr. Christiansen's quick departure where my aunt's body should go or about her death-preferences. I was relieved when the social worker let me know that my aunt had pre-purchased a plot and casket, had provided the mortuary with her royal blue crepe pantsuit with gold buttons to wear inside it and had requested that the cemetery provide a rabbi to conduct a brief graveside service. Although it's not strictly traditional at a Jewish funeral, my aunt had even pre-purchased yellow roses from the cemetery flower shop when she'd chosen a plot on a hill overlooking L.A. River, the freeway, Warner Brothers, and beyond the studio lot, her house on Hollywood Way.

My aunt's house—demolished to make way for a three million-dollar black McFarmhouse a week after the McDeveloper bought it—had been a small bungalow with an exaggeratedly sloping shake roof and a red brick chimney¬—one of a dozen historic "fairytale" structures rumored to have been built as off-studio dressing rooms for Warner Brothers. The house had just the right amount of Hollywood whimsy for my aunt, a dancer who wanted to be a movie star who became a studio secretary. "I spent my life tapping," my aunt would say. "First with my feet and then with my fingers."

My aunt's greatest movie roles were her only two movie roles. She was one of a dozen beautiful young women dressed in skimpy gold lame who pranced around the movie star. She was the shocked-mute sales girl in the department store scene of a slapstick comedy. She worked as an extra, then moved from the set to the typing pool. My aunt typed, then "coordinated" film and television scripts at Paramount, Universal, Warner Brothers, Technicolor, NBC and Disney. Rain or heat-wave, my aunt wore heels, Chanel knock-off suits, and Max Factor's Ruby Red lipstick, designed especially for Marilyn Monroe. And she always subdued her curls—a natural chestnut dyed blonde and finally a natural silver—in a tight chignon.

The evening of the day my aunt died I sat in her velour wing chair with the hand-crocheted yellow lap blanket she'd made and she kept folded over the left arm and listened to Freddie's nasal snoring as my aunt's absence and darkness filled the room.

I was sure I'd been exposed to Covid. I'd touched things in my aunt's hospice room—the bed rails, the restraints, her hand, then touched my face with my gloved hands. I'd removed my face shield and kissed my aunt's cheek through my mask after Dr. Christiansen left and before the social worker came in. I didn't wash my hands after removing the mask and discarding it outside her room. I'd touched Sunny Morning Elder Living things—pens, papers—and surfaces and breathed Sunny Morning Elder Living air as I made my way—tears-blinded—to my aunt's apartment, And I didn't wipe down any of the surfaces inside with antibacterial and anti-viral wipes when I'd come in.

Covid virions had probably attached their fiendish spikes to the cells in the moist surfaces of my sinuses and were already rolling deep into my lungs, penetrating my alveoli and replicating.

I opened my laptop and found a DIY online advance directive form and specified my wishes—you guessed it—No CPR, no ventilator, no feeding tube — completed it, and sent it to the Sunny Morning Elder Care social worker as an attachment, then opened the middle drawer of my aunt's secretary and found the red pen and the opened package of blank notecards. On one of them I printed,

'No CPR, no ventilator, no feeding tube"

I signed my name and stuck it next to my aunt's "No CPR" card with the same flag magnet on the refrigerator.

I'd have to figure out to whom I should bequeath Freddie and the money my parents left me later.

10.

I spent my rest of my first night in the world that no longer contained my aunt trying to fall asleep in my clothes on top of the green bedspread that smelled of

Arpège, Aqua Net hairspray and Downy Infusions Lavender Serenity fabric softener, the yellow crocheted lap blanket draped over my shoulders and Freddie's curved back pressed against my stomach.

I'd already called my roommate Hans and told him my aunt had died, that the facility where she lived had been quarantined with me inside it, and that I'd reimburse him for his Lyft, gas and food to L.A. and the drive back to Goleta if he could please come pick up his car and also bring some clothes, my Valium, my electric toothbrush and my earphones.

Before the lockdown order, I'd planned to stay in the apartment/condo at Sunny Morning Elder Living only until I'd figured out what I needed to do about my aunt's estate. But a crisp manila folder in the middle drawer of my aunt's secretary labeled, *"FOR MY NIECE MS. ASCHER LIEB AFTER MY DEATH"* in the same red ink as the cards on the refrigerator revealed that I was non-essential.

My aunt had taken care of everything pertaining to her death and estate ante mortem, and what I needed to do was close to nothing. The folder contained the cemetery/mortuary paperwork, her will—she left everything, including her Lexus and the Sunny Morning Elder Living condo/apartment to me—her Medicare and supplemental insurance cards and information, her OPEIU pension paperwork, a small investment portfolio—Disney, AMC Theatres and a few other stocks––the key to a safe deposit box at Bank of America branch in North Hollywood, records of a forty thousand dollar checking account and a term life insurance policy for seven hundred and fifty thousand dollars, her accountant's business card and the name of the lawyer who'd prepared her will.

Among the documents I found an envelope addressed to me. The greeting card inside had a reproduction of a hideous Red Skelton clown painting called "Balloon Man" —Google it—I'm not exaggerating—on the front.

My Dear Ascher,

If you are reading this I'm gone. I tried to think of everything but there are few things that you or the lawyer who helped me will have to do. His name is Zack Nelson and he has an office in Encino. He's very nice and about your age. And single. Anyway, please make sure Eternal Home Of Peace orders enough death certificates. Get ten of them just to be safe. You'll have to send them to Social Security, to my credit card account, to Sunny Morning to take possession of the condo, to utilities, to the bank, and the life insurance carrier.

I always keep a month's plus supply of Freddie's food and medications in the kitchen. The vet's name and phone number are on the refrigerator with some other FYI's for you. Just make sure it's not the other vet if you take him in. Freddie hates him. In case you forgot, Freddie has a treat after his morning walk, after I have lunch and after the afternoon walk. When the treats run out please do not buy the rawhide ones. Rawhide is very bad and can block a dog's intestines. Freddie gets his seizure pill (a tablet cut in half) twice a day in a little ball of cream cheese.

Don't feel bad about me. I am not afraid to close my eyes and sleep and I am not afraid to go. Yes I have regrets but that's the way it is. I know you love Freddie and that you'll take good care of him. My only worry is that you won't find your way and that like me you'll be alone. Please, take care of yourself and try hard. Your parents loved you so much. They were so proud of you. I am so proud of you too. You are the best and most important thing in the world to me, Ascher. That's why I bought the plot in the cemetery next to mine for you. The papers are in my safe deposit box at the bank. We will be together again.

Until then and always you have all my love,

Aunt E.

11.

I studied the peach-colored cottage cheese ceiling above my aunt's bed until it became a pockmarked Martian landscape across which my dead, plank-stiff, aunt— dressed in her blue pantsuit—floated horizontally. As my aunt solemnly progressed above me over the jagged topography, the sheet the cemetery men had wrapped around her wafted behind her like a sail in the thin Martian atmosphere.

My aunt had been beautiful. She was thoughtful and generous despite a lonely life, unforgiving jobs and a tragic romantic breakup—the details of which neither she nor my mother would divulge.

I did not deserve to have been important to my aunt.

I'd done nothing to earn her love. What the fuck was my aunt proud of? My 3.2 GPA? My degree in journalism from Sea View Community College? My glum self-centeredness? My habit of always doing the minimum, or the way I slid by first with my parents' help, and then with hers? Maybe my aunt was proud of the way I always used my parents' death as an excuse for fucking up.

I realized then that my aunt's closed-eyed corpse's drift across the ceiling and the somber U-turn it executed parallel to the crown molding had to be an important message.

Not a farewell, but my dead aunt's way of making me understand that she didn't take care of her death-plans, bank accounts, investments and pension in advance to spare me pain. But that she did all that because the only person she had in the world who might have helped her with them—me—was the opposite of graceful, joyful, honest or reliable and couldn't be trusted to do anything right and wasted the love she had received.

Alone and ashamed doesn't cover what I felt as I turned away from the ceiling to cry into the not-Covid-disinfected yellow blanket as Freddie farted and chased something infuriatingly out of reach in his dream.

12.

The apparition of my aunt has not returned, though I still wait for it every evening.

My aunt resides inside the silver framed photographs next to my great-grandmother's candlesticks and brass menorah, the Royal Albert Old Country Roses china plates, cups, saucers, and the sauce boat in her china cabinet. On the morning of her funeral I removed one blurred, black and white photo of my aunt smiling under a jaunty hat and placed it on the kitchen counter with a yellow artificial rose from the fake bouquet in her bathroom and lit a battery-operated tea light—the only candle I could find in her apartment—.

The bereaved—Freddie and I—and the others—the Sunny Morning Elder Care social worker, the Activities and Enrichment Directors, the Sitting Yoga Instructor, a few computer-literate residents from the independent living section I'd never met, and two white-haired former studio friends "attended" my aunt's hastily-arranged Zoom funeral. Freddie looked smart in his purple bow tie. I wore the same jeans I'd worn the day before—no one could see—a pearl necklace of my aunt's that I found in her dresser and the black turtleneck sweater Hans brought with my other things he'd left for me in a trash bag outside the lobby door when he picked up his car.

Though my aunt had already provided everything the cemetery required when she "pre-purchased" her plan, her burial plot and mine—her death outfit, her social security number, the date and place of her birth, her father's name and her mother's maiden name—and though Dr. Christiansen as attending physician had certified her death and released her remains—prior to the funeral the five-o'clock-shadowed sixtyish cemetery man with the black satin kippah bobby-pinned to his black toupee inquired from behind his N95 how many death certificates I wanted to order. They would cost twenty-two dollars each, he said, and explained that I'd need them for Social Security, my aunt's insurer, the DMV, her pension, the will, tax returns, the condo, blah, blah, blah—everything my aunt had already told me in her note. I said I'd like to have ten, then upped that to a dozen to be mailed to my aunt's address.

What was supposed to happen at a Jewish funeral happened except the actual presence of mourners, the cutting of a black mourning ribbon pinned to my sweater—a symbolic rending of garments and token of my broken heart—and the shoveling of earth into my aunt's grave after her casket had been lowered into it. On my computer screen I watched the man in the toupee lift the shovel and I wanted to be the one removing dirt from fragrant, reddish pile on the grass that I now knew grew directly over my future resting place. And I wanted to be the one tilting fresh shovelfuls over the yellow roses on her casket lid.

Everything had already become completely terrible before funeral and after the ordering of the death certificates when the man explained that I was required-by-the-state-of California to "Zoom visit" my aunt and officially identify her "remains" so he could permanently close her casket.

The man asked me to hold my driver's license close to my computer camera. That accomplished, he carried the iPad through an empty chapel to the curtained room where my aunt's plain wood casket sat on a long white table covered with a long white tablecloth. The man moved his iPad along the open box starting at the foot, then finally angled the iPad screen close to my aunt's face.

I don't remember what the man said other than asking me if the body in the bright blue crepe suit with gold buttons whose once-lovely and loving face had hardened into a mask of sneering anger was Miss Evelyn Paula Mendel.

It was. A forever-frozen-in-rage Miss Evelyn Paula Mendel.

"She's so angry," I said. "Oh my God. Just look at her face."

"No, no," the man turned the iPad away from my aunt's body toward his own face—close enough for me to count the glistening hairs of his Uni-brow. "Death and sickness can alter a person's expression, Miss. That's all. And the lighting is not good in here. She's at peace, I know. Believe me, Miss.

I did not believe him.

Miss Evelyn Paula Mendel was not at peace. She was at something else, something I hoped was not permanent and was merely purgatorial or transitional. Something I hoped that did not reveal anything about the state of my aunt's soul—a thing that I did not believe existed.

Would my aunt's expression have appeared softer and more forgiving if I'd been in the coffin-room with her? I told myself the lighting was harsh, that her makeup had been applied badly—her lipstick was almost brown for fuck's sake—and that computer distortion and rigor-mortis had produced the pure dead fury of the eyes-shut visage that met my gaze.

13.

The morning after my aunt's funeral Freddie and I returned from his walk—I was allowed to leave the premises to exercise him twice a day––we reentered the Red Zone to find that big yellow caution tape X had been affixed to Golfing Gary's door, paper bags had been placed outside all the other doors, and a glossy beige cardboard box had also been left at my aunt's door.

Or was it my door now?

Freddie went crazy snuffling the aromatic edges of one of the paper bags. I picked him up, unlocked the door, picked up the bag, then nudged the box over the threshold with the toe of my flip flop. Inside, I put Freddie down, sloshed the hand sanitizer that Sunny Morning Elder Living had distributed to residents—and that I'd put right near the door as Dr. Gupta had suggested—onto my palms. Then I lifted the potentially-infected-with-Coronavirus bag onto a paper towel I'd placed on the counter.

Had I decided to live? I still don't know why I bothered with any of it, but I took off my surgical mask and threw it in the trash bin and immediately scrubbed my hands with soap and hot water in the kitchen sink for a full twenty seconds, making sure to lather and rinse the area underneath my aunt's ring. I'd learned from MSNBC that Covid virions hung in the air and could live for hours on any and all surfaces, so I put on my aunt's purple kitchen gloves before I opened the stapled-shut paper bag. Inside were four pairs of disposable gloves, four blue surgical masks, and a goldenrod sheet of paper reminding all Sunny Morning Elder Care Living Red Zone residents to call the Activities Director if the nurse failed to visit them twice daily for wellness and temperature checks, if they had any questions regarding symptoms or the Red Zone quarantine and to Have a Sunny Day!

I applied another blob of hand sanitizer onto the palms and between the fingers of the kitchen gloves and opened the other, heavier bag. The tuna sandwich inside was exactly like the tuna sandwich that had been in last evening's bag—two slices of thin white bread smeared with a gray fish paste flecked with relish with a limp iceberg leaf draped on top, the bread cut into neat triangles and wrapped in plastic, a lukewarm container of low-fat pineapple yogurt, a bag of potato chips, three individually-wrapped butter mints, a hard-boiled egg in plastic wrap, a freckled banana—also wrapped—a paper napkin, packets of salt, paper, sugar and Sweet & Low, a tea bag and a plastic soup spoon.

I unwrapped the sandwich and tore off a soggy corner for Freddie as a post-walk treat, then closed the box and put it in the refrigerator. Freddie licked the invisible crumbs off the kitchen floor, then followed me as I pushed the beige box across the carpet to the foot of the yellow chair. Then Freddie settled into his bed and began another long, hopeless stare at the door.

I regarded the mystery box. What could it possibly contain except more death?

I closed my eyes and hoped that when I opened them the box would have disappeared itself just as mysteriously as it had appeared. When it hadn't, I squinted at it until became an anonymous block of alabaster that had tumbled into my aunt's apartment by accident.

I switched on the latest Covid news on CNN—"Rand Paul tests positive for Covid." "Diamond Princess cruise ship passengers offer insight into virus." "Gun sales surge," then ordered two Starbucks venti lattes with extra shots and a cheese-burger and fries from The Counter to be delivered by Uber Eats in fifty to seventy minutes in front of the closed lobby door.

I wasn't hungry and I couldn't shake my anxious wakefulness. And I was afraid to take Valium. Maybe caffeine that wasn't delivered to my bloodstream via my aunt's tea bags and food that wasn't Sunny Morning Elder Care tuna would burn away the arctic fog of grief that made—even Freddie—seem vague.

I checked the emails on my phone, canceled all my current paper-writing jobs with a concise, dishonest email about having contracted COVID and removed my Craigslist ads.

I expected to feel unburdened, but I didn't.

I put on a fresh mask and gloves from the paper bag, walked outside to the front of the lobby and accepted the burger and coffee from the Uber Eats guy who'd texted me. I startled Freddie awake when I reentered the apartment and tracked jacaranda blossoms onto the carpet, but the smell of the food calmed him. I put the bag on the kitchen counter on a paper towel, disposed of my mask, washed my hands, then flossed and brushed my teeth, took a long shower and washed my hair with my aunt's lemony Jhirmack Silver Brightening Ageless shampoo. I turbaned one of her yellow towels on my head, put on some fresh sweats, got one of the venti lattes and carried it to the table by my aunt's chair.

The box waited like a dozing predator. The lid was decorated with picture of a stone plaque with a Star of David entwined in the branches of a tree with "Eternal Home Of Peace" printed in the center in a curly font. I shoved the box with the toe of my flip-flop the way you'd shove a caged snake to make it angry.

The box resisted. There was something heavy inside it.

14.

An hour and a half later the box had not been opened.

I'd used up the minutes shutting down my paper-writing PayPal account, eating the burger and fries—except for the bits I gave to Freddie—and drinking the latte numero duo I'd over-reheated the microwave and that burned my tongue.

I sucked ice cubes while I re-read the clown card my aunt had written to me just in case I'd missed something, then slid it back into the envelope and closed the secretary drawer.

I listened to the "Dirty John" podcast but knew where everything was going right away.

A tap at the door at noon interrupted my exhausting, claustrophobic wakefulness. A woman in Sunny Morning Elder Care Living peach scrubs and outfitted with an N95 mask, clear plastic goggles, and a surgical hat asked me how I was feeling and read my temperature with a wave of a large, no-touch forehead scanner.

She told me my temperature was 97.8 and addressed me by my aunt's name.

I explained who I was, why I was there, and lied that I felt great.

Was I supposed to say that I'd hallucinated the ghost of my dead aunt on the ceiling and hoped for a repeat apparitional visit ASAP? That I was ninety-nine percent sure that my mucosa and alveoli were already cooking up a lethal Covid dose? That I was unable to sleep? That I was freezing and totally spaced out? That since my aunt died, I'd been stuck in an out-of-life, wide-awake-but-still-dreaming paranoid paralytic state?

I didn't tell the nurse that from the moment I saw the cemetery box, I hadn't been able to stifle the notion that after her Zoom funeral had ended, the Eternal Home Peaceniks had removed my dead, angry aunt from her unpeaceful grave, cremated her and placed her remains—or–what might be worse—placed the remains of some other incinerated person inside the box that lay in wait for me on the carpet.

The nurse wished me a sunny day and I shut the door hard enough to scare Freddie into a fit.

None of this was the nurse's fault. But as Freddie's limbs twitched and he peed on my sweatpants, I couldn't help wishing that the woman in the peach scrubs with the touchless thermometer would have a sunny fucking day herself.

15.

The "Snapped" episode in the marathon I'd been watching all afternoon as a break from CNN shimmered on the television. The murderess was serving her philandering orthodontist husband a tall, refreshing cocktail of orange juice and antifreeze, Freddie dozed next to my aunt's sweater on the bed and I was doing an inventory of contents of the cemetery box, arranging the items in a Stonehenge circle on the cemetery-green bedspread.

The good news was that unless the Zoom funeral had been a hoax on the level of Piltdown Man—my angry aunt was still tucked safely inside her box in her plot at the Eternal Home Of Peace Cemetery and the heavy thing in the box was not a cremated anything.

It was a tall, seven-day memorial candle "to be lighted upon returning home from the funeral OR as soon as possible thereafter which may be relit if there is need to accommodate travel or safety." Alas—I'd discovered on a card in my aunt's secretary drawer—Sunny Morning Elder Living strictly prohibited the lighting of candles in residents' apartments and I—for at least the next three quarantined weeks—qualified as a "resident."

Besides the tall glass candle, Boxhenge consisted of a translucent business card with a man's name—I figured it was the toupee guy's—above the words,

"MEMORIAL COUNSELOR,
Eternal Home Of Peace Memorial Park, Crematorium and Mortuary, Eternal Home Of Peace Drive, Glendale, California.

- Another card embossed with a star of David explaining that earth from Mount Zion in Israel had been placed under the pillow upon which my aunt's head rested in her casket.
- A Yahrzeit calendar noting future dates of the anniversary of my aunt's death according to the Hebrew calendar.

- A small booklet of memorial prayers in English and Hebrew.
- Acknowledgement cards for thanking funeral guests charitable contributions given in my aunt's memory.
- A Family Care Services sheet listing "referral services available to the bereaved in the coming months."
- A mourning pin with black ribbon tail that scissors had roughly shredded.
- A faint carbon copy of the Consent To Release Remains form that authorized Sunny Morning Elder Living and the attending physician to release the remains of Evelyn Paula Mendel to Eternal Home Of Peace Cemetery/Mortuary, all organ donation declined, autopsy declined and with my shaky signature.
- A booklet from Social Security.
- A brochure from the Valley Haverim Chevra Kadisha Burial Society.
- A card with my aunt's name typed in that listed the numbers of her interment space, lot number—whatever that is—and the section name of the cemetery—King David—where she was interred.

Did my aunt receive boxes like this after my parents died? She never told me. I crawled over Boxhenge and searched her dresser, secretary, cupboards and clothes closet. All I found was a hoard of toilet paper rolls under her bed and a dark blue envelope inside a brown accordion folder stuffed with ancient canceled checks, faded family photographs that had belonged to my grandmother, and out of date appliance instruction booklets on a high shelf behind a pair of rain boots in the closet. The blue envelope contained a carbon copy of a contract and a receipt for two "smart cremations" and two ocean "dispersals."

The head-on with the truck carbonized my parents, the truck driver and the errant bird. Therefore it was convenient that in their wills they'd requested that their cremated ashes be thrown into the sea—the seething Pacific that turned my aunt's face gray and made me puke before the boat had traveled one of the three roiling nautical miles away from shore that the state of California required for the scattering of human ashes.

I remember the brief farewell to the lumpy sand that had been my parents as a queasy dream. Angry green sea met storm-black sky. The engine's thrum and gasoline stink hung over the yellow roses my aunt tossed into the ocean and which immediately drowned below the disappearing sand the cremation company representative in the blue windbreaker dumped from one, then the other bulging plastic bag.

The event was generic and non-religious—maybe purposefully atheistic or deity-denialist—I don't know. I assume the godlessness had something to do with my parents' wishes or lack of them. My parents' shocking accident and their sea-burials were also topics my aunt had never discussed with me. My parents celebrated Hanukkah and we had Passover and Rosh Hashana dinners with my aunt at my observant grandmother's house, but my parents never attended synagogue and I never learned Hebrew or had a Bat Mitzvah or attended religious school. I was unfamiliar with some of the stuff the distracted, masked rabbi said at my aunt's funeral except for the earth-shoveling part which I recalled from my grandmother's memorial at a steeply sloping Jewish cemetery next to 405 Freeway when I was eight.

The doomed husband on T.V. chugged his lethal cocktail and grinned at his widow-to-be as she cleared away the brunch dishes and broke the fourth wall by winking directly at me.

I had no experience with memorial candles, burial societies or mourning periods. Of the prayers in the pocket-sized booklet, I only knew the 23rd psalm. When the man on television collapsed on the floor and white foam oozed from the corners of his mouth, I switched to CNN's Covid report, got a latte from the refrigerator, got back on the bed and unfolded the accordioned Valley Haverim Chevra Kadisha Burial Society brochure.

16.

The evening wellness check revealed another lower-than-normal temperature. I had no physical symptoms that I chose to report to the nurse—a different woman this time. But I'd learned from CNN's always cheerful Dr. Leana Wen that how I felt didn't matter—a Covid-positive person could be asymptomatic and still be a "super spreader." Dr. Gupta had added that public health officials suspected that "super-spreader events" might be one reason for the pile-up of Covid bodies in hospital morgues. "Overwhelmed hospitals have been storing the dead in refrigerator trucks," Don Lemon said as his image dissolved into a close-up of an large white, ominously unmarked truck on a New York City street, then switched to a shot of the truck's interior in which with white-plastic wrapped, stiff Covid corpses had been stacked six high.

"Human beings were created in the image of G-d," the burial society brochure began. "Just as G-d's light fills the world, so does the soul, neshamah, fill the body. Just as the Holy One is pure, so is the soul pure. After death and until burial the soul remains close to the body, often troubled or confused."

I imagined the doors of the morgue trucks being shut and the troubled, confused souls of the refrigerated dead circling above the bodies like fireflies.

"Mourners refrain from conversation around the corpse and refrain from eating or drinking in the same room as the corpse," the brochure noted. "A window may be opened, the corpse may be placed on the floor with feet toward the door to help the soul journey toward the Divine. Candles may be lit, mirrors covered to remove obstacles to the soul's departure. From the moment of death until burial, the body is never left alone. A watcher or shemirah, remains in the room or just outside it to ensure that the soul does not feel abandoned…"

"Funerals are no longer permitted in New York," a more bloodless than usual Anderson Cooper said as I gave Freddie his dinner. I turned off the T.V. and looked up the Eternal Home Of Peace phone number but saw that it was too late to phone the memorial counselor, so I switched on the crystal lamp, got Freddie leashed, put on my mask and a hoodie, left the building and entered the empty, infectious, full moon-lit world.

I followed Freddie like a somnambulist along the faintly glowing sidewalk and tried to picture my aunt's confused, death-released soul. Was her unmoored spirit a small, white cloud? Something with wings like Harry Potter's golden snitch become ectoplasm? A weightless, crystalline tear? An invisible, lidless eye expelled during my aunt's agonized final gasp? Did it float shakily above Dr. Christiansen's head and mine and then dutifully follow the gurney into the funeral van the way Freddie was following me? A spark? A shadow?

I waited for a white Tesla with illegally tinted front and rear windows to run the red light, then let Freddie tug me across the street into the park.

The intermittent sigh of cars on the freeway, the creak and rustle of the arching sycamores and the yips of coyotes penetrated the opaque silence. I let go of Freddie's leash. He stayed close, though—a once-dumped dog doesn't have the urge to run away—and busied himself with nosing the grass and peeing against the wide tree trunks.

I was certain that I'd blown everything. That I'd fatally fucked up. And that I would forever occupy an enormous desolateness much bigger than the absences of my parents and my aunt.

I had abandoned my aunt's soul.

I didn't believe that the soul was real—but what if it was?

Even if "soul" was merely an idea or a metaphor—I had to know if my aunt's evicted, disoriented soul had suffered alone at the mortuary until her burial, or if the cemetery had—as the brochure said would upon request—provided my aunt's wrecked body and her anxious, untethered spirit a companion during its final unhappy hours on earth.

17.

I moved the cemetery box from its place next to the purple dog bed. The only illumination was the watery light of a muted, five-o'clock shadowed Jimmy Fallon delivering jokes from his laughter-less breakfast nook. I dug out the translucent card with the memorial counselor's name and an 800-number embossed on it above, "Available 24 Hours," and called the number on my cell phone.

I heard a click, a thudding silence and then a series of tinny rings that repeated until the I heard a different click that signified that my call had been disconnected. I got that day's second latte from the refrigerator, sipped it cold, redialed the number and was disconnected four more times until the fifth when after many rings a slurred female voice said, "Mortuary."

"I'm sorry to bother you so late," I lied. "But I have a quick, urgent question for the memorial counselor about a family member who was recently, um, at the mortuary. Her name is—I mean was—Miss Evelyn Paula Mendel."

"Can you please try again during regular business hours? The voice was tired. Defeated. Flat. "I'm the only one here right now it's insanely busy."

"Please," I said. "If you work nights then you can tell me what I need to know. My question concerns the night before her funeral."

"Sorry, I can't. I'm swamped and I'm a mortician, not a memorial counselor, Miss." There followed an exhale and after that I got to hear the sounds of an "insanely busy" mortuary—total fucking silence—then the electronic sputter of the final disconnect, and after that, the infuriating recording advising me that, "If I'd like to make a call, please hang up."

18.

I'd set my cell phone alarm and also my aunt's crystal bedside clock for 5:45 A.M. I took Freddie out for quick walk, then put on the nice black sweater I'd worn for the Zoom funeral with jeans and sneakers instead of flip flops, turned on CNN for Freddie so he wouldn't feel lonely, took a fresh blue surgical mask from the brown paper bag, and stepped out of the locked down Sunny Morning Red Zone.

As I quietly closed the unmarked exit door behind me, a crouching unmasked man in a stained, peach colored chef's apron, wearing surgical cap and smoking a huge joint startled me. I pretended he wasn't there and he pretended that I wasn't there as I freed my aunt's blue Lexus from its assigned handicapped parking spot, escaped onto Riverside Drive and drove toward Glendale. There was no traffic except a ghostly cortège of Von's delivery trucks rumbling eastward. I imagined the trucks were stuffed floor to ceiling with barrels of hand sanitizer and mountains toilet paper. Then the vague white paper mountains turned into stacks of the plastic-wrapped Covid dead. I was nervous. I needed to be back inside the apartment before the seven A.M. wellness check.

I made it to Eternal Home Of Peace Memorial Park in eight minutes—turned into the curving driveway past the tall, wrought iron gate and stopped the car at a "All Visitors Must Stop Here" sign. A woman in a black pantsuit and black cloth mask with a blue Star of David on it slid open the window of the kiosk and leaned out, her eyebrows furrowed with worry or annoyance.

"Good morning, Miss. Do you have an appointment? All cemetery visits are by appointment only during the lockdown."

I grinned inside my mask so that my voice would sound sufficiently warm and friendly and so my eyebrows would not look like hers. "No graveside visit." I lied. I'd planned a stealth, in-person stop to my aunt's grave after the other thing if there was time. "I have a quick, extremely urgent question for Mr. Sprague," I explained. "He recently handled a family member's funeral and there's something I need to discuss. I'm sure it will only take two minutes, max. I called last evening but couldn't get through or leave a message." Mr. Sprague was the name on one of the cards inside the Eternal Home Of Peace box——the one that promised Mr. Sprague would take care of all my pre-and post-need needs, night or day.

"We're closed to the public," the woman said. "May I have your name?"

"Ascher Lieb," I said, "I'm the niece of Evelyn Paula Mendel."

"Just a moment, please." The woman's head and shoulders disappeared behind the kiosk window which seemed to close itself.

I gazed above the stop sign at the cemetery grounds, the flats and slopes of living green interrupted by rectangles of markers and toward the area that I thought might contain my aunt.

The little window scraped open and the woman spoke again through her mask. "Please park your vehicle in a 15 minutes Only spot in the lot to your right." The woman pointed to the only parking lot, the one I couldn't miss right next to the entrance. "Then proceed to the main door and push the buzzer marked "Chapel and Flower Shop." Mr. Sprague knows you're here and he will let you in."

The kiosk window closed like a goat's horizontal pupil. I parked in the fifteen-minutes only space on the right side of the lot which was empty except for two House Of Peace vans, climbed the steps to the brown tinted-glass doors, pressed the brass button I had been told to press and felt, but did not hear it buzz.

A tall, powder blue blob floated toward me behind the glass, then it assumed the shape of a tall thick man in surgical booties, gray dress pants and a buttoned-down white shirt and tie under a semi-transparent powder blue surgical gown. The man held a file folder in one gloved hand and unlocked the door with the other.

"Please come in Miss Mendel," the man said from behind his white, valved mask. "I am very sorry to hear that there was a problem your memorial experience. How can I help?"

Mr. Sprague or whoever this was retreated across the dim, empty room to a spot a good nine feet away from me. I stayed in front of the black window of the empty flower shop.

"The memorial experience was fine," I said, involuntarily seeing my aunt's dead, anger-disfigured face. "I have a question about the services my aunt pre-purchased. Did she pay for a watcher before the funeral? And was her body ritually washed?"

One of Mr. Sprague's eyebrows lifted slightly as he opened the folder and thumbed through the papers inside. "Let me see," he said as the stone floors and walls ping-ponged his words and elongated their sounds. "We offer traditional tahara through Valley Haverim Chevra Kadisha and the service of a shomer, but our records show that your aunt did not request either. Is this a problem? Did you request these services for her and did she not receive them? Covid is forcing us to curtail some services and is stretching us to our limit, but mourners can still request those for their loved one." The man closed the file and looked at the brass clock on the wall.

It was 6:22 A.M. and I was a fool and a fucking lunatic.

19.

I jogged around my aunt's Lexus, alone in its fifteen-minute spot, behind the closed-windowed kiosk and went up the cemetery road. The air that leaked into the sides of my paper mask smelled like mown grass and the sea. One of those cards in the box said that my aunt was buried in the King David section of the cemetery. I ran past Ruth, Isaiah, Moses, then followed a sign to King David on a narrow, ascending concrete path.

The "King David" death pasture was above the mausoleum and looked as though it had been recently cut from the hillside, bulldozed flat and grassed. The slender trees required the support of fat wooden poles and rubber tubing to hold them upright. I stepped among the rows of markers—a few had pebbles on them left by visitors—then froze as four grazing deer silhouettes materialized and then evaporated about five rows ahead of me in the whitening morning light. I moved to the rectangle of fresh dirt where they'd been grazing and knew I'd found my aunt. Brown and wilted yellow roses were strewn across the dirt and over the temporary plastic marker that contained a paper with my aunt's name and the date of her death typed on it.

I had four minutes.

I used one to stretch out on my future burial plot and press my left hand through the masticated roses into the disturbed earth of my aunt's grave, and another to gaze at the veils of sky and cloud through which my aunt's soul—if she had one—rose flaming into clarity like a missile.

20.

I returned the Lexus to my aunt's parking spot at 6:55. The lot was empty except for two vans in the "Vans Only" spaces where the House Of Peace van had parked to picked up my aunt's body.

Because my aunt's was a handicapped space, it was only three steps to the door and I was inside the apartment before the morning wellness check. My mask hid my flushed cheeks, but my temperature was elevated—99.0. I explained that I'd just returned from a five-mile run and was overheated. The nurse told me to call the Director's office right away if my temperature went up. She seemed too harried to notice the black wool turtleneck I had on, or to tell to me to have a sunny day.

I hadn't had a sunny day for a long time.

My aunt's death had resuscitated memories of my parents' accident that I thought I'd euthanized, cremated and dissolved inside the thumping, caverns of my heart. The real memories—did I mention that my parents had their fatal crash while driving back to L.A. after making an emergency Big Bear Lake summer camp delivery to me? I'd gotten my first period and was too embarrassed to ask my camp counselor for sanitary pads—and the false "eyewitness" memories of the accident I'd constructed had become zombified. They jostled me as I showered, used the toilet, brushed my teeth, walked, sat, chewed, swallowed, held my breath or breathed. They stood between me and the T.V., the computer screen and Freddie's face. They surveilled me awake and asleep until the small apartment was crowded with bad luck, broken-mirror images of my parents' shocked faces as the panicked dove—in my fictional reenactment, it's always fat—flies into the car, my startled father swerves into the truck and car and truck, bird, father and mother blow up.

My maybe-case of Covid, my aunt's absence and her no-show ghost took up space, too. What day was it anyway? That day like the other days was dizzying in its dullness as it replicated the previous lockdown days' cold cereal, paper bowls, plastic spoons, cartons of low-fat milk, navel oranges, boxed and airlessly wrapped egg salad, turkey or tuna sandwiches, child-sized bags of pretzels and chips, "not for individual sale" containers of warm green Jell-O, yellow pudding and yogurt, televised toilet paper brawls in Walmart and Costco, sanitizer panics, extreme close-ups of empty supermarket shelves, and the hourly death graphs with bars aligned into a rising, swollen curve.

Each morning was a new old hole to scramble out of until evening was achieved. Each night was another head-first dive back down. I was stuck playing an endlessly repeating 3-D game of Snakes and Ladders with light eaters.

I was haunted. I was the dead living. I was the alive dying.

What the fuck was I supposed to do?

If I couldn't evade merciless dead, maybe I would have to join them.

21.

No, I didn't off myself. Come on.

I am responsible for Freddie now. And I don't do big gestures. I'm a coward, remember? A crawler into holes. An avoider. A liar and an evader.

Which is why after that evening's wellness check —my temperature had dropped to 98.6—and a soft door knock, contact-less delivery of an arrangement of fern fronds and peach-colored chrysanthemums—I think they stick the stems in orange food coloring—with an "In Deepest Sympathy from the Sunny Morning Elder Living Family" card stuck on a plastic stick—I stayed locked-in and—out of desperation–-I excavated the Valley Haverim Chevra Kadisha brochure from the bottom of the cemetery box, put it on the secretary where I would have to see it, took a Valium and slept.

I passed the next morning's wellness check, bit my tongue when I was wished a sunny morning and—still symptom-free—seized the still-feral day by sneaking out of the Red Zone and driving Freddie to "The Great Wall of Los Angeles," a mural on the western concrete wall of an L.A. river flood channel in North Hollywood. The saturated colors of the chronological segments depict California from prehistory to the 1950's, but Freddie and I walked north to south and time-traveled in reverse, beginning at the Holocaust and Joseph McCarthy and ending at mastodons, the Chumash Village and Chumash spirit animals. Freddie enjoyed the aromatic rot smell rising from the cement river bottom, the new tree smells, and the droppings from birds and dogs he didn't know.

Maybe it was the Valium. I zoned out driving the way back to the condo and found myself turning into a eucalyptus-shaded cul-de-sac I hadn't visited since before my parents died. I parked across from the small ranch house that had been ours—now a just small section of a lot-hogging, style-jumble of enlargements, additions, bulging bay and ceiling-high French windows and "features" including a second floor with fake balconies. I squinted until I'd decapitated the second story and blotted out the rectangle of plastic grass and the French-windowed tumor that had replaced the lawn the lemon and persimmon trees.

A slight wind twirled a paper mask abandoned on the sidewalk in front of the house and my scalp tingled. I pulled Freddie close, shut my eyes and waited for the coming lightning to split my now Frankensteined house in two.

But the heavens did not open. The haunted house within that monster house was not expunged. The front door of the house opened and a stiff-legged, long-haired, dirty-white dog with brown stains under his eyes and wearing a pink collar limped down the steps. Freddie growled as the dog stepped onto the plastic grass, then stood absolutely still and gazed fixedly at Freddie and at me while she squatted with difficulty and peed.

Answering the summons of the old place failed to provide an epiphany and did not free the tortured spirits of my parents from the endlessly repeating re-enactment of their deaths inside my head.

The girl who lived there with my parents isn't me. When my parents died, she died, too.

I stopped at the Starbucks drive-through on Laurel Canyon for two more venti lattes and a Puppuccino for Freddie. During the slow crawl to the window, I wondered if my dud of a home visit was the result of garbled communication from the ether. Still—the message my aunt's ghost communicated as she crisscrossed the ceiling had been clear—I was worthless. That was probably the only lucid message I would ever get.

My aunt's soul was wherever souls go and I couldn't rely on nudges from the universe-at-large to lead me. I had to figure out what to do for myself. I paid for the order, accepted the coffees and the cup of whipped cream and drove on too-quiet streets past empty sidewalks toward Sunny Morning Elder Care Living.

Being worthless didn't mean I couldn't do worthwhile things, did it? I resolved to accomplish something—not making the world a better place, not having world peace begin with me or filling the days of others with sunshine. Just one small, good thing each day—besides walking, feeding, medicating and playing with Freddie—until Covid sickened or killed me or my dead aunt returned from the death-world with an urgent update.

My problem then—besides the idea being total cliche—was finding even one good thing to do. The pandemic shut down meant I couldn't show up at the zoo and offer to clean the cages. I couldn't work in a hospital gift shop or read to the blind. Short of donating my body to science or leading an uplifting impromptu acapella Zoom hootenanny for the exhausted staff and quarantined residents of Sunny Morning Elder Care Living, I had nothing with which to refill the world's dwindling stores of sunshiny benevolence.

Then I remembered the brochure. I could donate my body—temporarily and not to science—to something else.

22.

I kicked my flip-flops under the table, slipped on the bracelet and the tag and positioned myself—toes toward door and arms at my sides like the mannikins in white and gray wigs in the training videos—then covered myself up to my chin with the sheet that had been left on the table.

I pressed my thighs together, but there was no way not to feel too wide. The stainless steel's cold percolated through my leggings, the back of my t-shirt and chilled my spine—which I imagined was the same mayonnaise white as the tile. There was nothing to do but defeat the impulse to hug myself, close my eyes and wait.

The air conditioner wheezed off and ticked. Without its hum, the quiet became subaquatic deep. A silent avalanche.

I'd missed the turn-off to the cemetery and had arrived late. I'd had just a few seconds to glance at the tub, the sink, the table, the spotless steel pots nested one inside the other, the clay pot of earth, the Q-tips, the scissors, the white laminated sheets printed with words in English and Hebrew, the folded white linen garments, the cloths and blue plastic aprons, the baggies and the three blue plastic painters' buckets on the floor.

Nothing I'd seen warmed me. Nothing made me think that this great idea of mine had been good.

The unyielding steel pressed against my back until it hurt—which I took as signal from my body that it was time to chicken out. I was half-sitting up and about to sneak into the hallway and invent an excuse later when the heavy door slowly inhaled inward and the women entered.

I flattened myself beneath the sheet and told myself that no going through with what I'd insisted on doing would be worse than the dread I felt. I tried to even-out my breathing as rubber soles sighed across the floor and the long sleeved, ankle-length plastic aprons crackled.

The tap hissed. Water rushed against metal during the repeated fillings and pourings I didn't count. I knew there would be twelve for the four right-to-left hand washings. I heard the snap of latex and the murmur of linen, the clack of the plastic buckets placed under the table.

Then the thin sheet covering me rose like an exhalation. Gloved fingers turned my plastic wrist band and touched the tag I'd tied around my toe.

A marker squeaked and I imagined my name and my parents' names—Ascher bat Michael v'Pauline—materializing in English and Hebrew on the dry erase board.

The square of cotton that drifted across my masked face smelled like laundry soap. My forgiveness for what was about to happen was implored.

My great-grandmother's engagement ring—the one my aunt wore–-was corkscrewed off my finger.

I smelled the acetone before I felt the saturated cotton ball dissolving my black nail polish—first on the right hand, then those on left, then the right toenails, then the left.

"'And the angel raised his voice and said to those standing before him, saying, "Take the filthy garments off him.' And he said to him, 'See, I have removed your iniquity from you, and I have clad you with clean garments.'"

I felt the proximity of warm bodies. I felt the light pressure of hands on my right shoulder, right arm, right hand, chest abdomen, as a cloth was pressed against my right foot and moved between toes—then the left foot.

I heard the buckets lifted from the floor and then a murmuring female voice—

"T'horah hi, she is pure.
T'horah hi, she is pure.
T'horah hi, she is pure."

23.

But I was in.

Not losing my shit while playing dead and being practiced upon had been the last requirement. I'd taken a required Covid swab test in the driveway at Cedars Sinai—negative—received the first of a series of Hepatitis B vaccinations, completed the online application and the Zoom-interview. I'd pretty much memorized the instructions and prayers in phonetic Hebrew from the booklet I'd received as a PDF attachment. I'd also studied the updated Covid guidelines issued by the National Association of Chevra Kadisha.

I—a profane, unobservant, atheist Jew, frequent liar and grieving loser—had become the newest member of Valley Haverim Chevra Kadisha, a Jewish burial society divided into two groups—one male and the other female—on-call twenty-four-seven and performing mitzvot at no cost to the bereaved out of two rooms in the mortuary of House of Sepulchers Memorial Grove in Woodland Hills—and sometimes at other cemeteries when the need arose.

The cold table I'd placed myself upon and which smelled faintly of lemon and bleach is in the windowless, fluorescent-lit tahara room—sink, counter, tilting steel table with a drain, body-cleaning supplies, dry erase board and a tub. The other room is where the shomer or shomeret—depending on the deceased's gender—guards the body until burial.

I hoped that washing, purifying and dressing corpses in almost monastic silence so as not to further confuse their already-muddled souls might be a way to do good—or as the instruction booklet described it—to perform chesed shel emet—an act of true and disinterested kindness—and would harmonize with my antisocial tendencies and meet my current fucked-up needs. I doubted there was a "volunteer activity" as anonymous or free of the obligation to engage in agonizing chitchat or deal with bureaucratic bullshit as purifying the dead.

Yeah—I was scared shitless. But I hoped that doing this would somehow bring me closer to my aunt, and maybe move her away from rage and closer to something approximating peace.

24.

My aunt's death had fractured Eternity and caused a —so far—unfixable leak. Sunny Living Elder Care Red Zone Covid Time oozed from one annihilated lockdown day to the next like lava toward a multi-million-dollar Kona house. The always-present, troubled reproachful absences of my aunt and parents refused to fade. But a world without their anguished ghosts in it seemed worse. I hated the idea—suggested by the accountant—of going through my aunt's things, of dismantling her apartment so it could be sold, and of throwing away everything that belonged to her. I refused to discard her costume jewelry, her makeup, her tubes of Preparation H, her walker, her old, unopened packages of support panty hose, her handkerchiefs, her Tupperware, her scarves, or the yellow shower cap with a few of her silver hairs still inside it. I kept my aunt's place—except for the trash bags full of my stuff—almost exactly as she had left it when she'd been rolled in a wheelchair—struggling to breathe–– toward hospice.

Her "No CPR, no ventilator, no feeding tube" card was still magnetized to the refrigerator next to mine. The frequently-perused clown note was snug inside its envelope in the manila envelope in her secretary drawer. The unburned memorial candle stood next to her silver framed picture, the battery-operated tea light and the more recently added vase of now-dried out orange mums and brown ferns on the counter. The dour cemetery box sat right next to Freddie's purple bed. I slept on my aunt's green bedspread under the yellow crocheted blanket with Freddie pressed against my chest dreaming and farting. I awoke each morning not knowing where I was or how I'd tumbled a place so lightless, bottomless and so bereft of sky.

I'd passed through twenty-two lockdown days of wellness checks, sandwiches in paper bags and bags of fresh surgical masks and individually wrapped toilet paper rolls—included by popular demand––inside. Three more Sunny Living Elder Care Red Zone residents had been removed by emergency medical technicians from the Glendale Fire Department. Three more caution tape X's marked the raw-liver-colored hallway's always shut doors.

My parents' accountant—who became my aunt's after the accident–
–had decided to wait out the pandemic in his Mammoth ski cabin and only replied to emails once a week. When I'd contacted him about the absent death certificates, he'd answered five days later, "during a global pandemic there is no rush on anything," and advised that I, "shouldn't hold my breath."

My aunt's safe deposit box in the shuttered bank was safe from me.

And—bummer of all bummers—although dying of Covid 19 in my aunt's apartment would have demonstrated a gorgeous karmic symmetry and solved most of my guilt problems—I was not only burning my candle at both ends—there was no candle Whatever afflicted me was likely permanent, incurable, not fatal and all my fault.

On the plus side, Freddie had been almost seizure-free. But his Hochiko-level grief-filled-waiting-for-my-aunt-to-come-back-staring-at-the-door-sessions never let up.

I'd expected—not hoped for—frequent day and/or night texts from the Chevra Kadisha leader I only knew as "S." summoning me to the mortuary, but I'd only had to pull my hair into a pony-tail, put on long-sleeved top and my one pair of nice pants and drive my aunt's Lexus to Woodland Hills twice.

The world was less solid each time I entered it. To walk Freddie, to step around the building to the locked doors of Sunny Morning Elder Living and pick up a food delivery, to gas up the Lexus and—when under the low black dome of night I parked under the headache-bright security light in the mortuary parking lot—I got out of my aunt's car to meet my first body.

My hands shook as I tied the closures of my long apron, put an N95 over my surgical mask, a shield over my N95 and pulled on my cap. I did not faint upon entering the tahara room and seeing the readied wooden casket, the white, folded linen garments, the lumpy shape under in the sheet waiting patiently for me on the cold table. I washed my hands in the prescribed manner—by pouring water right to left from a double handled pitcher at the sink, then waving them in the sour and frigid air to dry. And I didn't feel sick as I put on both pairs of gloves and stood with the three other masked and shielded women near the body while the deceased's name and her parents' names were inscribed on the board and the dead woman's forgiveness was implored.

I held onto edge of the metal table as the sheet was lifted—and kept holding it before a fresh square of cloth was placed over it and the dead woman's face was unveiled.

Like my aunt's—her face was not at peace. This was the face of suffering and sorrow.

Lukewarm squares of wet cloth gently were applied to it, then to the bald head and neck. Then came pouring of water upon the right arm, right side of the body, then the left arm and the left side, the pale cavernous mastectomy scar across the breastbone—only the area being cleansed was uncovered to protect the woman's modesty.

When it was over, I removed my PPE and disposed of it in a plastic box marked "Used PPE" and reentered the starless, spongy darkness still wrapped in death's wordless silence. Was the stunned spirit of the purified, maimed-by-life woman I'd helped dress in white linen, pocketless garments and placed in her coffin settling in for the long night, the shomeret's head bowed in prayer beneath a dark heaven?

25.

My second body was inside a plastic pouch and belonged to muscular woman about my age with short straw-colored hair. The tahara was abbreviated because she'd died of Covid and the men's group needed the room. The leader—her glasses behind her shield and gray hair under her surgical cap——had wiped down the sink, counter, and the table with a bleach and water mixture.

The special circumstances meant that we worked separately, distanced and more quietly than we had before. One member sprayed the length of the body bag with a special disinfectant, opened the bag and treated the inside with the spray. I filled the buckets and added bleach to each one as another member removed the bag, packed the mouth with cotton pads. The pouring of an unbroken flow of water was slowed to prevent splashing.

When the body was dressed and placed in the coffin, two of us left the room while the others remained to clean up.

Despite the disruptions, I'd felt confident during the first two procedures. Confident enough about the second body that I did not think once about its soul.

26.

I smooth my hair and watch myself in the audio-muted rectangle on the black Zoom screen and wait for the meeting to discuss whatever the fuck happened to me during the purification of body number three to convene.

I wish I knew.

Which tahara had been the aberration? My cool efficiency with body number two or my total freak-out with body number three?

A white sunbeam slices through the half-closed blinds behind the empty chair and table in what looks like a classroom.

I try to make-out the construction paper cut-outs stapled to a pocked brown bulletin board visible next to a window as if decoding them would reveal my doom in the Old English sense of the word—my destiny.

It's hard to make out the pre-fab Hebrew cut-out letters in faded primary colors I couldn't read if I could see. But I do make out a dwarf Moses, hands raised over his head next to a bush made of green tear-drop shapes erupting into canary yellow tear-drop flames. The short woman in the blue mu-mu and yellow crown must be Queen Esther. The brown circles next to the gray menorah are either potato pancakes or UFOs.

A woman's torso, then her head and shoulders fill the screen and the sunbeam ignites her long, corkscrewed pomegranate hair. "You must be Ascher Lieber." She settles into her seat as gracefully as a flamingo folding itself into its mud nest after descending from the gold-flecked, purpling air. "Lieb," I say. "Lieb, not Lieber." I can hear the smile in her voice as she addresses me from behind her pink cloth mask. "Welcome again to Valley Haverim Chevra Kadisha. I'm Sharon."

So, this is the "S." who texts me. The fine lines radiating from the corners of Sharon's concealer-smoothed and precisely made-up eyes announce that Sharon is in her late forties or maybe fifty. An amethyst Star of David flashes and her long-sleeved pink cotton sweater brightens as the pesky sunbeam lands again. Sharon looks down at something which I assume is a detailed report about the you-know-what—the catastrophe.

I straighten my mask—a cheap Amazon.com blue paper one—, rub my left eye though I'm trying not to, and repudiate my instant, unbidden, ungenerous, bitchy assessment of Sharon's fashion and mask choices—the bubblegum pink polished fingernails—rhinestones glued in the middle of each one—the bubble gum pink sweater and her hair's incendiary redness.

"How are you doing, Ascher? Feeling better?"

Who am I—a schlump who is opposite of fashionable or even put together—to judge what another woman wears? "I am feeling much better," I lie. "And I'm so, sorry. And so embarrassed about what happened that I don't know what to say—"Then— despite holding my breath and looking away from the screen and telling the bad feeling overtaking me to stop—I cry.

Sharon winds and rewinds a ruby curl with a bedazzled finger until I'm hiccupping and dabbing my unmade-up, too-small agate green eyes with a tissue. "I want you to know, Ms. Lieber, that what happened to you is completely normal and happens a lot."

"What happened to me?" I want to shout. To be honest, I find what Sharon said hard to believe. I want to ask her what exactly happens a lot and is completely normal. I want to ask why there was no footnote in the PDF booklet mentioning that what happened to me might happen so that when it happened, I could have at least been spared the shock and humiliation.

"I don't know what to say," I say. "Except that I hope you'll give me another chance and I feel really horrible about falling apart and I apologize for—" For losing my shit, I keep myself from saying out loud. For failing to complete the greatest act of kindness, for failing to comport myself with dignity and modesty while in the presence of the dead, and for upsetting an already unhappy soul—for swirling into a massive panic attack that required rebreathing my own air from a paper bag that smelled like tacos and that someone at the mortuary retrieved from the trunk of his SUV, for throwing up into the bag, for requiring a lie down on the plastic covered couch in the mortuary office.

For as usual totally fucking up.

27.

The sunbeam hits a rogue hair on Sharon's plucked right eyebrow making it shimmer like a hot wire. "Really, Ascher. There's nothing to worry about. May I call you Ascher?" I nod and imagine that behind her mask, Sharon's teeth are perfectly aligned and are a pure, appliance-white. "Perfectly normal," May-I-Call-Her-Sharon says. "There is no wrong response to death or to the mitzvot we perform. In my view, fearing death is another form of k'vod ha-met—of respecting the dead," Sharon explains.

Well, then, if fear, if paralyzing dread, if existential, vertiginous death-nausea is the exact right thing, then I have nothing to worry about and this is Sharon-Of-The-Most-Perfect-Choppers' and the other members of Valley Haverim's Chevra Kadisha's lucky fucking day.

I fake-grin behind my mask to calibrate my voice. "Thank you for your understanding. I really appreciate it. I am sure it won't happen again."

"I'm sure it won't, too," Sharon says, "But I think it would be a good idea for you to take a break and take a step back for a while and reassess."

The jolt I thought I'd evaded had arrived.

"Just continue to study the booklet and the supplementary materials, immerse yourself in the steps, the prayers, and the background articles and feel free to text me with any questions. And if, after your period of reflection, you decide that this work is not right for you, that's fine, too." Sharon moves her face closer to her computer screen. "Whatever you choose, Ascher. I hope your time with Valley Haverim Chevra Kadisha has been as meaningful, life-affirming and sustaining for you as it is for me."

I'm supposed to say something. I don't.

Sharon's eyebrows scrunch together as if she is trying to read a blurry chyron crawling across my forehead and displaying my private thoughts. "Each person who's drawn to what we do has deeply personal reasons. Don't worry, Ascher. I'm not going to share mine with you and I am not going to ask you about yours."

28.

I wasn't there for someone.

I need to be there now—there being the kicked bucket, the bitten dust, the state of pushing clouds.

Needing to earn forgiveness for the unforgiveable is why I took up death-work, Sharon.

And despite what Sharon says, I cannot take a break.

I'm sure, too, that Her Pinkness of Valley Haverim Chevra Kadisha would not have approved if she'd known who I really am and now will never permit me to return.

I nod at the crouching guy in the same peach-colored kitchen apron and hair net smoking a blunt outside the hall door and he nods back as Freddie pulls me around the independent, the assisted, the barely-living and the hospice sections of Sunny Morning Elder Care and into a sunset that burns like an above-ground nuclear test.

I hate summer.

It isn't here yet, but I can feel it out there. Summer is the worst, and if the Covid body count keeps rising, there will be no escaping Shark Week, re-runs, special summer game shows and the shitty movies on Lifetime. There's a reason the Summer of Love closed with a mock funeral, then devolved into the Manson race-war, spree murders and ended with swastikas on foreheads or that Meredith Hunter was killed at Altamont only four months after the Woodstock peace-fest. I know because I ghost-wrote a paper about the sixties and because of a freshman essay I did on William Butler Yeats. All things—especially the supposedly blissful, care-free, perfect things like summer—turn to shit.

Or maybe it's me and I have pre-summer-onset SADs—seasonal affective disorder plus sorrow. Freddie aligns his ass to true north to take a dump and I am grief-frozen. I've slithered from "Doing Good" to "Lost" on the Snakes and Ladders board and am sliding to "Bereft".

I am character–, skills– and imagination-deficient. I have a knack for failure and for lies.

I'd written "freelance writer" instead of "forger" in the "About Me: Occupation" section of the Valley Haverim Chevra Kadisha intake form. I omitted mentioning that I was a plagiarism-enabler. An unencumbered-with-ethics problem-solver who'd write your job application essay, compose the poem or short story your English teacher had assigned, pen your college admissions essay or your freshman paper—often a slightly altered previous forgery—and for a bigger fee, I'd take a whole online course plus exams in your name.

I'd included my one legit job, though it had ended when my employer, editor in chief and publisher of Mission City Lifestyle Digest, deemed that I was not "essential" during the pandemic. My "work" consisted of lifting biographies almost verbatim from the websites of the realtors, interior decorators, yoga instructors, coffee roasters, chefs, landscape designers, plastic surgeons, gynecologists specializing in vaginal rejuvenation and orthodontists that were published as "profiles" among full color ads for "The Tri-Counties' Best"—who happened to be the same realtors, decorators, yoga studio operators, coffee roasters, restauranteurs, landscape designers plastic surgeons, vaginal rejuvenation gynecologists and orthodontists—that made up ninety percent of the "magazine" which was delivered for free to medical and dental offices and upscale salons and businesses throughout Santa Barbara, Montecito and Ventura counties.

Except for the humiliation, leaving Mission City Lifestyle Digest had felt good and meant that I could stop pretending—except to my aunt—that I was a working "journalist." But instead using my newly freed-up time to drive to L.A. and check up on my aunt, I retreated into my room in the Goleta house I shared with three electrical engineering/video game designer roommates—my sort of boyfriend Hans and his friends Garza and Bree. I wrote papers, ordered food and coffee, and watched the novel Covid 19 virus mutate on the television news. The shaky, hand-held videos of nursing homes exteriors, the aides' paper gowns inflating and deflating as they rushed hospital beds carrying people who might or might not be dead to waiting ambulances became slick, hours-long Covid-19 Town Halls featuring Don Lemon, Dr. Sanjay Gupta, Anderson Cooper, Dr. Leana Wen, Dr. Fauci and always the computer-generated, brightly colored Covid virions, their lethal, fleshy spikes glittering as they danced behind the talking heads.

A sickness had infected me and it wasn't the virus.

I was light-averse and could not sleep. Then—with the help of my friend Valium—I couldn't stop sleeping——until the urgent call from Sunny Morning Elder care woke me.

It's not just the governor's stay at home order. Each thing—waking and sleeping, trying and failing, lies and truth—returns me to my absent aunt, to the locked-down Sunny Living Elder Care Red Zone and to death.

29.

I stand in my mask, sunglasses, pajama bottoms and a faded turquoise Sea View Community College Krakens sweatshirt neck deep in the pit of my own black shadow outside the shuttered Sunny Morning Elder Care Living lobby. Freddie digs a hole next to a broken sprinkler as I wait for a contact-less delivery of rawhide-free dog treats, dog pate, tampons and Midol from my Instacart shopper, Zvi, who texted five minutes ago that he was on his way.

Freddie moves to a withering gardenia bush, smells it, and pees on it and looks at me suspiciously. Maybe he's figured out that my aunt is not coming back and he blames me.

A red compact car slides into one of the six handicapped spaces in front of the lobby and a middle-aged man wearing a red bandana over his face opens the car door, steps around the hood to hands me a stapled red and white CVS paper bag.

"Lieb?"

Weird, but Freddie doesn't bark. Even weirder, he dances wide-eyed and joyfully around Zvi's white Crocs and wags his tail.

"Yep," I say. "Thanks very much." I am about to step six long paces away from Zvi when he kneels close to Freddie. "Cute dog."

Before I can warn Zvi about Freddie's anxieties and his triggers Freddie is on his back and receiving a tummy rub from Zvi.

30.

Freddie was morose after Zvi drove away, so I made sure we visited all his spots including the rose bush and a pink, a yellow lantana quivering with moths and bees and some shrubs along the driveway that are his new fave.

Freddie is glum as I lead him around the back of Sunny Morning Elder Care Living and as we enter the hallway and return to my aunt's apartment/condo. He

swings his tail only once as he watches me put the plastic bag on the counter, remove the prescription eye drops, the eye patch and the ice pack. I put the pack in the freezer, look at the little box containing the eyedrops and struggle to read the tiny print until I realize that I still have my shades on and take them off. The bag crinkles as I take the dog chews out. "Oh look!" I say to Freddie in a super cheerful voice. "Oh my goodness, what can this be? Is this a special treat for Freddie?"

Freddie's ears go up.

"Wowie zowie." I rip open the bag of chews, take out an inch-long dehydrated apple and chicken "sausage-chew," and make a big deal of delivering to Freddie in his bed. "Here comes good boy Freddie's treat."

Freddie lifts his chin, opens his mouth and then looks at me with distrust. Instead of accepting the bone-shaped treat, he wrinkles his nose to expose his teeth, produces a low, rumbling growl and lunges toward my hand.

I drop the chew and back away.

Freddie growls—meaner and louder

31.

I decide from the safety of the bed that the only thing I can do about Freddie's idiopathic hostility is to avoid pissing him off. He could be in pain from an illness or injury I can't see—and if he's sick or hurt, he'll definitely bite. Until he calms down or I can get some canine sedatives, there is no way I can check, or lift him into the car for a distanced visit to the vet.

I turn off the lights to calm Freddie, wash down a Valium with a cold latte, then have to pee. I slow-walk to bathroom without waking Freddie or inspiring the baring of his sharp, microbe covered teeth.

32.

A yowl reaches me before I can finish washing my hands for the full twenty seconds. I open the bathroom door and a bar of light falls across the carpet.

Half in darkness—or light depending on your outlook—his black eyes shining with rage—Freddie snarls and scream-barks at a small, floating-halfway between-carpet-and-ceiling no-color, glowing like neon globule.

A series of smart knocks rattle the door—the evening wellness check.

Freddie redirects rage from the thing to the door.

The shimmering whatever-it-is-trembles before I turn on the lamp and it disappears.

"Coming," I use my outdoor voice, smooth my hair and put on a paper mask. It's a nurse I think I've seen before who has the no-touch aimed straight at my forehead. "How are we feeling this evening, Miss Mendel? You look pale."

"Okay," I say, having given up on trying to get the Sunny Morning Elder Care Living staff to stop addressing me by my aunt's name. "Except we have a pesky migraine."

"98.8," the nurse says, her eyebrows slightly lifted. "Still normal. But if you feel feverish or develop any symptoms, please call the director's office right away. How long have you had the headache?"

"It started a little while ago," I lie. "I made the mistake of ordering Chinese take-out and I forgot to tell them no MSG."

The nurse tilts her head to the right. Is she trying to see past me into the apartment to check if there are take-out boxes on the counter or the table? Or is she looking for something else?

"One of the residents who shares this hallway mentioned hearing voices. Is there any chance you had or have a guest, Miss Mendel? Maybe the take-out delivery person stayed for a visit?"

"A guest? Someone said I had a guest?" I sound shocked. Offended.

"Maybe I had the TV on too loud, but, the only ones here are me and the dog. And I always go outside the building to pick up my take-out orders. No one ever comes in here. Right Freddie? That's against the rules."

Freddie paws the carpet and snarls.

"Freddie has idiopathic epilepsy," I say. "Sometimes he barks at nothing. Maybe what that person reported hearing was him."

"I'm sure it was," the nurse says, "We're still under strict quarantine, as I know you are well aware."

"Yep," I say. "Completely well aware."

"Have sunny evening, Miss Mandel. And you, too Freddie."

33.

I press my ear against the door to check if the nurse is still on the other side listening for the sounds of human contraband. I hear the air conditioning crackle, a tiny cough, then fabric whispering against the door's surface.

I wait for a count of ten, then tiptoe to the bed—keeping clear of Freddie— as he warily tracks my movements. I switch on the TV with the remote, flip to CNN and turn the volume up in case the nurse returns. "The coronavirus has infected 1.7 million people and killed more than 110,000 worldwide." The numbers appear in blue above Don Lemon's head. "And the United States has reached a grim milestone. We now have more than half a million cases and the most coronavirus-related deaths in the world."

One of Don Lemon's waxed eyebrows is thicker than the other and the animated computer-generated Covid virions are a nasty yellow and an angry candy apple red.

34.

I wake up hungover from murky, Valium not-dream. Freddie is snoring and curled against me on the bed. Did I put him here? I can't remember. What I do remember is the glowing blob and leaving my aunt's lamp on when I went to bed.

Will he snap at me if I move? I'm afraid to find out. I look at my cell phone. 6:24 A.M.

I have a half hour before the wellness check that will be early because of the nosy nurse last night.

I scan the ceiling. My aunt is absent.

So what was the blob? A shadow-trick, a waking dream? A hallucination?

Did Freddie really see it too, or did hear something—probably the nurse in the hall?

What's worse? That it was there or wasn't?

35.

A different nurse performs the morning's wellness check and informs me that my temperature is 98.5 and asks me about last night's "migraine." I tell her it's gone, urge her to have sunny day and shut the door before she can foist another sunny fucking day on me.

CNN tells me that Italy's Covid death toll is the highest in the world. Los Angeles County hospitals are seeing a steady increase in the number of patients. 2,500 people are confirmed to have been infected in the county, with 342 new Covid cases reported in the past two days. The US Department of Homeland Security's National Operations Center has temporarily moved to an alternate location after an employee tested positive for coronavirus, according to a source familiar with the situation.

I need a source familiar with my situation.

A direction source.

A source of illumination.

I wash my hands, then my face with cold water and my aunt's slippery bar of Dove soap, and look at myself. A toothpaste smudge on the mirror rests like a white feather on my left cheek.

I look the way you'd expect. Like shit.

36.

I walk around to the front of the building to receive my PostMates delivery of four fresh lattes and two chicken burritos.

I receive the plastic bag and the cardboard cup holder from a woman who wears black leggings, a lime green track jacket and a mask with a photo of the lower half of a ginger cat's face printed on it.

As I turn toward the Red Zone/independent living section, a Eternal Home Of Peace Cemetery van like the one that took my aunt away—maybe the same one—rumbles through the Sunny Morning Elder Care Living driveway and into the dimming and Jacaranda petal-strewn street.

37.

The fateful timing of the my creepy-cat masked food delivery means something. Maybe it was destiny blowing a smoky "Surrender Ascher" in my face. Well, not blowing. My aunt explained to me that the sky writing effect in "The Wizard of Oz" had been achieved by a needle injecting black ink in water.

Or maybe I'd surrendered unconditionally already as my continued occupancy in my aunt's—and when the death certificates arrive, my––apartment/condo in the independent living wing of the Sunny Morning Elder Care Red Zone—demonstrate.

The Eternal Home Of Peace death van?

That was a fucking portent. A pointed, concussive kick to my head telling me to give up. To give in.

The mocking, opposite-of-serendipitous, unpeaceful van was what I wished for, wasn't it? A reliable source that turned out to be a ticking directional signal pointing me deathward.

38.

Freddie settles into his bed, stares at the door, then at the spot where the globule was and begins today's somber wait-fest for my aunt.

I lock the apartment/condo door, step through the hallway to the exit.

The blunt man isn't there.

There are no Eternal Home Of Peace or any other vans in the van parking area. I pop the Lexus' trunk and throw the two fat rolls toilet paper I carry inside, lock the car and make a mental note to order some bottled water and protein bars on Amazon Fresh.

A woman on CNN said this is the thing to do during a global pandemic.

So there—I've done it.

Freddie's panicked, high-pitched barking assaults me as I cross the threshold into the hallway—I know the sound of separation panic when I hear it.

I run toward the old, freaked out dog howling behind the avocado door and the places where sunlight meets the wall glow like blood.

38.

"Freddie," I say before the door is even open, "I'm back, kiddo. Calm down, Fredster. I'm here— I will never ever leave you."

The barking ceases the moment I enter the apartment. But Freddie isn't in his bed.

Is he having a seizure?

I step into the kitchen. Freddie is not crouching by his water bowl or hiding under the tiny table. He's not on the green bedspread on the human bed, either. I kneel and look under it, just in case.

"Hey, Freddo," I say and turn to the only other place a grieving dog with epilepsy and separation anxiety might hide in this glorified studio apartment—the bathroom.

"I'm coming in," I warn Freddie," I hear a whine and then snuffling sigh and push the door open.

Freddie's teeth show, his ears are back and he sits inside a shaggy bathroom-rug and toilet paper cocoon.

He growls, but not at me. His wild gaze meets mine for just a second, then returns to the object of his fury.

39.

"Ssshh," I say. "Everything's okay."

It isn't.

The not transparent, not opaque, heavier than mist but the opposite of solid, vibrating slightly as if it has a pulse, fading in and out, there and not there, globe, smudge, light-streak, whitest pearl of blackness, less than shadow, silent alarm and violator of pandemic lockdown protocols that broke into the apartment/condo last night and is camping out in my aunt's cheery and now disorderly bathroom.

I glare at it—hoping to drive it off—but it stays put.

Shit.

40.

Although there are glasses and iced and running water available the kitchen, I swallow the Creamsicle colored Valium tablet dry, wrap the doggie-sedative I found among the bottles of Freddie's pills in cream cheese and give it to him.

I turn up the volume up on CNN to cover the sound of Freddie if he barks again, put my aunt's white sweater—her Arpège-scent is fading—in his bed, place Freddie on top of it, pat his head, then sit on the floor beside him because I've pushed my aunt's chair against the bathroom door.

I wait for the Valium to numb my dread and defang my panic—but my problem is stark and its implications unpleasant.

If the bathroom lurker isn't real, I'm psychotic—which means I'm fucked.

But since Freddie saw it, I'm leaning toward real—which means I'm fucked.

41.

The insistent knock on the door startles me from sleep.

Shit—it's evening wellness check and sandwich drop-off time.

Freddie stays in his bed, his eyes aimed on the bathroom and reflecting the bluish flickers of the television screen.

"One minute," I address to the door. "I just stepped out of the shower. Would you mind coming back in a few minutes?"

"Back in five," the muffled voice says from the hall.

I stand up stiffly and really have to pee. I step warily to the chair, pull it away from the bathroom door, hold my breath and listen.

Nothing.

But there's a hair-thick glimmering filament below the jamb.

I open the bathroom door, but I don't go in because of the faint, folded handkerchief-sized glow oscillating near the ceiling that disappears when I switch on the light.

My pulse beating in my ears—I use the toilet and wash my hands, then turn the light off—and despite not wanting to, I check the ceiling.

The luminous gray thing's glow is weak and emits a lepidopteran sadness.

42.

I receive the sandwich and pass the wellness check. I think fuck it and give Freddie half of the gray roast beef and decomposing cheddarish slice on limp whole wheat. I switch all the lights on before I take Freddie out for his walk. It's uneventful except for his lack of pep and the moment we turned a corner into the shadow of that new condo building under construction when something sort of glowed above and behind Freddie's head.

Did it follow us back onto the locked-down, yet porous Sunny Morning Elder Living Care premises?

I've looked over my shoulder, checked under the bed, every shadow and cranny—whatever that is—but I haven't worked up the courage to turn off the lights.

Maybe I should call Hans. But I learned the hard way that Hans's default settings are less emotionally and/or physically available than my dead aunt's. So I watch the "MayDay: Why Planes Crash" marathon on the Smithsonian channel, and read some articles that might be useful when I join a new burial society—and then I see this–

–

"…The disembodied soul….is now seeing without physical eyes…The Kabballists call this frightening process Kaf HaKela — it is like being thrown with a sling from one end of the world to another."

I think-test the concept by applying it to my parents' and aunt's souls and to those of bodies one, two and three and try to imagine them motion-sick and blindly "seeing" the living world flaring in and out of focus.

What do these bumbling and boomeranging souls seek?

What is their urgent errand? Their message?

By the way, I never loved you.

I loved you more than you can ever know.

Hey you—at least I think it's you—I'm sorry.

You know what? I'm still not sorry. I regret nothing.

I left the hose running in the pool when I died, please turn it off right away.

I had a hair appointment for next week, could you tell them I'm not coming?

The key to the safe deposit box is rolled up in a pair of red wool socks in my drawer.

I'm not who you think I was.

I lied to you. To everyone.

I wasn't a nice person.

I was a crook.

I killed someone.

This is stupid.

I don't need to know what the fresh dead seek for me to do them good or to perform tahara.

But was what I saw on the ceiling my aunt's still striving and disapproving soul—or my grief-fantasy?

I'm left with two staggeringly consequential, personal and embarrassing questions with no one—or no One—to answer them—

If the soul is real—then do I have one? And whose confused, distraught spirit is waiting for me in the bathroom?

43.

It is two A.M. Freddie snores rhythmically into the yellow blanket on the bed on which I've placed the picture of me and my parents at Disneyland and my aunt's silver-framed photo.

I have no photos of bodies one, two or three—so I improvised by putting the Valley Haverim Chevra Kadisha brochure next to three Post Its—with Body One, Body Two and Body Three written on them.

I turn off the crystal lamp and the apartment goes black. I hold my aunt's yellow plastic flashlight, but decide not to turn it on as I open the bathroom door. The luminous object hangs desolately above the yellow floral shower curtain like a chrysalis. "Auntie Evelyn, is that you?" Nothing. Not even a subtle brightening or darkening or tiny flutter.

I try again, more casual this time as if I'm speaking to a barista in Starbucks. "Whoever you are, I've been thinking about your—uh—situation and I'd like to help. But I need to know how. If you're able, please follow me."

I leave the bathroom door open, feel my way to the bed, sit cross-legged next to Freddie embarrassed by and afraid of my foolishness.

44.

Freddie is deep inside a flatulence-inducing dream and my left foot has fallen asleep when a splotch of darkness a few inches above the bedspread reveals itself to be less dark than the rest.

Am I even awake? Is what I'm seeing some sort of satanic Tinker Bell or something worse—a phantom predator escaped from the chaos in my head?

Freddie groans—which I take as a sign that the thing is real—that's how lost I am right now.

Tears fill my wide-open, not-seeing eyes. "I realize I could be totally off," I whisper hoarsely at the smudge. "You are probably just a completely random physics mistake. Or I could be going crazy— and if I am, I apologize for dragging you into my shit. But in case I'm not––I put some pictures and names on the bed on the off chance that one of them might be you."

45.

I've pretzeled myself in the dark so long and my pupils are enlarged enough to make out the faint numbers on my aunt's microwave—3:00A.

What I can't make out is the you-know-what that may or may not be surveilling me.

Is the unidentified winged soul or not-soul still in the building? Or has my presumptuousness driven it away?

I unbend my legs—careful not to bump Freddie—and extend my hands palms-down above the objects on the bed-become-Ouija board. I don't know what I expected, but I see and feel exactly nothing—no thickening or thinning of the darkness, no slight electric charge or change in the air's texture as my palms linger over the Post-Its, the picture of my parents and me, then the photograph of my aunt.

I slide my hands farther into the shadows and pause over the Chevra Kadisha brochure.

Is the darkness slightly cooler here? Maybe.

My palms circle body number one's Post-It, then the one for body number two.

I hold them over the last little square of paper.

A hint of light—well, not even that—something not-dark glints above the third Post It and the air beneath my hands goes from a diaphanous cool to a crystalline cold. A cold like the cold of the sharp, clear, water droplet that splashed into my eye during the tahara that gave me so much trouble—body number three's.

Rachel.

Her name was—is—Rachel.

46.

I was upright and open-eyed for the seven A.M. wellness check. I walked Freddie in the clothes I tried to sleep in—which were the clothes I was wearing yesterday and are the clothes I'm in right now.

I spent the hours between three and six-thirty A.M. awake and in the company of two refrigerated, flat lattes and one question with two variations—

What does Rachel want?

What does Rachel want with me?

Did I mention that Rachel is taking a break? Or maybe she's dissolved permanently into the light of day—or just into The Light. She wasn't able or willing to put me out of my night-time misery by blinking the information I need in Morse Code.

Still, Rachel's distraught and sorrowful vibe was relentless and I'm sure that something in Rachel-World is terribly wrong.

Why she picked me must have been our close proximity to her the tahara room. That she didn't choose one of the more obviously competent others must indicate her disorientation.

I'm confused and flying blind, too. I get it.

But how do I understand an almost-Jane Doe whose full identity and particulars are hidden and maybe unknowable?

So far I've come up with one thing—totally iffy—that I can try.

I order four fresh lattes with two extra shots each and another CPK pizza, then go online and buy a shitload of stuff on Amazon Prime.

47.

The man inside the kiosk barely lifts his eyes from his cell phone long enough to nod toward the parking lot. The cost of overnight delivery of my scrubs, oversized sunglasses and the other stuff I bought was worth it—the blue of my stiff new scrubs is close enough to the House of Sepulchers blue the morticians wore when I saw them on my way to the tahara room.

I know that tahara is performed in the mornings—but because of the high Covid death rate, I waited until almost five to come knowing that a body can come in at any time. I park about ten spaces away from the unmarked House of Sepulchers Memorial Grove lighted mortuary entrance—my aunt's blue Lexus won't be what anyone coming or going sees first.

I have to be back at Sunny Morning Elder Care Living before the seven P.M. check. Sharon can't ever know that I made this visit. I cannot run into anyone from Valley Haverim Chevra Kadisha. But I'll have to risk the presence of a shomer or shomeret and hope that he or she remains behind the closed door while I'm on the premises.

It's not Shabbat so I can't help imagining my former colleagues and my replacement in the tahara room this morning efficiently and without error or panic purifying a female body and softly reciting the Song of Songs— "How beautiful you are, my love, my friend…"

They are not my friends. They do not know my name and I don't know theirs.

Only Sharon knows and she's not permitted to reveal that information. The full name of the deceased is also a secret—burial society members are forbidden to reveal anything about the dead in their care.

Which is why I need to see the mortuary records—which may not work because Rachel is such a common Jewish name. How many Rachels are buried here? How many disembodied Rachel-souls worry in this place?

I need my Rachel's middle and last name to locate her death certificate—a copy of which—I discovered last night—can be purchased online. From that I can find the cause of her death, where Rachel died and exactly when. Knowing who paid for her burial and who requested her tahara might be useful, too, along with an obituary if anyone wrote one. And if Rachel was married, her maiden name could lead me to her husband, her relatives, and maybe to her children.

48.

I turn off the engine and switch from my blue paper Sunny Morning mask to a hard- core N95. I take off my new shades and adjust the neoprene straps of my anti-fog, tinted goggles, tuck my hair inside a yellow surgical cap, kick off my flip flops, put on socks and slip the powder blue booties over my new black medical clogs.

The booties are wrong—the mortuary people wear waterproof ones—but these were all I could get right away.

Once out of the car I walk with my head down and pretend to look at my phone. I stay in the shadow of the building and pass the other two cars in the lot—one must belong to the guard—and carry a cloth Trader Joe's shopping bag over one arm. I found the bag in my aunt's trunk. A new jacket made of sweatshirt material that matches my scrubs spills over the top of the bag and protects my laptop from view.

What if Home Of Sepulchers has updated the entry code since I've been here? The code Sharon gave me—183662—is based on the number eighteen—Chai or "life"—and its multiples, which have special meaning in Judaism.

I enter the number-sequence—there's a soft buzz and the door sighs inward.

Now comes the scary, irrevocable part. I hold my breath, step into the hallway and carefully close the door—visible to anyone leaving or entering the building.

But the doors to the tahara room, the break room, and the two unisex restrooms are closed. The boxes of PPE and the biohazard receptacle for their disposal are where they were when I was last here.

The mortuary office door is slightly ajar, but the interior is dark. Both preparation rooms and two unmarked doors are closed, but muffled music and bluish light bleeds from the beneath the door of Room Two.

My booties silencing my footfalls, I advance toward the office. The aura surrounding the Preparation Room Two door darkens as someone inside approaches it.

I run and almost slip ass-first into the tahara room and pull the door shut just as Harry Styles singing "Watermelon Sugar" spills into the hall and heavy work shoes in waterproof vinyl covers thwap-thwap across the blue resin flooring.

I wanted to be here—but not here. Not in this room or inside this seamless gloom made darker and more airless by my goggles and my mask.

The footsteps stop.

I hear a door open and shut.

I shuffle from the tahara room door to where the stainless-steel table should be and collide with its stubborn coldness. I press my hands on the grooved surface just in case the vertigo and the other stuff that swallowed me the last time I was here try to swallow me again.

The pipes inside the wall behind the sink register a toilet flush and a faucet's whine. A metal trash receptacle rattles, a door opens and clicks closed, and I count twenty-seven weighted footsteps until the radio is muffled once again.

Go, I tell myself.

Coming here was a horrible mistake. A sick joke. A manic overreach.

Who am I to think I can I fix anything for anyone or uncover even a minuscule truth?

The impervious-to-air-and-water and bodily fluids, to-death-and-life, to-mourning-and-joy mortuary table's metallic cold is familiar—it is the piercing chill of Rachel's dead hand in mine.

49.

It felt as though it took forever to leave the tahara room. I was—as I'm sure you've come to expect—the total opposite of brave. But instead of silently hauling ass to the exit door—I skidded into the empty mortuary office where I crouch now.

Whoever is in Preparation Room Two was still preparing someone and still listening to oldies. As I slid by the door, he was atonally singing along to Cyndi Lauper's "True Colors." Though I'd learned that Jewish law forbids cremation and requires a closed, plain wooden casket—I knew from the cemetery box and my parents wishes that many non-observant Jewish families request incineration and ash-scattering, or an open casket in which the body of their loved one must be—as my aunt was—dressed in fancy clothes and subjected to a number of cosmetic procedures. But at least my aunt had avoided the biggest Jewish Death-No-No, embalming.

Jewish law requires that we return to the earth as we arrived at birth–-pure. Not altered. Not fucked with in any way. Plain-clothed. Barefoot. Completely biodegradable and with nothing—nails in a coffin, for instance—that won't become dust.

But I need a little time.

So I hope that whoever is being worked on in Preparation Room Two or his or her family requested the whole forbidden shebang—an ultra-fancy box that needs its handles polished and its sides shined before the ornately prepared and refrigerated body can be casketed on silk pillows just so. A three-piece suit or fancy dress and jacket—complete with socks and lace up shoes or stockings and heels—that require pulling and tugging and the manipulation of many closures, buttons and zippers. A face that needs not just make-up but some serious reconstructing, hair resistant to being coaxed into a public send-off-worthy coif and hands too stiff to fold.

50.

I make it to the office and wait for my eyes to adjust to dimness and for my breathing to slow. Now I bootie-step across the noise-eating industrial carpeting to the biggest desk in the room—Danish modern dark wood in a corner under the only window—the blinds are closed––with a really nice ergonomic adjustable desk chair in front of it facing a large computer screen and keyboard. The glowing screensaver—a golden Star of David—wafts across the screen. I sit in the very comfortable desk chair sideways so I can half-see the door and touch the computer keyboard.

The House Of Sepulchers Memorial Grove log-in screen replaces the screensaver. I take a chance and type in the door code Sharon gave me, but it's two digits short. I add two more eighteens—36—then try more multiples of eighteen, and just eighteen. Nothing works.

I know that after a certain number of attempts the log-in will freeze. I can't have that happen and this is taking too long. I'm sweating so much that my googles fog. The filtered air I breathe inside my mask feels low on oxygen. My gloves make my fingers clumsy. I leave the desk and go to the large metal filing cabinets along one side of the room. They're locked.

I return to the big desk, open the drawers and look for the key to the file cabinet as "London Calling" by the Clash reverberates from the opening door of Preparation Room Number Two.

I step to the almost-shut office door and try to make out the footsteps and their direction, but it's hard to hear through this door. I open it a crack and squint into the hall.

A large navy-blue humanoid shape and the white-vinyl boot covers below it flow past me.

Is he receiving the delivery of a new body? Are more people coming?

No. He'd be heading toward the exit to do that and he's going to the john or to the break room or to whatever is behind the unmarked door. And—I realize—he could also be turning the corner and entering the mortuary lobby—a place I never went to. But why would he? It's after hours.

People die all day and all night—especially now. That's why.

I peek again and see him pause before an unlocked door to what I thought was the refrigerator room or storeroom, unlock it and enter.

Why would he go into the refrigerator room without the body?

I am so out of my depth right now that I'm drowning.

I look at the big desk. The screen-saver has replaced the log-in screen again and the glow of the Star of David dances along the surfaces of the other three desks, the water cooler and the table piled neatly with brochures, and cemetery boxes like the one I got from Eternal Home Of Peace—except these are blue.

I hear a door being closed and more footsteps, then the music dulls.

If I had any luck—which I'm sure I do not—I've just now officially used it up. I give it the nitrile gloved finger and that's when I see it.

A gunmetal gray thumb drive that is just a nugget-shaped shadow in this dimness against the dark wood.

I slide the drive out of the port, kneel on the floor, pull my laptop from my bag, insert the drive into the port—open Finder, open the drive, then copy the files to my computer while listening for the lumbering man to reenter the hall.

I know I'm luck-deficient, but I can't help it—I wait until I think I have all the files, remove the thumb drive, reinsert it in the computer on the desk and—though I know I've already used up any luck I had–-silently count to eighteen and open the door.

51.

I slip into the first of the two unisex restrooms, prevent the door from making noise as it closes, then force the wadded contents of the paper towel holder into the toilet and pull the flush handle. I hope a clog-induced overflow might distract anyone entering the hall as I try to get out.

I pat my bag to make sure my laptop is really there—it is.

I open the door. Music still seeps from Preparation Room Two. The hallway is empty.

The toilet gurgles, the water in the bowl rises over the toilet seat and pools on the tiled floor.

This is it—I tell myself. Run.

52.

I'm driving east on the 101 Freeway and almost to Encino when stopping at the big CVS in Encino that used to be a Barnes and Noble to buy a pair of sweatpants and a sweatshirt and throwing my new scrubs and my mortuary PPE into one of their Dumpsters feels like a smart thing to do.

I exit at Havenhurst and drive into the lot past a row of Dumpsters along the chain-link fence, each trash receptable padlocked shut. Three shirtless men are igniting newspapers and pieces of broken-down cardboard with a blow-torch near below the middle one.

So much for the Dumpster idea.

The Starbucks and the CVS windows are boarded up with "BLACK LIVES MATTER" spray-painted on the boards. I drift inside the sealed Lexus toward the Ralph's market at the other end of the lot and park under a skinny tree. I shove my booties, gloves, clogs, N95 and googles over my laptop in Trader Joe's shopping bag, zip up my blue sweatshirt jacket, brush out my hair, put on my surgical mask and check the rear-view mirror.

With my hair down and wearing the plain surgical mask——if you don't look closely and why would you, especially with everyone distanced six-plus feet away?—I'm a nondescript woman in a navy-blue track suit.

Nothing about me screams mortuary.

I don't need to buy sweatpants or a new sweatshirt. All I have to do now is get to Sunny Morning Elder Care without being stopped by the police, their sirens screaming and lights spinning as they rush to apprehend the file-copier and toilet vandal who just hit—of all places–-a fucking morgue.

It's getting late but I open the drivers' side window and mindfully take in big mouthfuls of the smoky—the fire by the Dumpster is roaring now—crepuscular air and hope my heart rate slows.

One of the men is halfway up the fence and trying to break a branch off the coral tree behind it. A second man carrying a machete in one hand scales the fence one-handed and—as the first man pulls—severs the branch with a clean cut.

The men gracefully join the branch on the ground, make quick work of hacking it into camp-fire sized pieces, then feed them to the flames reddening their sunburned faces.

I'm shaking.

The world is a grotesque dream. And except for Freddie—and maybe Rachel—I'm stuck inside it alone.

53.

I can hear Freddie's howls when I open the hallway door at seven-fifteen.

A sheet of paper taped to the door at eye-level informs me that I have been "declared not present" during this evening's "mandatory" seven P.M. wellness check and sandwich giveaway—which is a "serious violation of quarantine protocols" and caused a spewing of Red Zone red tape and activation of Sunny Morning Elder Care Living resident code violation response procedures and also a noisy pet citation.

The dark clouds of a Sunny Morning Elder Care bureaucratic shit storm have gone from throwing shade to a category four:

"Dear MISS MENDEL"—my aunt's name is printed in black marker in the blank space on the form—"Sunny Morning Elder Care Living Residential Supervisors regret to inform you that you have been deemed absent for the required—"7 PM–again PM is inserted—"wellness check and nutrition delivery…"

The date and time are scribbled in and also a phone number I am to call "IMMEDIATELY."

I fish my laptop out of the Trader Joe's bag and put it on the floor, then take off my jacket, throw it, my scrub pants, the cloth Trader Joe's bag and the rest of the stuff inside it into a trash bag, take a shower, put on my flip-flops, leggings and a different Krakens sweatshirt and walk Freddie. I give him his treat and his meds, order another pizza and more lattes, check that my laptop is still on the floor and take a Valium.

I scratch Freddie behind his ears while we watch some CNN together waiting for my food and coffee delivery, and when Freddie seems calm and the world's machete-sharp edges have worn down, I turn off all the lights and check for Rachel.

54.

Rachel doesn't make herself known right away.

She waits until I've given up on her and for the most inconvenient moment to show herself—during an episode of House Hunters International called "Man-Cave in Managua"—and while I'm lying my ass off to the Sunny Morning Elder Care Night Residential Supervisor, Quarantine Dominatrix and Chief of the Red Zone Pet Police.

I know I should welcome or at least acknowledge Rachel's tentative, grayish, not-radiance manifesting above the refrigerator. But the bitch-voice on the phone barks about "notations of lifestyle guideline infractions in your residence file" that include "loud and unrelenting pet vocalizations" and "inappropriate interior noises." I don't lie when I explain that Freddie is grieving the loss of my aunt, and that fresh disturbances like the new Sunny Morning Elder Care Living industrial vacuum cleaner scare him and trigger his seizures. "Which is a huge disappointment to me," I explain, "since my aunt chose her apartment/condo because of Sunny Morning Elder Care Living's 'pet friendly always' promise. I've already contacted my lawyer regarding this callous breach of the letter and spirit of her contract, and you and your superiors should be hearing from him tomorrow."

I hear crackling, then the yapping resumes. "Residents of nursing homes are required by a County Department of Public Health mandate—which is law—to remain inside the premises and to comply with twice-daily wellness checks. You failed to comply."

"I fell asleep with the television on and while wearing earphones so I did not hear the knock on the door. You can't tell me that this sort of thing doesn't happen all the time. I dare you to swear that the elders in your care don't ever snooze through their wellness checks. Go ahead. I'm waiting."

The light-blur flickers above the refrigerator.

"The automobile registered to your apartment/condo was not in its assigned space at seven P.M., Miss Mendel." Bitch Voice is triumphant. "And I have a cell phone photo with a time stamp to prove it."

Boom.

"I loaned the car to a friend who was kind enough to offer to do some errands for me. Is the car under quarantine, too? Do you need a notarized affidavit from my friend? Maybe time-stamped?"

"You were not present for the wellness check," she growls. "You did not leave a note on the door explaining your failure to comply as directed on page ten of the resident lockdown handbook."

What handbook?

Blah blah fucking blah. Woof.

"I'm here." I say. "I've been here all day. I was here all day yesterday, the day before that and all the days and nights before. I've been here so long I don't know what day it is. I leave only to drive my car so the battery doesn't die, to receive deliveries orders in front of the building, and to walk my aunt's dog —mine now—two times a day. That's allowed, right?"

"In the future. Sunny Morning Elder Care Living would appreciate it, Miss Mendel, if you made yourself available to Sunny Morning nursing staff promptly for all required pre-arranged morning and evening wellness checks and compliance with any and all lockdown and other procedures."

"I'm available now. Why not send someone to check my wellness now?"

"We cannot do that, Miss Mendel," Bitch Voice says. "I'm sorry."

"Okay," I say. "You want to know what I think happened? I think the nurse got distracted and walked past my door, then marked me absent. Maybe it was the end of shift. Or time for a break. But if anyone had actually knocked at my door, the dog would have alerted me. This whole conversation and the bogus notations in my file are incredibly insensitive considering that I just lost my aunt. I'm sure my lawyer will be interested when I tell him about this little chat." I end the call and silently wish my harasser a sunny eternity in Hades.

Despite my bluster, I'm sure that no lawyer—especially the lawyer my aunt mentioned in her note—Zack Something—would be interested in my Sunny Morning Elder Care Living troubles, especially now that new, big yellow Death X appeared three doors down while I was away. And making a pest of myself is a bad idea.

I'm caged in here with the residents in the Covid hot zone, and the night residential supervisor and everyone else who works here is caged, too—and living on contactless-delivery take-out and the Sunny Morning Sandwich diet.

My hands resume shaking, but it's too soon to take more Valium. I wish I hadn't missed that wellness check. It could bite me later on. And if someone at Home of Sepulchers somehow connects me to Valley Haverim Chevra Kadisha and the vandalized restroom—well, I'd be totally fucked.

I'm guilty of trespassing and records-stealing. And sabotaging a toilet. All because of my feeling that the something or someone—who could have been a trick of light or shadow above the refrigerator and who is not there now—is worth the risk.

55.

I turn up the volume of the T.V., wait until the voices lull Freddie to sleep, then put on my flip flops and my mask, tiptoe into the hallway and open the door to the parking lot.

The aproned man in the surgical cap—his eyes are slits—crouches next to the step in the haze of his skunky, aromatic blunt. He nods and I nod back. "You wouldn't by any chance have an extra to sell, would you?"

Two writhing smoke-snakes slide from his nostrils as he produces a joint the way a magician materializes a stunned rabbit or dove—not from a pocket or a mirrored box, but out of the smoky air itself. I hand him the ten-dollar bill I stuck in my sweatshirt pocket and I'm inside in the hallway and back in the apartment in less time than it takes to say "Sunny Morning Elder Sandwich Care—Some Call It Living."

I switch off the lights and look for Rachel, but she's not here. I turn on the crystal lamp,

roll up two of my aunt's yellow towels and stuff them along the bottom of the front door, then seal the edges with masking tape. Standing on the rickety kitchen chair, I tape a gallon bag around the ceiling smoke detector. A book of matches—"The Smoke House Est. 1946"—from my aunt's everything drawer, in my hand—I check on Freddie.

His sleep-breathing is deep and even.

I take the matchbook and joint into the bathroom and check for Rachel behind the shower curtain. Zero again. I, switch on the light, shut the door, stuff another towel along the bottom of the door, turn on the fan and run the shower.

I sit cross-legged on the yellow rug, strike a match, light the joint, close my eyes and inhale.

56.

My courage weed-fortified and my hands steadied, I tear two slices of cold CPK pizza from the box, put them on a paper towel next to the crystal lamp, open my laptop and review the folders and files I stole–
–

- DC RorderFrm.
- GenRelsFrm.
- CoronerLACFrm.
- AuthForDispw/woEmb.
- DisclPre-need.
- DeclDispCremated Rms.
- SCaCremAuth.
- PriceList.
- FnralAttendance.
- VAFlagFrm.
- VAPreNeedElig.
- VAMarker.
- PrayerBk.
- Disc.PreNeedFnrlAgmt.
- VtalStats&Rel.
- PreNdVital&Rels.
- IntrnmtsRcnt.
- Intrnmts6MS.
- ContractsRcnt.
- SupplyOrdrs.
- EmployeeRcrds.
- Invoices.
- Crmatns.
- LicenseRnwl.
- DeathCertRepts.
- AutopsyPprwrk.
- SSSbenefitfrms.
- Unionfrms.

- ChvraKdisha.
- Chapls/Rbbis.
- Flrl. Kinko/FedX.

"Disp" is probably disposition; "Decl" means declaration. "DC" must be death certificate. What is "Rel"? Relative? Why would there be a form for a relative? I take a bite of cold, dry pizza. Maybe "Rel" means "relations" or "release." "C" must mean "County"—L.A. County Coroner form. I don't want that. I'm not interested in cremations. I don't think Rachel was a veteran, so I skip the VA stuff, then click on the "InttrnmtsRecent" folder. I can't figure out "GenRlsFrm" and some the other files in the folder, so I return to "IntrnmtsRcnt "and search for Rachels—

Meyerson, Rahel A.— Close. Is the c missing or is this the name?

Weskinski, Rachael—Not sure.

Faller, Rae E. —I don't know. Long shot.

Zigg, Rachelle—Maybe.

The name used during tahara was her Hebrew name, so I look up variants of the Hebrew—Rachel—means "ewe"—that she might have gone by. Rahel, Rachael, Rae and Rochelle, Rachela and Rachelle are possibles.

I get a cold latte from the refrigerator and check the space above it for you know who——then try to figure out what to do first. Do I go through every file on the drive? There are hundreds. Do I skip the files and check online funeral notices for Rachel and its variants that were posted around the time of her tahara? Jewish law requires burial within twenty-four hours of death, so Rachel would have been buried the afternoon of or the day following her tahara.

57.

I start with an online death-records search for the possible-Rachels I found in "InttrnmtsRecent." I discover for-money records sites, free death indexes, and links to Ancestry and other genealogical and records sites, but the data available stops long before this year's deaths.

My aunt's death certificate still hasn't been issued, or if they have, they haven't been added to the online database or mailed to me. Rachel's would not be handled faster than my aunt's.

I turn on a repeat broadcast of CNN news. A baggy-eyed Chris Cuomo announces from his fancy white basement that sick with a high Covid fever he hallucinated his dead father and shivered so violently he chipped a tooth.

I—fever-free at my last wellness check and who was negative on my pre-Valley Haverim Covid test—return to the files I copied from the thumb drive not knowing if I should hope or fear that soul-Rachel is probably real.

I start with Rachelle Zigg.

It is after midnight when I hear Sara McLachlan is singing "Angel" during that unbearable, endless SPCA commercial featuring abused, thirsty and starving cats and dogs. I kill the T.V., then stand up and stretch. I've read pre-need forms, pre-pre-need forms, authorization to accept or decline embalming forms, burial benefits allowance forms and vital statistics forms—which only at the very bottom of the pages revealed to me—after a long time of not noticing—that these are actually "authority to release remains" forms.

Vital Statistics forms contain all sorts of information about the "decedent" and some about the "informant" who "authorizes the release of the remains of the decedent indicated to Home Of Sepulchers Mortuary and its assignees, and to do everything according to Jewish law… [and] agree[s] there will be no embalming, no autopsy, no public viewing and no cremation…"

Rachelle Zigg—no middle name or nickname—died at 8:23 A.M.

three months prior to the death of the Rachel I seek. Rachelle Zigg was ninety-three, born in Lithuania, had no record of U.S. military service, was a widow, with six years of formal education and her race was Caucasian. So much for hardworking, long-lived Rachelle. I hope she is at peace.

I check Rae E. Faller next—Nope. Rae died five months ago.

Many sections on Rachael Weskinski's Vital Statistics form are blank: Her place of birth is Poland but her middle name, marriage status, her parents' names, and her next of kin are empty boxes. And her "informant" is not an M.D. at a hospital or hospice care center like the others, but an Isaac Kahn whose address is close to hers.

But despite the omissions—what I need to know about Rachael Weskinski is here—Rachael died less than a day before the tahara I helped perform.

I smother my impatience and move to Rahel A. Meyerson's Vital Statistics form to be safe. Rahel died in January—too long ago to be the owner of the soul haunting me.

My heart knocks against my sternum—Rachael Weskinski must be my Rachel.

What happened to trouble her so deeply?

58.

After the morning wellness check—I was behind the avocado door a full two minutes before seven and flung it open at the first footfall I heard—I take Freddie back to the Great Wall to walk, to free myself from Sunny Morning Elder Care Living's gravitational force, and to think.

Freddie examines every pee-bleached patch of dirt, the plastic microwave containers that someone filled with water and left for the squirrels, and lifts his nose into the urine-scent wafting from the squat tents erected along the chain-link fence.

No one followed me here. I backtracked, made some evasive moves and U-turns on the way—but I'm still nervous. And I can see the Lexus parked in a row of empty parking spaces across the flood channel and most of the one-mile walking path around it.

I'm free and I'm alone.

The police have not knocked down the green apartment door. Neither Sharon nor House of Sepulchers Memorial Grove Mortuary has gotten in touch. I'm pretty sure my spectral, angry aunt has departed permanently— though Freddie still watches the door and listens for my aunt's footsteps and the sound of her key in the lock.

And there's been no sad glimmer of Rachael. She might be hunkered down wherever souls go for a break or she might be permanently AWOL. Did Rachael Weskinski's yearning, vacillating soul just want to make sure that someone besides the Isaac Kahn person listed on her Vital Statistics form knew that she once existed?

We've completed the circular path. I lift Freddie into the passenger seat, pour some of my bottled water into a paper cup I saved for this purpose and watch droplets settle on his whiskers. An orphan myself–-I can't pretend I'm not one any longer—I understand Rachael's need to be remembered—if that's what this is about—and would be happy to leave stones at her grave, to burn memorial candles in her memory, and say her name while reading prayers in phonetic Hebrew on the prescribed days.

But why would she pick the only unobservant Jew-atheist in the tahara group? Maybe what Rachael wants is not about memory or prayer.

I don't drive directly to Sunny Morning Elder Care Living. I go south on Coldwater Canyon. During a red light at Ventura Boulevard, I check the rear-view mirror for police officers in plain clothes driving unmarked cars. All I see are drivers in truly plain clothes in a black Range Rover, a dark blue Tesla, a beat-up pick-up truck with ladders in the back, and a white SUV with a child-passenger hypnotized by a cellphone.

The light turns green, but I can't bring myself to turn in the direction of the Red Zone.

I follow Coldwater Canyon as it rises into the hills.

59.

I go east on Sunset, then turn onto Fairfax. After crossing Melrose, I pass burned-out and boarded-up storefronts. I turn into the Farmers' Market, take a ticket from the kiosk and park in one the many empty spaces near the closed fresh fruit shop. I give Freddie more water and a half of a small Milk-Bone, then leash and carry him to the sidewalk.

Freddie trots ahead of me to Third where we wait at the light. The Whole Foods Market is boarded up and the Farmers' Market exteriors are graffitied with black spray paint. As we cross the street, I check the map on my phone screen, keep going past CVS toward Wilshire, then stop so Freddie can examine some fossilized gum at the base of the bus bench before we pass the rust, sky blue and moss green doors of the Park La Brea garden apartments. When the light changes at Harper I lead Freddie briskly past the place I want. I carry Freddie into the 99 Cent Store on Sixth where I buy two more bottles of water, some discount dog treats and a plastic shopping bag, then exit the shop. Freddie I and backtrack north.

I stop and pretend to adjust my flip-flop while checking to see if anyone is following. There are two boys with a basketball, a woman in a green babushka and a floral housedress under her coat and pulling an empty shopping cart. Also some people taking cell phone pictures of a local T.V. reporter doing a live report outside the Whole Foods Market.

I check the address and lead Freddie toward the glowing line on the cell phone map labeled Partridge Place. It's just a short alley no wider than a driveway between a private parking lot and a building with a boarded-up Ramen place on the Fairfax side.

I look around again for the watchers whose smoldering gazes I feel burning into my back.

But no one loiters close to me or stares. No one glances at me or at Freddie. Though I saw some outside Canter's, there are no LAPD officers—traffic, uniformed or plain-clothed—studying my movements. I might as well be on the dark side of the moon—that's how disconnected and invisible I am despite the constant-and-insistent-since-my-illicit-visit-to-House-Of-Sepulchers-Mortuary feeling of being too visible and always seen.

I doubt that my body is capable of casting even a thin shadow at noon. Am I real?

I mean, if no one sees you, are you there?

The filthy sidewalk that sticks to the soles of my flip flops could rumble open and swallow me and Freddie and the world would not register even the tiniest disturbance.

The universe has other problems at the moment and does not give a shit about us.

Well, being a non-presence has its benefits.

I dawdle at the edge of the parking lot and stare. There's a bent restaurant chair near the chain someone has strung across the entrance. The parking spaces are empty except for a white ambulance, a dusty school bus, and three black Kias. I lead Freddie the few steps to Partridge Place and speak into my phone as if I'm answering a call, then pretend to take a selfie with Freddie as I take photo bursts of the ambulance and cars. A swirl of air loosens a cloud of blossoms from the Jacaranda tree beyond the parking lot as I lead Freddie into the alley that is Partridge Place.

Four brown doors—each with its own number—interrupt the building's brown brick wall. The number listed on the Vital Statistics form as Isaac Kahn's Partridge Place Los Angeles, 90036 address is the third door—the one with a faded blue and white decal in the shape of a shield stuck on it and a small, brass mezuzah on the jamb.

After I found Rachael Weskinksy's Vital Statistics form, I checked out Los Angeles Isaac Kahns on Facebook, LinkedIn, Instagram and Google. I can't imagine that any of the Isaac Kahns whose profiles pictures and photos feature cute toddlers and fit wives in pencil skirts and Lululemon yoga outfits live in the windowless room or rooms behind the door off the Partridge Place. Ditto the Isaac Kahns who are lawyers in big firms downtown and in Beverly Hills. The Isaac Kahn realtors and the Isaac Kahn who is a magician at the Magic Castle and does private parties are maybes—the magician might use the windowless space for rehearsals or for private shows, and one of the realtors could be between residences. Maybe one of the two personal trainer-Isaac Kahns uses this space as gym or studio. The Isaac Kahn who's a chef might be okay with this set-up—but the solar-panel installer who works in Simi Valley would never live in the Mid-City.

Freddie lets me know that he's had it by barking as I fake-chat with an imaginary friend on my phone, then he refuses to move past the Ramen place and exerts a surprisingly strong counter-pull to my tug of his leash.

My plan—only formulated when I parked at the Farmers' Market—was to check out the Kahn address, then walk to Rachael Weskinski's address to see for myself where she died and presumably lived. I carry Freddie toward the Lexus wondering why Isaac Kahn lives where he does and why he was the person who released Rachael Weskinski's remains to the House of Sepulchers Mortuary.

60.

Freddie curls up on one of my aunt's yellow towels that I've folded across the passenger seat and his eyes promptly close. My aunt was picky about her car and—as if her return is imminent—I've been trying to keep it clean. I'm dying for a latte, but everything is closed. I decide to do a drive-by of the address for Rachael Weskinski listed on the form, but I drive north on Fairfax first. The heavy sensation that I'm being followed has returned—.

I drive past Canter's, then take Rosewood to La Brea and go east on Third. Seeing Canter's again revives a dormant memory the time my parents received a meal check with a red star printed on it. The star entitled the recipient to a free salami from row of them suspended behind a white-aproned man behind the deli counter. I think I was nine or ten—the memory is hazy and my parents' faces are clouded. More than clouded—the centers of their faces are fuzzy black holes like the ones produced by damaged macula. What can it mean about me and my relationship to my parents that the only sharp, luminous thing I recall is the prize Hebrew National salami—liverish and leathery inside its wrinkled shrink-wrap—being ceremoniously removed from its hook and placed in my father's upturned hands?

The Lexus floats down Third Street as if it is driving itself and everything feels weird. It isn't just the shuttered and gutted businesses, the absence of traffic or George Floyd's agonized face, "BLM" and "I CAN'T BREATHE" painted on walls, sidewalks and pavements. The world is sorrow-deadened, grief-crushed and drained of color like an inside-out garment. The street I want is a block away. I pass it, then double back and slow as I pass the faded, paint-peeling-from-the-white-stucco, two story Art Deco apartment building on Silver Street.

I drive to the end of the block, turn and park around the corner. I open the passenger door and Freddie growls when I try to leash him. I open driver and passenger windows an inch, pat his head, beg him not to bark, and lock the doors.

61.

I feel even more exposed without Freddie. I put in my ear pods and pretend to listen to music and walk on the sidewalk opposite the white apartment building with green trim whose street number matches Rachael's address. There's small "Studio Apt. For Rent" sign in front I didn't see until now.

The street is palm trees, occupied parking spaces, two- and three-story apartments and duplexes built too close together—most of them Spanish style with tile roofs—the top floors of the silvery medical dental buildings on Wilshire visible behind them to the south. An observant Jewish man in a blue surgical mask like mine, a white shirt, a wide-brimmed black hat and with white tzitzit hanging from below the jacket of his black suit strides past me without lifting his eyes. Then a woman wearing the same blue mask, a black beret and a long powder blue, long-sleeved dress and pushes a baby stroller behind him and who must be his wife passes me. I'm sure Freddie would have barked at the stroller and disturbed the child inside it and hope he is sleeping--not barking—inside the car.

I cross the street and stand in front of the white two-story building. Four units are visible in the front and when I step a few paces to the side, I can see that there are four in the back. The two street-facing, ground-level apartments have patios. Hanging and potted plants crowd the patio on the left. Wind chimes tinkle and Reggae floats out of its partially-open sliding doors. The patio on the right side has a dead Ficus in a pot and a chaise longue with a striped beach towel thrown across it. The second story apartments have balconies narrower than, but directly above the ground floor patios. The balcony on the left has a barbecue, a rickety black metal table and one of those rattan hanging chairs they sell at Pier One. The balcony on the right is empty except for a folded aluminum hair leaning against the closed sliding door. Vertical blinds block the view to the interior.

I open the green, port-holed entrance door and enter a small lobby.

There are eight mailboxes on the wall, a hallway leading to the apartments in the rear and a broad, white stone stairway to the second floor. All the mailboxes have embossed plastic labels except a blank one—probably Rachael's. One mailbox has "MGR" above "C. Ruez." I go to the door that matches manager's mailbox number and which is the source of the Reggae and the clink of wind chimes. Despite the note on the door—I knock.

I reread the "Do Not Disturb FRI 7 PM Thru Saturday 7 PM" note while waiting for the occupant to open the door, then realize that it is Saturday and 4 P.M. I knock again anyway, listen for footsteps, and decide on the lie I'll use if and when the door opens. It doesn't. I knock one last time and the door opens.

A copper skinned man with glossy black hair and prominent cheekbones above his black cloth mask furrows his brows at me. "This better be good," he says. "Like a dryer fire. Or a plumbing back-up. Didn't you read my sign?"

"I'm really sorry to bother you," I say. "I am only in L.A. this afternoon and I saw your studio for rent sign and I'm moving here and would really like to see the studio now for just a minute or two, if it's possible."

"I'm closed," the man says. "It's Shabbat."

I wasn't expecting Shabbat. "Could you possibly just give me the key and stay where you are? I'll peek inside and if it's okay and I can write you a check for the first and last month's rent and give you a deposit. I'm beyond desperate for a place."

"Tell me why you're desperate. Make it fast."

"I live in Santa Barbara. Or I did. My aunt got sick and I came to L.A. to take care of her and then she died. I've been living in her apartment in a retirement community with her dog, and I just got a new job. I'm a journalist," I lie. "I need my own place. I saw the sign driving by and—well, that's it. I'm very sorry to disturb your Shabbat."

"I'm sorry about your aunt," he says. "And it's not my Shabbat. I work in a Jewish bakery and Friday sundown to Saturday sundown is my time off. It's twelve hundred a month, plus utilities, plus first and last month's rent and a cleaning deposit—plus a pet fee since you have a dog, and there are forms you'll have to fill out. I'll need some pay stubs, too. And there's only street parking which gets hairy on garbage and street-cleaning days. Still want a look?"

62.

After leading me up the stairs—Rachael must have been in pretty good shape to manage them at her age—the manager unlocks the freshly painted, ivy green door of apartment five. I can smell the paint and Lysol through my mask as I enter a large white room with wood floors. There's an arched opening to a green-tiled galley kitchen and an open glass-handled door to a pink-tiled bathroom with a pedestal sink. The manager opens the vertical blinds and unlocks the sliding door. "It's small, but it's got a balcony."

I step onto the balcony, hold the rough stucco's edge, and look down at the dead Ficus and chaise longue on the rectangular patio below when the patio—with the potted tree and chair upon it—detaches itself from the earth, spins and rises to meet my gaze.

I close my eyes, take a deep, masked breath, and retreat inside. "The balcony has possibilities," I say.

Carlos stops texting. "Yeah," he says. "You could fix it up nice."

I step into an old-fashioned kitchen empty except for a white paint-speckled tomato-shaped plastic oven timer on the green tile counter. As I open and shut the cupboards I wonder if Rachael's vestigial presence caused my dizziness and if I will feel her more strongly in here.

I cradle the whimsical oven timer that must have been Rachael's—and hope to feel some vestige of Rachael's presence.

I don't.

"A lot of cupboard space," I say returning to the living room. "The light is great and there's only one shared wall, right?"

"Right. The couple that lives next door is pretty low key. But they do have a kid. A baby. They're out of town for the weekend."

"I love the high ceilings. Actually, I love the whole place. I feel so lucky that I drove by when I did." I smile behind my mask until eyes are at maximum crinkle.

The manager nods. "I'm Carlos by the way." There's an awkward moment that would have been filled by a handshake and that makes me realize that last human being I've touched was Rachael on the tahara table. "Yeah. It's a nice little unit. The cleaning and the painting were just finished yesterday. It became available kind of suddenly. You are lucky."

"I'm Evie, by the way." I lie. "There's no catch is there? It's not haunted is it?"

"No catch and none of the cleaners or painters reported any paranormal activity. But I guess you should know that there is something pretty sad," Carlos's eyebrows meet in the middle. "Full disclosure—the old lady who lived here died from a really bad fall."

"Wood floors can be slippery," I say. "Especially with area rugs. I always told my aunt to be careful about area rugs." I remember the dark bruising I saw on Rachel's body and feel lightheaded.

"No, not a rug."

"The bathtub?" I lean against the cool Van Gogh swirls in the freshly painted wall.

Carlos slides the balcony door shut, locks it, then tugs the clattering metal blinds closed. "She went off the balcony." He makes a diving motion with his hand.

"You mean she jumped?" It hadn't occurred to me until this moment that Rachael's death could have been a suicide. "That's terrible."

Carlos shrugs. "The police said it was an accident. I think maybe she was standing on her aluminum chair to change the exterior fixture's bulb and the chair gave way."

"Horrible," I say.

"But I don't know," Carlos says. "She kept to herself. She never smiled or said hello. Never let me do anything for her, never let anyone inside the apartment. To be honest, Evie, she wasn't a very nice person. I can't say that any of the tenants miss her."

63.

I find myself inside the Lexus, which must have backed itself into my aunt's parking spot. The trip from Rachael's studio apartment to Sunny Morning Elder Care Living is –blurred–as if I traveled through smoke. Was I followed? I can't recall checking the mirrors or the other cars. All I saw was Rachel's naked, bruised tahara body falling from her balcony to the murderous pavement below, then jerking into reverse and ascending balcony's edge only to plunge again—the repeating soggy slap of body meeting cement the only sound I heard.

Freddie is eager to get out of the car and happy to be leashed. No lunging or snapping. Dazed, I let him pull me around the block and enter the apartment a good hour before the wellness check.

My temperature is normal. I receive two rolls of toilet paper, a roast beef-flavored sandwich and a carton of lime yogurt and I thank the nurse. I feed Freddie his supper, give him a corner of the sandwich and his pills in a ball of cream cheese, cancel the check I wrote to Carlos that I tore from my aunt's checkbook and on which I forged her signature—the bank hasn't received a death certificate yet, so the check was good. I leave a message for Carlos at the number he gave me— "It's Evie. Evie Mendel. I thought it over and I'm sorry, but the idea of living where someone died a horrible death is kind of freaking me out. Thanks again for showing me the place on your day off." I turn off my cell phone, take a Valium and scrub my hands and face with hot water and soap, then put on my thickest sweatshirt and reheat my last latte.

I consider turning off the lights and waiting for Rachael to appear. Instead, I sit in my aunt's chair under the glow of her crystal lamp, wrap myself in her yellow blanket and try to thaw the deep, clarifying chill overtaking me since I learned about Rachael's fall.

I swallow the steaming, flat-foamed latte and listen to Freddie breathe and think about Keats. While doing research on a for-money English paper, I learned that consumptive, death-doomed, never to return home, sleepless, night-sweat drenched-cold Keats would listen to the sleep-breathing of young and healthy travel companion, Joseph Severn.

A doctor, Keats knew too much. He regretted traveling to Rome—the warm climate was believed to be his only hope of recovery, but he knew he would never again see the woman he loved. Keats's time in Rome was an emotional death and severing of worlds. Keats understood finality, that dying meant disappearing, that death was complete undoing. "Here lies one Whose Name was writ in Water," is the epitaph he chose for himself.

Was Rachael sick? Did she know she was dying and chose to hasten her vanishing?

The soul that invaded this small apartment and that summoned me during her tahara belonged to a person who died because she killed herself, because her own reclusive stubbornness caused her fall, or—and though Carlos didn't suggest it—I felt it as a sharp pain inside my skull as the ground below her balcony rose up—the not very nice Rachael Weskinski fell because she was pushed.

64.

After taking possession of the Postmates-delivered four venti lattes and two spicy chicken ramens, I decide to winnow the Isaac Kahns to the one who matters—the one who knew that Rachael Weskinski fell to her death on Silver Street and knew to whom her remains were to be released.

I review my cell phone photographs of Partridge Place, then enter Isaac Kahn's address into Google maps and click Street View.

The photograph was taken before Covid 19. The jacaranda tree is not in bloom and its frothy leaves are yellowed. An unmasked man pushes a flat-tired bicycle toward Wilshire. A female jogger is an elongated blur the foreground. I enlarge the image. There are four SUV's, three compacts, a white pick-up with a ladder in the back, a Volkswagen with a Domino's pizza sign on the roof and a yellow sports car near the entrance. A white ambulance like the one I saw is parked in almost the same spot.

I zoom in on the ambulance, which was photographed from the rear. Below the row of red and white lights, the back doors display a shield outlined in blue with "HATZALAH" in red and beneath that, "EMERGENCY MEDICAL SERVICES" in black above a zig-zagging red heartbeat-line design.

This shield matches the decal I saw on Isaac Kahn's door.

Does Isaac Kahn run a private ambulance or medical transport service out an office behind the brown door? It makes sense that someone working close to Rachael's apartment would have answered an emergency call about her fall.

Who called?

The neighbor upon whose patio she crashed? Probably.

The manager, Carlos? He mentioned police, not EMS.

The person who pushed her?

Someone walking by who saw a human-shaped shadow drop to earth?

Isaac Khan might know some of it. I search "Isaac Kahn Los Angeles Hatzalah" and find nothing. But the Southern California Hatzalah website has photos of ambulances just like the one in the lot.

I learn that Hatzalah means "rescue" in Hebrew. I search some more and learn that volunteer Jewish EMS services use the name all over the world—not just in Southern California. This Hatzalah group operates in the Fairfax district and in North Hollywood seven days a week, twenty-four hours a day and serves the observant Jewish community. I check the "contact" page to find their address—but only a P.O. box in Culver City is listed. There is nothing on their website about Partridge Place.

I add the Hatzalah phone number to my contacts, spread the yellow blanket on the bed and then lift Freddie on top of it, scratch his head until his eyes close, brush my hair, get a fresh mask, touch the Lyft icon on my cell phone screen and type in Isaac Kahn's address.

65.

Though my interactions with the Sunny Morning Elder Care Living wellness checkers have been cool since my blow-up with the resident supervisor, I don't want to attract the wrong kind of attention and be forced to move. It's weird—but my aunt's apartment is a comfort to Freddie and to be honest—having my aunt's things around just as she left them is a comfort to me, too.

Plus, the place is mine and it's where Rachael chose to make herself known.

I have to stay.

And I don't want my aunt's Lexus missing from its parking place, especially at night. Using Lyft means that anyone checking on me will see the Lexus in its assigned parking spot and assume I'm inside Sunny Morning Elder Care Living as snug as a sedated Covid patient on a ventilator and locked down tight with Freddie, my sandwich du jour and the yogurt or the pudding.

I tiptoe out the door and into the empty, ember-red hallway, listen for Freddie—he's quiet—then exit the building—. The blunt man is not here. I sidestep along building, then past the lobby, and wait in the shadow of the construction site as watch the vastly oversized Lyft car's icon jump across the cellphone map. As soon as the silver Camry rounds the corner and slows, I'm opening the back door and sliding into the back seat. As I secure my seatbelt, I look out the window. If there's a Sunny Morning Elder Care Living spy in peach scrubs lurking on the dark, empty street—he or she is a ghost.

My Lyft driver is a henna-ed young woman in a hot pink cloth mask and a multicolored striped sweater that I remember not buying at the GAP because it made me look fat. It still would. The sweater has the opposite effect on her. "Partridge Avenue. Past Third, right?"

"Yep," I say. "It's off Fairfax. A tiny street. I'll let you know when we get close."

"Okay." The driver makes a U-turn then heads south. "Do you

mind the radio?"

It's a Christian rock station. A woman backed by orchestra sings, "Let every lie be silenced and all depression cease. Let every dark assignment bow down at Jesus' feet…" "It's fine," I tell the driver even though it isn't.

I'm proof that lies can't be silenced and that depression can't be permanently stopped or cured——I've been trying and failing to do both since I was twelve.

Laurel Canyon is almost empty, which gives the driver the opportunity to indulge in active vehicular aggression and to show off her tailgating skills. On the sharp curves, the radio praises Jesus and the air-freshener tree hanging from the rear-view mirror swings like a scythe.

I steady my cell phone and enter "Weskinski" and into the Yad Vashem database of Holocaust victims which I hope might lead me to Rachael's relatives. For "Last/Maiden Name" I entered Weskinksy, too. I still don't know if Rachael was ever married. Because of the "ski" suffix, for "Place" I choose "Poland," then click "Search."

The alternating dark and light blue rows of "Victims/Individuals" page fill the screen, above them "Last Name," "First Name," "Birth Year," "Place of Residence," and "Fate" headings. I locate no Rachaels after whom my Rachael might have been named, but I find two Weskinski variants that might be close enough—

Washkinsksi, Mordecai. 1901. Nisko, Poland. murdered.
Weshkinski Ida. 1898. Lwow, Poland. murdered.

Looking up Nisko and Lwow on Google takes me to the Nisko transport, the Nisko Plan, the Lwow Ghetto, the Lwow Pogrom, and then to the Belzec Killing Center:

Bełżec camp guards included German Volksdeutsche and up to 120 former Soviet prisoners of war (mostly Ukrainian) organised into four platoons.[5][25] Following Operation Barbarossa, all of them underwent special training at the Trawniki SS camp division before they were posted as "Hiwis" (German letterword for Hilfswilligen, lit. "those willing to help") in the concentration camps as guards and gas chamber operators.[34] They provided the bulk of Wachmänner collaborators in all major killing sites of the "Final Solution"…The more detailed description of how the gas chambers at Bełżec were managed came in 1945 from Kurt Gerstein, Head of the Technical Disinfection Services who used to deliver Zyklon B to Auschwitz from the company called Degesch during the Holocaust.[37] In his postwar report written at the Rottweil hotel while in the French custody, Gerstein described his visit to Bełżec on 19 or 18 August 1942.[28] He witnessed there the unloading of 45 cattle cars crowded with 6,700 Jews deported from the Lwów Ghetto less than a hundred kilometres away,[38] of whom 1,450 were already dead on arrival from suffocation and thirst. The remaining new arrivals were marched naked in batches to the gas chambers; beaten with whips to squeeze tighter inside.[39]

Hilfswilligen. Technical Disinfection Services. Batches.

The driver makes a hard left onto Hollywood Boulevard after the light has turned red. I shove my cell phone in my pocket and I close my eyes.

Could Rachael have been a Holocaust survivor? Were the murdered Washkinskis—that sounds like a sick trapeze act—her relatives or her parents? I saw no tattoo on Rachael's left arm during her tahara—but I remember from a pricey paper I did—"Genocide in the Twentieth Century: A Definition and a Reckoning"—that only Auschwitz, Birkenau and Monowit indelibly quantified their prisoner/victims. Being a concentration camp survivor might explain Rachael's "not-nice-ness"—her distrust of people and her reclusiveness.

Or maybe Rachael was afraid of something or someone in the present. Maybe a young extermination camp guard settled in L.A. and Rachael—despite all the years since Poland—recognized him. I imagine Rachael—still bruised, since that's the way she was when I saw her—reaching for a quart of milk, then knocking if off the refrigerator shelf as the universe engineers a cosmic convergence and the former Nazi guard—now old and maybe a school bus driver or mail carrier—he's a helper, right?— picks it up for her.

As he hands her the milk carton, the murderer's still air-blue eyes meet Rachael's suspicious gray ones and she registers the horror of who he is and the former guard realizes that this old woman is trouble.

The Lyft driver runs the red light at Santa Monica Boulevard and I tell myself to get a grip. This Nazi-guard-milk-carton thing is pure, ludicrous Lifetime movie bullshit.

I know nothing more about Rachael alive or dead than I did before I got into this car. It is unlikely that a Polish former concentration camp guard knocked the frail, old, and apparently unfriendly woman over her balcony's edge. And if there were such a guard, why would he bother? There are so few Holocaust survivors left that any accusation from Rachael would be her geriatric word against his. Witnesses are dying. Would Rachael have lasted long enough to be threat to a former Nazi or anyone?

The Lyft driver lurches ahead before the light turns green, speeding up Fairfax until she's forced to halt in a line of cars stopped behind a large group of protesters ahead.

I get out of the Camry as the driver suggests that God bless me. Always a liar, I thank her for a great ride, give her a five-star rating and a twenty-five percent tip.

I walk toward Partridge Place and the crowd, reminded that I—suspicious, not-nice and self-isolating—have not had a real, honest, in-person conversation with a living human being in months.

I need to find Isaac Kahn.

66.

"I'm sick and tired of Black people killed for the crime of being Black." A masked and goggled Black man in cranberry pants and a sweatshirt talks into a bullhorn as the protesters—fists raised—march eastward. "I'm sick and tired of being sick and tired. No justice, no peace!"

Stragglers, LAPD officers in riot gear carrying shields, television reporters and camera operators pass through the intersection. "Say their names!" the man's voice reaches me. "Breonna Taylor. George Floyd. Ahmaud Arbery. Elijah McClain. Trayvon Martin…"

I want to join them. I want to shout those names.

I don't.

I cannot speak.

Everything—sky, ground, protesters—is whirling—dissolving.

I make it across Third, sit on the edge of the bus bench and cover my eyes with my cold hands.

I feel the way I felt on the cremation boat, in the tahara room and on Rachael's balcony. I flatten my hands over my face. I lower my mask, breathe, re-mask my face and open my eyes.

The protesters have almost reached La Cienega. The world unblurs and solidifies around them. Horizon and sky return to their previous arrangement.

What just happened?

What the fuck is wrong with me? Since I can't really be sea-sick, am I earth-sick? Do I have Covid?

Maybe I'm just afraid.

Afraid of what, though?

Everything I dreaded might happen has already happened.

Because of me, my parents died in the accident.

I broke up with Hans because of Bree after he broke up with me—because of Bree.

Because of me, my aunt died alone of pneumonia or Covid and/or something else that the never-arriving death certificate will someday explicate.

How can I be afraid when I've already lost everything?

I guess I could lose a limb or my right hand. The Big One could finally finish slouching its way to the greater Los Angeles area and bury me under a high-rise building.

I could go blind. Stop hearing.

I could no longer be able to get or to keep my grip.

I could stay lost forever.

Something bad could happen to Freddie.

My pulse whooshes under my temples.

As soon as I get back to Sunny Morning Elder Care Living, I need to write my will and make sure that if anything happens to me, Freddie will be cared for.

I dig a Valium from the bottom seam of my purse, chew it, wait for its pure bitterness to replace the tablet's no-taste on my tongue, then stand up and turn toward Partridge Place.

67.

It's only a few steps to the Partridge Place. I arrive in front of the boarded ramen place and look for anyone who might be following me, then fake talk into my cell phone while I check out Isaac Kahn's grim brown door and the parking lot.

The chain is coiled on the blacktop. The three dirty black KIAs are filthy. Four news vans—KCAL, KNBC, KNX and KTLA—are parked along the wall under the jacaranda tree. A man wearing earphones, wrap-around mirror shades and a faded-to-pink red Angels baseball cap dozes in the bent chair next to the chain. Maybe he runs the lot or is here to watch the vans.

The ambulance is not in its parking space.

I consider walking to Sixth and back, or returning to the 99 Cent Store. I decide on Sixth and start walking south. If the ambulance is not here when I get back, I'll take it as a sign from an anonymous source that I'm fucking up. Again.

68.

LACMA is being torn down, but Levitated Mass, the three hundred and forty-ton boulder perched above a descending and ascending V-shaped, cement walkway remains and is visible from the street.

An irregular grey blot against the ice-colored street-lights and buildings on Wilshire, the granite hump emerges from the lunar gravel behind the fence I lean against to distance myself from groups of protesters returning to their cars and zigzagging joggers.

I've wanted to see the installation since I did an art history paper comparing it to Magritte's "Le Château des Pyrénées," his painting of a boulder with a castle carved out of its top suspended weightlessly between a clouded blue sky and a dark, turbulent sea. I know from looking at photos and reading about it that the LACMA boulder rests upon gill-like shelves in the walls of the passage—which at its nadir transforms the boulder into crown or cover. A sloping, elongated opened tomb of Jesus with the guardian stone returned, Levitated Mass is an Ozymandian, elegiac joke. At least that's what I wrote. I heard from my annoyed client that the paper had earned an "A"— a huge red flag to his teaching assistant.

Magritte's friend commissioned the painting. He requested a rock––apparently a symbol of hope—floating in a "dominion of light." But a humongous, illumination-obstructing, dead-centered mineral is neither hopeful nor enlightening. The three hundred-plus tons of obdurate, in-your-face, igneous gloom I'm staring at through prison-bar fence is proof.

Magritte's boulder's light-eating density and scale diminish or swallow sea, sky, earth and people. The castle is a hubristic frill atop an unknowable, eradicating thing. Boulders—like Sisyphus' crushingly indifferent and relentlessly encroaching wheel—are always about blotting out—the way death blots out my parents' faces whenever I try to remember what they looked like.

69.

Bucket List update: I have faced-off with the megalith and received the megadose of indifference it was designed to deliver.

Well, fuck me.

My bare feet are numb and dirty in my flip flops as I edge the mini-boulders that are people sleeping under bus benches, against the bases of street lamps and in front of the garden apartments whose windows are golden geometries radiating delicious smells that my mask cannot deflect entirely. Each apartment is a tamper-proof, fenced-in, sealed, two-tiered box of fragrances, voices, movement, food, sensation, touch, arguments, grief and maybe love.

So solitary that my skin tingles—I cross Harper on the red light during a long lull between cars, then walk to the edge of the parking lot.

There it is—the white Hatzalah ambulance, its engine rumbling, brake lights glowing, and back doors opened toward the door to Isaac Kahn's office or apartment.

The only illumination comes from a streetlight halfway down the block, the headlights of passing cars, a sickly LED security light above the corner of the building near the ramen place and the ambulance's headlights bleaching the brown door. I feel as though I'm the only person awake in the world as I tiptoe past the sleeping parking lot man and duck behind the third Kia as the brown door opens. A face-masked and long-bearded man with a stained, white cloth apron over black jeans and black t-shirt, and elbow-high, thick black potholders protecting his hands and forearms carries foil-covered pans to the back of the ambulance. The man wipes his forehead with one of the potholders as he reenters his open doorway. After few seconds, he returns with three more pans and slides them into the back of the ambulance.

Okay. The chef. What's he doing? Taking food to his fellow EMS workers?

Isaac Kahn balances a huge, plastic-wrapped stainless-steel bowl on top of a lidded, rectangular plastic tub with something that looks like chopped salad inside it. He lowers the bowl and salad container into the ambulance, shuts the doors, jogs to his apartment and the brown door thumps shut.

The ambulance's engine is still running—which means that Isaac Kahn is about to drive somewhere with the food.

Do I watch him disappear or try to talk to him now?

70.

I step along the rumbling ambulance until I'm facing the curling Hatzalah decal in the center of Isaac Kahn's pockmarked door. There are four small screw-holes in the jamb, but the mezuzah I saw in the picture is gone

Chef Kahn's peephole gives me the evil eye. There's no bell or buzzer.

I look over my shoulder——no one has entered the parking lot—then make a fist and knock—not hard enough to wake the attendant, I hope—but loud enough to summon Isaac Kahn. The door absorbs the blows, but nothing happens except the arrival of a tall man—surgical mask around his chin, frown hardening into a grimace and his photo IDs bouncing against his blue fleece jacket as he cuts through the alley carrying a video camera, tripod and microphone toward the news vans.

Bad timing. But the photographer glances through me, not at me––stows his gear in the van, gets inside and starts the engine. Maybe I really am invisible.

The lot attendant grunts in his sleep and sirens spin and echo along Wilshire. Using their wail and the ambulance's engine noise as cover, I hit the door hard with both fists and try to bury my dread.

71.

Light surrounds the figure in the doorway—Isaac Kahn is negative man-shaped space bleeding light.

"Yeah?" A not friendly one.

"Excuse me," I say, "Are you Isaac Kahn?"

"Why are you asking?" Isaac Kahn pulls his mask back up and over his forthright nose.

"I'd like to ask you about Rachael Weskinski. I'm her niece. From out of town."

The black hole that is Isaac Kahn's head tilts to the side the way Freddie tilts his. I hope he is not scream-barking or seizing right now.

"Rachael Weskinski," he repeats. "Oh. Her niece?"

"I live in Santa Barbara. Because of the pandemic I didn't get word that she died until this week. I'm Ida."

"I don't have much time, but sure. Come in." Isaac Kahn retreats more than the mandated six-foot distance and motions me through the dusky entryway toward the light—a bendable three-light pole lamp I'm sure I saw on Amazon.com. Isaac Kahn has a slight accent that I can't place.

"In" is a windowless, rectangular space with a polished cement floor, a blue futon and a cluttered, fake wood laminate coffee table on one side. Wire restaurant shelves, a stainless steel work table and two stainless steel carts stand near a deep double sink and huge restaurant stove along the other wall. Oversized stainless-steel bowls and mostly green vegetables are pyramided on the table which isn't that different from the table in the tahara room.

Isaac Kahn has a black ZZ Top beard and obsidian pupils and his feet are sockless inside his rubber clogs. He stands between the wall with the futon and the wall with the kitchen.

"How did you get my name?"

"From the mortuary," I answer—sort of telling the truth. "I'm just trying to find out about my aunt's death. I know she died without family present and for my peace of mind I need to know what happened. Anything you can tell me would help."

Isaac Kahn doesn't suggest that I make myself comfortable on his futon. The chill of the cement floor rises to my ankles like icy water in the hull of a sinking ship. "I'm not an M.D.—I'm an EMS. Your aunt's fall caused serious injuries and trauma to her head."

"Was she alive when you arrived?"

Isaac Kahn strokes his beard before he speaks. "I didn't find her–—I answered a call. And yes, she was alive, but gravely injured. I tried to stabilize her."

"A 911 call?"

"No. Someone called the volunteer medical response group I work with. I was on duty and close to her address, so I took the call."

"Why would someone call you and not 911?"

"I don't know if your aunt requested that Hatzalah be called or not–—she was unconscious when I got there—but usually we get called on Shabbat or on a holiday or when going to the hospital might conflict with a patient's observance of religious law. When language or modesty is an issue."

"So they called you, you found her on the ground injured and unconscious, and you called 911?"

"Yes. Los Angeles Fire Department paramedics arrived about ten minutes after I got there—response times have slowed during Covid. They took her to Masada General. Its E.R. is excellent it's a Level One trauma center." Isaac Kahn looks at the square black Fitbit on his wrist, then folds his arms in front of his chest. "I am truly sorry about your aunt's death. I did everything I could. I'd been called to her apartment a few times before and I knew that she was troubled. But right now I'm running really late."

"Just please tell me how she seemed on the earlier calls and why you didn't you take her in your ambulance to the ER. Then I'll leave. I promise. Oh, and was it a man or woman who called?"

"Your aunt had a couple of panic attacks. She was anxious about something. Sad." Isaac Kahn steps toward the steel prep table. "Moving her after that fall could have injured her more. Paramedics were set up to transport her more safely than I could have alone. And the call came through our dispatcher, so I don't know." Isaac Kahn looks toward the door.

"Thank you very much" I say. "May I ask one last question?"

Isaac Kahn nods as he pulls plastic wrap from an oversized roll and smooths it over a container.

"You're a caterer? What kind?"

"Sort of. I work with another Kosher chef who's waiting for me right now."

72.

The compact car that picked me up in front of the boarded-up Trader Joe's on Third is the color of cement, proceeds at or below the speed limit and stops whenever the light turns red. I sit on the stiff, clear plastic seat-cover that protects the gray upholstered back seat from me and protests if I move. The hunched, barrel-chested Lyft driver leans into the steering wheel as he turns onto Crescent Heights—which he views though bright yellow anti-glare night glasses. The all-news radio station plays at high volume—I try to tune it out.

The gray fabric pockets behind both front seats bulge with plastic bags—the thin, supermarket kind for fruits and vegetables, each folded in half, then folded again and rolled into cylinders secured with rubber bands at each end with one in the middle. I can't tell if the driver is a doomsday prepper, a hoarder who ran out room for bag storage inside his home and uses his vehicle for the overflow, or if these are courtesy bags intended for passengers to use for purposes I do not understand. Car sick bags maybe? Souvenirs? Faux sage smudge purification sticks?

The driver hasn't spoken since he said, "Sunny Morning Elder Care Living." The driver has not unglued his eyes from the sulphurous road ahead and has not once glanced into the rear-view mirror to observe me.

My head is full and I am grateful for his lack of interest.

I found the right Isaac Kahn.

He lives alone. I saw no female clothing on the rack, nothing feminine in the place. But he could be gay and in a relationship with a man who wears clothing the same size as his.

I need to find or speak to the Hatzalah dispatcher.

I have to check out Rachael's neighbors.

Isaac Kahn said Rachael had been anxious "about something." Panicked. Was hers the nameless, shapeless terror that ambushes from the inside out? Or was she scared of something or someone beyond herself?

I could tell Isaac Kahn was being careful about what he disclosed. But he answered my questions and didn't overtalk or over-elaborate––that's what liars often do.

The driver slows to a stop at the red light on Sunset and looks straight ahead, then directs his vehicle northward, only turning his head once to glance at the glowing map on the cellphone in its dashboard holder.

He slows again behind a line of cars at the traffic light by the Canyon Store. The brake lights' radiance transforms the agaves planted along the edge of the road into pinwheeling red sea stars.

I haven't been to the ocean since my parents' ash-scattering at sea.

The light changes, turning starfish to dirt plant.

Whoever called the Hatzalah dispatcher instead of 911 delayed Rachael's arrival at the E.R. She didn't have a chance.

73.

I ask to be let off a block away from Sunny Morning Elder Care Living. I'm not sure where the night supervisor's office is, but suspect it's in the wing where the offices are and where my aunt died.

I don't want her or anyone to see me get out of the car.

"Have a good evening, Miss." The driver addresses his reflection and adds that if I want a "baggie" I can go ahead and take one—just one. I decline his offer, thank him, watch him drive away, then give him five stars, a twenty-percent tip and notice that he's wearing the same yellow-tinted glare deflecting glasses in his Lyft profile photo.

My sweatshirt hood pulled up on my head, I stride past Sunny Morning Elder Care Living's locked lobby, careful to avoid the light-haloes and light-pools above and below their illuminated sign and near the front entrance.

I proceed along the side of the building along the driveway toward the parking lot. It's familiar and dark with only a few steps to go before I'll reach the unmarked door, enter the red hallway and greet Freddie. I unshrug my shoulders and unclench my fists, then pause where the building ends and the dim parking lot begins.

I pause and look around the corner to check if the parking lot is clear. The lot is full. The night is quiet except for the rattle of the Sunny Morning Elder Care Living ventilation units on the roof.

I step forward.

Something cuts off my air and jolts me back into the dark.

74.

A big hand squeezes my left shoulder. Another big hand presses hard over my masked mouth— a ring digs into my bottom lip. I can feel the callouses on the wide thumb pushing down on the bridge of my nose and I smell grease and potato skins.

The hand releases my shoulder, then a thick, muscled forearm hooks me in a chokehold. I lose my flip flops. My heels scrape the driveway as I'm dragged behind a row of shrubs and shoved down in the dirt.

I try to pull the arm off my neck, to scratch the hand smothering me with my fingernails—but there isn't enough air and the darkness is thick.

The man is panting.

Is he going to rape me? Kill me?

Is this strip of dirt along the Sunny Morning Elder Care Living driveway where Freddie likes to take a shit the place my apparently prophetic dread has been taking me since my parents died?

75.

The man leans over me and has me pinned behind the razor-thorned bushes whose new orange berries I only noticed yesterday. He's on his knees—with one hand clamped over my masked mouth and nose, the other pressing my thigh into the cold ground.

"Just stay quiet," he rasps. "Don't move."

I squirm. He pushes harder. I stop squirming.

A car door slams in the parking lot. An engine starts. The leaves and berries and thorns turn white under the headlights as the car turns into the driveway, then rolls past the shrubs. During that moment of illumination, I can only see the low, black sky.

I hear the car turn into the street. The man's hard breathing replaces the car's fading sounds.

He coughs. "I'm sorry Miss." He releases his grip on my thigh and lifts his hand off my mask.

I pull down my mask and gulp air heavy with his sweat. As soon as I catch my breath, I'm going to scream and run—and then call 911.

"I knew she'd see you, so I had to get you out of the way." Something metal clicks, a lighter sparks and ignites. The blunt guy immerses the tip of his cigarette in the blue part of the flame and takes a deep, sucking drag. His eyes are bloodshot. His face looks wet. "Sorry if I was rough or if I scared you, Miss." He looks as if he's about to cry. The hand holding the cigarette wobbles.

"You?" I roll away from the man and the shrub. "What the fuck?"

"I was out in back having a smoke under the break room window. It was open because the super says she hates smells near the microwave. I heard her tell someone that she saw you in front of the building. That she was going to catch you this time in the parking lot and make sure you were kicked out. I just wanted to help you is all."

I slide away from the blunt guy on my ass, facing him as he leans against the thorn bush, his legs stuck out straight in front of him.

"Don't move," I say, "I'm calling the police."

Nothing moves except the smoke spiraling from his nostrils and clouding his face.

I grab a branch and pull myself upright. Thorns dig into my palms and wrists. My heels burn, the seat of my pants feel wet—but I'm up. I slide my cellphone from my pocket. "Try to touch me, or come toward me or think about following me and the SWAT team will be all over you."

I sound like someone in one those cop shows my parents used to watch—totally fucking stupid. What SWAT team am I talking about? Do I even know how to speak in my own voice—or have I lost that, too?

The man sucks his cigarette, suppresses a phlegmy cough and releases more smoke. "I knew your aunt. She was a very nice lady."

My pulse thunders in my ears. I aim my lighted cell phone screen toward him as if it is a weapon or a shield, back away between two thorn bushes, then run—my cold wet ass and my back receiving by what I imagine to be blunt man's deranged and homicidal stare.

The pitted blacktop feels like pins under my bare feet. I look over my shoulder for his big, strangling hands reaching for my neck, but the blunt guy isn't there. I can't pick out his shadow or locate the flaring tip of his cigarette. I reach the place where he sits and smokes, open the door, push it closed and hear Freddie's bark-screams in the hallway. I make it to my avocado door, miraculously locate my key in my pocket, unlock the lock and tell myself that if I ever come back here–—, I will have a deadbolt installed—procedures or no procedures.

Freddie dances in circles around my filthy, bleeding feet. I lift him up, press him against my fluttering heart and kiss his weird little face.

76.

Freddie watched me swallow two dry Valiums and wash them down with water I sucked from the kitchen tap. He urinated by crouching on the pee pad I unfolded for him, then waited on the yellow bathroom rug while I showered.

His black eyes follow my hands as I dab antiseptic cream into the soles of my feet and then slide on a pair of fuzzy thick yellow socks I find in my aunt's drawer. I use most of my aunt's Band-Aid stockpile on my palms and wrists, then comb out my hair, put on clean underwear and leggings, my other KRAKENS hoodie, UGGS, and look in my aunt's secretary for her Sunny Morning Elder Care Living Resident Procedures booklet.

Freddie knew something was wrong when I lurched into the apartment stinking of fear, dirt and the metallic smell of human blood. Now instead of curling up in his dog bed, he jumps into my lap—a first—as I sit in the yellow chair and scan the index of the Procedures Addendum someone slid under the door at the start of lockdown and that I stuck unread in the back of my aunt's Resident Procedures Directory.

- Emergencies
- Fire
- Fire Alarms and Drills
- In-Room Dining
- Lost Keys
- Plumbing Issues
- Sunny Morning Elder Care Living Cares About YOU!
- Wellness Checks, Mandatory Twice Daily
- We're All In This Together!
- Visitors, Prohibited At All Times

The topic I want—Getting The Fuck Out—isn't there, so I turn to page A-6, Emergencies. I consider another Valium but wait because I'll be driving and my head feels like a helium balloon. I wrap the yellow blanket around my shoulders and around Freddie but I can't stop shivering. I pat Freddie's forehead and scan the list.

- In Case of Earthquake
- Kitchen fires
- Medical emergencies—Covid 19
- Power Outage—STAY WHERE YOU ARE!
- Other

I go to "Other" and find it—Family Emergencies/Absences:

"In the event of a family emergency—death or serious illness—residents must inform the Resident Supervisor on duty of any planned emergency absence and, if the absence is approved, resident will not be permitted to return to Sunny Morning Elder Care Living premises without documentation of a negative Covid 19 test taken within the prior twenty-four hours. Please note that all absences may be followed by a required quarantine period up to fourteen days. Absences are discouraged during lockdown and must be approved for the welfare of Sunny Morning Elder Care Living residents."

I can't tell the Resident Supervisor that my parents died—my aunt might have mentioned the car crash to someone here and word could have gotten around. My aunt loved to schmooze and always told the truth. At least I think she did.

77.

I shove a change of clothes, another pair of my aunt's fuzzy socks, some clothes, my toothbrush, my aunt's toothpaste, a bottle of Valium and my laptop into a trash bag, then collect six containers of Freddie's pate, his bottles of medicine, his cream cheese inside a plastic bag in which I put some ice cubes, the box of biodegradable poop bags, his treats, my aunt's sweater—filmed with his dark fur—and his bed into another bag and carry both to the green apartment/condo door.

I open the door inch and peer into the Masque of the Red Death-red hallway. It's empty except for the caution tape X on the creamed spinach door near the fire extinguisher. "Stay," I tell Freddie. He stays as I shut the door and carry the bags to the exit door.

I expect to see You Know Who crouched outside the door and smoking a blunt that—like the Hanukkah miracle—never burns all the way down. I imagine him exhaling through his nose and slightly open mouth, nodding as I carry the bags past him to the Lexus, open the trunk and lift them in—then flexing the muscles of his big hands.

But the blunt man has evaporated.

I reenter the building unmolested. I open the apartment/condo door, pick up Freddie and press him against my chest, the patter of his tiny canine heart slowing my percussive, rushing, human one.

I turn off lights and sit on the carpet facing the refrigerator in case Rachael intends to show herself. There are things I feel I should say in her presence—or to her presence. That I found Isaac Kahn, that I visited her apartment, that I stood on her balcony, that I learned things about her, and that thanks to the blunt guy I almost joined her on the other side.

"Please, Rachael," I say. "I'm trying my best, which I know isn't great. I have to go away overnight or maybe longer. I just wanted you to know."

I decide not to mention Isaac Kahn or her balcony and I wonder if Rachael hears me.

Has she faded into the shadows behind the refrigerator or has she departed to the world of souls? Is she indisposed? Pissed off?

Or does she live inside my head?

The thought burns through me like shame or electricity. I wait for the heat to subside, then turn on the lights, look around the apartment in case I've forgotten something. I turn on the TV and make sure to lock the apartment/condo door once I've leashed him and lead Freddie into the hall.

I'm outside. The blunt guy isn't in his spot. It's just me out here—a shadow carrying two flat-foamed to-go microwaved lattes in the cardboard carrier they were delivered in and following a strangely obliging and eager Freddie toward my aunt's car.

78.

I drive away from the brightening east, away from the blunt guy, the red hallway and all my questions. Freddie dozes on the towel on the passenger seat. My aunt's Lexus is the only vehicle stopped at the red light at the freeway entrance, but I wait for the light to change before proceeding. The sky is charcoal. The navy blue, brown and gray tents erected along the medium smolder like velvet under the street lights. I wait until I pass the 101- 405 interchange and drift past the Sepulveda Basin the flood channel to auto-dial the Sunny Morning Elder Care Living resident supervisor's number, suck up more latte and touch "speaker."

Three rings trill.

If the super-bitch night supervisor who wants to evict me answers, there's not much I can do if she says no. But why should I believe what the blunt guy said? Maybe that car leaving the parking lot saved me from him——and he wasn't saving me from anything. Sure, super bitch, must think I'm a huge pain in the ass—I am. But if I were supervising a place like Sunny Morning Elder Care Living, I'd be grateful to have at least one resident who is under eighty, in good health and doesn't need special assistance during the pandemic.

Two more rings, then crackling and a nasal female voice.

"Night supervisor." She sounds as if she's holding her nose and the two words are a question. But the heavy vocal fry tells me this is not her voice.

"Oh, hi," I singsong, pretending to be relaxed and super friendly. "This is Ascher Lieb from Evelyn Mendel's apartment/condo. Well, it's mine now but I have a problem…"

"How can we help you?" A microwave pings in the background. Is she in the break room the blunt guy mentioned? Maybe heating up this evening's box of Lean Cuisine?

"Unfortunately, I have a family emergency and must be gone from Sunny Morning tonight and part of tomorrow. Or maybe longer. I just don't know yet."

The microwave must have been opened because I hear the door being shut and then rustling. "Oh. Okay. Please hold on one moment while I retrieve your file and get an absence notification form."

She puts me on hold—which means being assaulted by a scratchy loop of Norah Jones's "Sunrise" at full volume on speaker.

Freddie sleeps through the Sunny Morning Elder Care Living unofficial theme song, I sip my latte, and the Lexus sails north on the almost-empty freeway. I think about the lies I'm going to tell the supervisor about my sick boyfriend in Goleta. Should I say fiancé instead? Yes. Fiancé is much better. The relationship it signifies is more profound and my obligation to lovingly care for him despite risking my own health is so much more compelling.

79.

The sky over that hill in Calabasas where someone always erects a huge inflatable pumpkin every October widens—a twenty-five-thousand-mile deep, Covid lockdown, black and blue bruise.

Freddie is awake and panting and I have to pee. Maybe I drank one latte too many.

I take the exit for Whizin's Marketplace.

The parking lot is empty. A big, illuminated sign advertises a "boutique experience" —wine and cheese, pasta, tacos, artisanal chocolate, coffee and pastry, hair spa, barre studio, a shoe store called "Super Souls," and a window display of shabby chic sofas buried under beige and gray pillows and cashmere throws. Like the boutique restrooms I'd hoped were open, the "experience" is locked and dark.

The sign reminds me that I am shabby but not chic—and hungry—I never ate supper and I need more coffee.

Freddie lifts his leg and urinates against a spikey succulent growing out of the cement below the "Market Square" sign. I lift him back into the car, get into the drivers' seat and locate the closest gas station on Google maps—a Shell—on Kanan Road.

After two minutes I see the cool brightness of big, modern station complete with a car wash and a Food Mart with the lights on. I lock Freddie inside the car, put on my mask and jog to the Food Mart door. A small handwritten sign—just a three by five card— taped on the inside says, "SORRY RESTROOMS CLOSED DUE TO COVID." I try the door anyway.

It's locked. Then I knock. I wave my arms. Then I rattle the door again.

Nothing happens. There's no sign of a Food Mart worker or a Food Mart night supervisor among the bright and orderly aisles of snacks, tissues, canned goods, Top Ramen and feminine products.

I look around for a private spot. Visions of the soft white rolls of toilet paper my aunt stowed underneath her bed swim before my eyes.

Because I've been keeping the car super clean in memory of my aunt, I don't think there's even one tissue or napkin in the car. The insistent signals coming from my bladder make me sweat.

I could drive up Kanan Road toward Malibu until the houses disappear, pull into a cutout—bare ass to the wind—and pee off the edge of a cliff.

I get my latte, pat Freddie, lock the car again, dump the coffee, walk to the gas pumps, take a handful of brown paper towels from the dispenser above the windshield sponge, then go around back where plastic crates are stacked against the wall. I pull down my leggings, squat and pee into the cup, throw the cup in a trash, and trot back to the car.

It's only as I turn onto the frontage road that I see the red-haired, mask-less man in royal blue overalls behind the Food Mart door. A port wine stain veils the right side of his face from chin to eyelid and he gapes at me open-mouthed like a fish.

80.

There's a car I don't recognize parked next to Hans's car in the driveway of the Goleta house—a blue Nissan Leaf. And there's a car I recognize—Bree's orange Subaru. I park behind Bree's car—boxing her in because she's parked in my space.

I put on my mask, get out of the Lexus and breathe in the familiar powdery mix of darkness and fog, eucalyptus and salt. I leash Freddie but let him sniff the row of clivia plants I planted until he chooses one to pee on.

If this is where I live? I don't know, but it feels good to be here.

I take the trash bags out of the trunk and lead Freddie along the flagstone path to an unlocked wooden gate, then around the back to the kitchen door. No one ever uses the always-dead-bolted front door of the Goleta house. I never asked Hans why—but no one does.

Walking alone with Freddie in the dark—even here where I know each flagstone by heart—the third one is imprinted with a lacy, fossilized fern—ignites the blunt-guy panic. I put down the bags, find the Valium bottle in my purse and chew one, then lead Freddie past the redwood picnic table, past Hans's barbecue and his smoker, around the avocado tree and the mismatched lawn furniture Hans and I picked up at a garage sale.

I have my house key in my pocket but the kitchen door is always open. Buttery light spills from the window above the sink. I cup my palm over the familiar scuffed brass doorknob and turn it.

81.

The kitchen door is bolted.

I knock and wait for Hans to let me in. The two trash bags deflate at my feet and Freddie strains at the leash toward a fresh skunk smell. Did Hans hear me? It's the middle of the night.

Does Bree and whoever owns the Leaf hear me? And now that I think of it—what about the people whose cars I saw parked on the street?

I imagine Bree on one side of Hans—both naked—and a shadowy human I can't identify—also naked—on the other side in Hans's water bed———and they're not sleeping.

I press my ear to the surface of the kitchen door and hear voices rising and falling. The sulphurous skunk-stink has become insistent. I remember a biology paper I wrote for someone on skunks. The scent of their anal-gland-spray can travel over three miles. And they can spray five times before they run out. Skunks are omnivorous and crepuscular. Well, it's not twilight now. Is this skunk rabid? What if the skunk is here to feed on the too-ripe avocados that accumulate at the base of the big tree in late spring and early summer?

Freddie whines and growls in the direction of the oily, musky smell. I take out my cell phone, go to Favorites and call Hans.

82.

The porch light—a dead-insect-filmed sixty-watt bulb—goes on. The lock clicks, the bolt scrapes.

My heart rat-a-tat-tats when I see Hans, whose new beard and the long hair he's twisted into bun on top of his head gives him a Wooly Willy look. He wraps one of his long-fingered hands around the doorknob, places his other hand against the jamb so that he fills the space between me and the dim kitchen.

What I heard through the door was definitely voices.

I stand on my tiptoes and try to look over Hans' shoulder. All I see are soft yellow blobs of light trembling on the living room ceiling. Candles.

"Are you going to let me join the séance or must the dog and I get totally skunked out here? Can't you smell it?"I chatter, "because if you can't, you might have Covid."

"I smell it," Hans crosses his arms across his chest and spreads his feet apart——a slender Mr. Clean with hair and no earring. "And Covid is a hoax. You do know that, right?"

Jesus, is he serious? "Stop shitting around, Hans," I say. "I need to go inside. I need to pee. I need to talk to you. And I need to sleep in my own bed. I don't feel safe where I've been staying." My voice quavers for real.

"This is a bad time, Ascher."

"I need some stuff from my room."

"It's not your room." Hans blinks. When Hans blinks, he's pissed off. "Your stuff is in the garage. You're welcome to come back and pick up the boxes next week. But please call first. How about Wednesday?"

"I'm paying rent for that room. It's mine." Freddie barks at whatever rustles under the avocado tree.

"I'm sorry Ascher," Hans says. "It's not possible for you to visit right now. If you'd called, I would have told you. We have people here.

We're in the middle of something. And we can't have a stranger and a strange dog disrupting things."

I ignore the "we." "The dog is only a teeny bit strange," I say. "The dog is wonderful. I love this dog. You will, too."

"I won't." Hans puts his hands in his pockets and curls and uncurls the toes of his beautiful right foot. The skunk smell is intense. Freddie whines and tugs at the leash.

"Hans, Please. Just give me fifteen minutes. I drove a long way to talk to you."

"No." Hans blinks again, and his long black eyelashes graze his cheekbones.

"Why not? Why can't I talk to you, Hans?"

"Because you never tell the truth."

My face gets hot. I touch the cool siding to fight my dizziness. "That's not true," I lie.

Hans blinks twice. "Okay. How did your parents die, Ascher? Tell me."

I've invented multiple versions of my parents' deaths. When I was in boarding school, Indonesian rebels murdered my anthropologist/CIA operative parents and the CIA covered up the assassinations. At Sea View Community College and after I'd written a for-pay history paper on the Rosenbergs, my parents were Israeli spies executed by the U.S.A. in secret. No one had heard about it because my parents' espionage convictions and electrocutions had been classified by the National Security Agency as five levels more secret than Top Secret. My mother's heart—like Ethel Rosenberg's at Sing Sing—refused to stop beating despite the three shocks administered in the electric chair and the two additional shocks that were required to kill her. Witnesses reported seeing smoke rise from her scalp when she died. This last, true-of-Ethel-Rosenberg grisly detail reliably rebuffed prying questions.

By the time Hans and I were a thing, I'd riffed on, reinvented, edited and polished the parental-demise-narrative many times and my dead parents had become white-collar, environmentalist whistleblowers in the witness protection program—not boring accountants—whose vengeful fracker-pursuers hunted them down and staged the car accident/murders.

A shrink my aunt made me see in boarding school suggested that these fabricated betrayals, murders and punishments were not about my parents at all—but guilty fantasies enacting the punishments I wished upon myself.

Fucking duh.

"Hans, let me in and I'll tell you the truth." Fat chance, but I'll come up with something.

Hans blinks, then exhales. Freddie pulls on his leash and I notice the dark blue tattoo on the top of Hans' left foot.

"What is that on your foot?"

"A tattoo."

"Of what?"

"An ayahuasca snake mandala."

Hans was not the man-bun, ayahuasca snake mandala tattoo type until now. Though the tattoo is a problem, his hairstyle could just be a Covid-shelter-at-home, no-hair-cut man-bun, couldn't it? "This skunk reeks, Hans. I'm going to pass out. I live here, Hans. I pay rent. Utilities. I paid first and last month's rent and a cleaning deposit. I pay for Wi-Fi and for cable. I've paid your rent—and Bree's—when you guys needed me to. I don't need anyone's permission to go inside. Get out of my fucking way."

83.

Hans watches me as I drag the trash bags and lead Freddie into the gray-tiled, ranch house kitchen which someone has obsessively decluttered. The only objects on the counter are a new, fancy juicer and a plastic, gallon-sized milk container three-quarters full of dark chocolate milk and the stack of red plastic cups next to it.

I release the trash bags to the linoleum floor, pick up Freddie and walk through the arched opening to the living room. Or I try to. Hans skates ahead of me and blocks my way.

"I don't want drama, Ascher. And I told you. We're in the middle of something private and you cannot go in there. Understand?"

"No, I don't." I bend down and try to look through the space between Hans's lets into the living room. "Is it an orgy?"

I see the back of Bree's head. Her long, straight, sun-highlighted hair absorbs the candlelight. She sways over something or someone. Hans presses his legs together.

"Tell me what's happening, Hans. Seriously. Is this an orgy? An all-night CPR class? What's going on?"

Hans reaches for my shoulders with both hands. Freddie lunges at his left ankle.

"He's very protective of me," I tell Hans. Unlike you, I think.

Hans puts his hands on his narrow hips, glances into the living room then back at me and blinks. "Okay, Ascher. You win. I'll give you five minutes. In the game room."

84.

Hans steps through the kitchen to the hall. I follow—still holding Freddie—his fast, little heart tapping against whatever is banging inside my chest.

Hans goes to the fourth door in the hallway and holds it open with the exaggerated politeness of a hotel doorman. It's a black-curtained room he set up for playing and working on video games. Hans rolls the balance ball from under from the height-adjustable desk below three large screens. "No thanks," I say. "Freddie and I will stand." Hans shrugs, and sits on the edge of the black leather couch which has one huge speaker on each side of it. Hans cups his kneecaps with his hands. "A lot of stuff has happened since you left," Hans says.

"Like what?" The skunk smell has joined us in the room.

"Well, Bree and I have shared some profound experiences together. Life-changing."

"Uh oh."

"You knew I'm working with Bree on a new game, right?"

I nod.

"Well, we were building it around ayahuasca visions and archetypes. So, we decided we should try it."

"And it changed your lives, right?" I mock.

"It detoxed our psyches."

"And detoxed the kitchen—I saw."

"Why do you always have to be so mean?" Hans blinks.

I didn't expect Hans to say that—it stings.

"What you're into is a fad, Hans. Like celebrity-vagina-scented candles. I'm sure you and Bree felt something, but you felt it because you wanted to."

"You're wrong, Ascher. Bree and I are vegalistas now. Healers. Ayahuasqueros. In our circles we help people purge their anger and delusions and get in touch with The Mother—you should try it. We can help you."

I ignore the last thing. "So, you and Bree are running ayahuasca circles in out of the living room?"

"Yes. And I asked Bree to marry me and she asked me to marry her."

I knew that was coming—but why now? I hold my breath so I don't cry. Having fiancés Bree and Hans administer a psychedelic that renders me defenseless against my guilt and shame is my nightmare. "Thanks, but no thanks. I'm going to use a bathroom—the one attached to my room—give my dog some water, get some of my stuff, and detox myself of you."

Hans folds his arms across his chest and blinks twice—his blinking has become a tic. Freddie growls at Hans or at the skunk smell congealing in the stuffy room. "We are all one vibration, Ascher," Hans intones. "Plants, stones, people and animals. Past, present and future. The living and the dead. Our ancestors and our future children. Bree and I are going to have four—Earth, Air, Fire and Water—but in Spanish. I really hope that someday you will unburden yourself of your bitterness and lies and die and be reborn like Bree and me."

85.

I liberate one of Hans' and Bree's trash bags from under the kitchen sink and fill it with clothes, books, framed photographs of my parents and my aunt, toiletries and the Valium stash I hid behind the heavy oak estate sale dresser that eluded the declutterer who purged my presence from the house and who must be Bree.

Reborn Hans has blinked his way into the living room to help his shaman wife-to-be enlighten the seekers dressed in white—I snuck a peek—who were puking all over their yoga mats. During our little valedictory chat, Hans gave me the fucking creeps and finished the breaking of my heart which he began months ago.

Freddie's leash in one hand, I drag the bedroom trash bag to the kitchen, tie it and the other two bags together, open the door, and pull the bags over the threshold.

I leave the door wide open as an invitation to the skunk.

I'm halfway down the flagstone walkway when I realize I've forgotten something important, drop the bags and go back with Freddie into the kitchen to get it.

86.

I drive above the speed limit and faster than the flow of traffic until I get to Oxnard, where I park at a combination gas station and truck stop. I get out of the car and open the trunk. The bags are where I put them, holding the plastic half-gallon container steady and upright. I lock the trunk, I put on my mask and take Freddie for a little walk to the edge of a flat black fallow field that begins where the parking lot ends. Freddie opens his mouth to taste ocean, humidity, diesel, exhaust soil, petroleum and scents too subtle for my human nose, then defecates exactly on the border of lot and field and doesn't protest being locked in the car. I enter the glaringly lit mini-mart with a lighted sign for Dunkin' Donuts and coffee and tell myself I'm shaking because I'm starving, exhausted and coffee-deprived—not because of Hans.

The restroom is clean enough. I take off my mask and wash my face, then dry it over the hand dryer which Bride of Frankensteins my hair–—I don't care. I buy two extra-large coffees to which I add sugar and cream, and a box of six assorted which turn out to be four crumb and two jelly doughnuts.

I inhale the jelly doughnuts immediately and give Freddie a little piece of crumb, then sip the shitty coffee as I then fill out the online form, enter my credit card number, and take the screenshots of my health insurance cards required by the twenty-four-hour pharmacy where I have a 4:30 A.M. appointment for a fast, no-contact, drive-up Covid antibody test. If everything works, I will return to Rachael's troubled and unmoored soul and be present for the Sunny Morning Elder Care seven A.M. wellness check fever-free, Covid-negative and with minutes to spare.

That is if the blunt guy isn't waiting for me outside the door.

87.

The blunt guy wasn't here, but his roach was. I thought about finding another way in and out of the premises—but there isn't one and fire doors don't count because they have alarms. I took a cell phone photo of the roach for use in what will be my blunt guy removal campaign, then carried it like a murder hornet into the red hallway and through the green door to the apartment/condo. I return outside—my heart hammering—to get the trash bags and the other thing from the trunk, then lock myself into the apartment.

When I open the green door after hearing the exactly-seven A.M. knock, Freddie is in my arms—I discover a new wellness-checking nurse—an African American man in the required peach scrubs whose eyes fix upon the birds' nest that is my hand-dryer hair. He hands me a paper bag with food in it and a box of tissues. "How are we doing on toilet paper, Ma'am?"

"We could use a few rolls," I lie and wonder why I did since my aunt's toilet tissue hoard is secure and untouched beneath her bed.

The nurse makes a note on his clipboard. "I see that you had an emergency absence for— he reads, "'… fiancé illness.' How's your partner doing? I hope okay now."

"He's stable," I lie. If the psychedelically-reborn and engaged-to-Bree Hans is "stable," then what does that make me?

"Just a reminder that you're now under a fourteen-day, post-absence quarantine inside your condo."

I slide my cell phone from my hoodie's front pouch and find the email from Chrysalis Pharmacy announcing that my negative Covid-19 Rapid Antigen test—which by the way really, really hurt my nasal passages or maybe it was my brain, that's how deep the long swab traveled.

"Do you mind if I take a look at that?" I place my cell phone in his upturned, wide, blue-gloved palm. "I'm Miss Lieb, Miss Mendel's niece. Miss Mendel died."

"I apologize for the mix-up, Ma'am, and I'm very sorry for your loss."

"Thanks."

"The supervisor will need a screenshot of your test results. Just email them to supervisor at sunny morning elder care living dot com." The nurse hands me my phone and points the thermometer at me. "99.6 Normal. You're all set. Until the supervisor approves and updates your file, you will be confined to your condo. But I'm sure that will it only be a couple of hours before you can walk your dog again. Have a sunny day, Ma'am. Oh, and I should be circling back with that toilet tissue you requested very soon."

88.

"You can take your sunny day and shove it," I silently reply and lock the door. Now I can't order Starbucks or California Pizza Kitchen. And I left the crumb doughnuts in the car.

I take screenshots of my Covid test results from the pharmacy—"A negative test result means that proteins from the virus that causes Covid-19 were not found in your sample" and email them to the supervisor.

Freddie stares intently at the door. "Auntie Evelyn isn't coming back," I say. "And I can't walk you right now, Freddie. I'm really sorry."

I put Freddie in his bed, unfold a pad next to it in case he needs to use it, then enter my aunt's tiny galley kitchen and open the freezer which mostly contains Marie Callender's frozen dinners arranged spines-out like books in a chilly rare book library—Fettuccini with Chicken and Broccoli, Country Fried Chicken and Gravy, Slow Roasted Beef Bowl, Roasted Garlic Chicken Bowl, Comfort Bake Vermont White Cheddar Mac and Cheese, White Wine and Butter Shrimp Mac and Cheese Bowl, and Kansas City Style Barbecue Sauce and Chicken Cornbread Pie.

Marie Callender's was my aunt's favorite restaurant. She loved the holiday meals, the huge rectangles of too-sweet, crumbly cornbread, the too-sweet cream pies beneath cumulus mountains of whipped cream and meringue, and the carrot-and-pea-studded viscous chicken pot pies. She always returned from the salad bar with her pyramid of greens and macaroni salad weighed down with kidney beans for protein—which she pronounced "pro-tee-in." Let's just say I was a picky eater and always had cheese burger fries since they didn't offer lamb chops or pizza.

I shut the freezer and open the refrigerator on the off chance I've forgotten that I stocked it with CPK pizzas and Starbucks lattes. I didn't. The paper bag the wellness checker gave me sits forlornly on the middle rack next to an empty Starbucks cup carrier and the plastic container I lifted from the kitchen of the Goleta house.

I take out the milk container, unscrew the top and sniff it.

Jesus fucking Christ.

I'd learned while researching a religious studies paper on psychedelics and spirituality that ayahuasca has a nauseatingly foul taste—but not this foul. I close the container and put it back on the refrigerator shelf. Were the rebirths of the cosmic truth-seekers whom Hans and Bree were supervising stillborn because they couldn't refill their plastic cups with this muck? Did they pay Hans and Bree for their aborted self-realizations, anyway? Or when they demanded their refunds, did Hans promise to make good on his previous promises the way he always did with me?

I take out the paper bag, peel off the white label with my condo number and my aunt's name printed faintly on it and unfold the top. Today's sandwich is egg salad with tiny packets of salt and pepper flattened into the moist white bread, a green apple, a hard-boiled egg even though the sandwich is egg salad, a bag of Sun Chips which don't deserve to be called "chips," and a container of watery orange Jell-o. I take the bag to the tiny table, tear the cellophane off the sandwich, scrape off the egg salad with a spoon, tear off the crust and save some for Freddie, eat the bread, pour the salt and pepper on the egg, try to eat it and gag, eat the Jell-o, then use my aunt's yellow pencil and her long, lined pad of paper with "Shopping List" and daisies printed at the top and make a list—

- Make a will.
- Get deadbolt(s) installed. Can I get Ring? An alarm?
- Buy pepper spray.
- Get blunt guy fired.

I remember the roach, find a baggie, put the roach in and seal it, then wash my hands.

- Dispatcher/Isaac Kahn—follow Kahn to dispatcher? Who called in Rachael's fall?
- Check on death certificates.
- Who are Rachael's neighbors?
- Do something good.

89.

Something in the periphery makes me look up from—I'll say it myself–—my manic list-making.

Freddie drools and quakes, his empty eyes fixed on my aunt's secretary.

I move toward him slowly, then kneel beside him to make sure he doesn't fall. Did I forget his meds? No. I gave them to him in cream cheese first thing, before I stood behind the door and waited for the wellness checker.

Freddie's body relaxes a little, but his blank dark eyes are still aimed at the space below the secretary. I follow his gaze to the grayish glow that is Rachael's unsettled soul.

90.

I've bathed Freddie and wrapped him in one of my aunt's yellow towels and he's in his dog bed.

My cell phone alerts me to a text message from the Sunny Morning Elder Care Resident Supervisor advising me that I will be permitted to leave the premises to walk my dog twice daily and to receive deliveries beginning at noon today and wishing me a sunny you know what.

It's only nine A.M., but I take a Valium, place an Uber Eats order for six venti lattes with extra espresso shots and three CPK barbecue chicken pizzas and specify noon delivery. Have I become a hoarder?

I pull on a fresh KRAKENS hoodie, close the drapes and sit on the carpet cross-legged to face-off with Rachael's presence. "Hi, Rachael," I say. "I'm here. Can you somehow let me know what you want me to do?"

The glow trembles.

"Did you kill yourself, Rachael?" I ask. "Or did something else happen? Did someone hurt you? Is that what this is about?"

Freddie opens his eyes, gazes at the glimmer, growls, then closes them and sleeps.

Rachael's is a weak, sad and desperate light—I feel it. But that's all I see or feel. What does Rachael want? In general and with me? My face gets hot when I think about what I am doing right now—trying to communicate with the soul of a dead woman I never met who is hiding out under my dead aunt's desk and who might have been murdered. Might have.

I go to the kitchen and tear off three blank pages from the shopping list pad, write SUICIDE on one page, MURDER on the next, and OTHER on the last one, carry them to the foot of the secretary and put the three papers on the carpet, the words facing Rachael. This Ouija-board thing worked once—maybe it will work again.

"Rachael," I say. "Can you let me know if any of these three papers is correct?"

I recross my legs. The tiny cuts on the bottoms of my feet sting and itch and my stomach growls every time I think about Hans or Hans and Bree.

My legs start to go numb. Freddie whines in a dream.

The smudge of light vibrates.

91.

The aura or death-shadow or whatever it is skims the surface of the carpet the few inches required to reach the spot directly above the paper marked MURDER and loiters there.

If my extremities hadn't already gone to sleep, they would have turned to ice. "Rachael, are you telling me you were murdered?"

The light-thing haltingly drifts above SUICIDE.

"Which one, Rachael? Did you kill yourself? Is that what happened?"

Rachael's glow moves again—becoming more transparent as it floats between MURDER and SUICIDE, then fizzles out.

Did I doze off and dream Rachael's flame-like presence? Her answers to my questions?

Or is Rachael taunting me? Fucking with me?

It would be a huge helping of cosmic justice for a ghost to lie to a liar—but the universe must have better ways to punish someone like me than by using someone like Rachael.

What if Rachael doesn't remember her death?

Then she could have chosen OTHER. That's why I included OTHER in the first place. To give her an out. A veil but also way to reveal something, but not everything. To afford her some privacy.

So why didn't she choose OTHER?

OTHER would have told me exactly nothing, but would have eliminated MURDER and SUICIDE—and would have made me think that Rachael's death was an accident. And would have freed me from the obligation to uncover the circumstances of her death.

I uncross my legs and rub away the pins and needles, stand, stretch and turn my back on the secretary.

Why is Rachael so evasive? So difficult?

Maybe what Carlos said is true and Rachael—whatever her problems and her sorrows—is just not very nice. Maybe she's selfish––a horrible person who became a horrible soul. Why not? Not everyone is nice.

Or maybe, as the tahara booklet explained, Rachael's soul is anguished. Confused. Lost. Terrified.

I sit down again on the carpet, pick up the pieces of paper, crush them into a ball and toss them toward the kitchen, then scoot close to the secretary. I lower my head until my eyes are opposite the spot where the pathetic little light-veil throbbed a few inches above the carpet.

"I'm trying to reach you, Rachael. I'm really trying—but nothing works." I speak slowly and loudly as if Rachael is deaf or submerged.

"I think you were in trouble and still are. I know you need something from me. And I've been trying to figure out what—but you make it hard. Hans said that I always lie—and maybe I do. Do you want to know why I lie, Rachael? Because people always insist that they want the truth—they demand it. But when you give them truth, they hate it. The truth pisses them off. They say they don't believe it—that you're a liar."

My heart struggles like an animal caught in a trap. "After the accident, I confessed to my aunt that I was the reason my parents died. She became furious and told me I was forbidden to ever say that again. She insisted that the crash was no one's fault. Not my father's—though he was driving. Not my mother's—probably too frozen in fear to take control of the steering wheel. And not the bird's. My aunt actually covered her ears with her hands when I told her why my parents were driving a Rite Aid bag full of Midol, Tampax Junior and period pads on that road that afternoon."

I learned to say what people want to hear—bullshit and lies with bits of truth mixed in. And I got good at it. But I want you to know that I am not bullshitting you, Rachael. That I promise never to lie to you."

"But I'm the reason my parents died. Me. Only me. That must be why I can't see what my parents look like. And my aunt died alone because I didn't hear my phone because I'd taken Valium. And I didn't visit her when I should have. But I'm here now, Rachael. Do you understand?"

92.

Rachael did not to respond—but she didn't flee.

I've begun to wonder if—like ancient starlight that takes millions of light-years to reach earth—Rachael's faint signal from wherever souls go is a distorted and obsolete residue.

And that Rachael is a ghost of a ghost.

I take possession of the handled plastic bags that contain my Uber Eats orders in front of the Sunny Morning Elder Care Lobby two minutes past noon, give the driver five stars and a twenty percent tip, and feel shaky as I enter the ruby hallway even though the blunt guy isn't lurking by the exit door. I take another Valium, eat a third of a lukewarm pizza, then drink the second of my six lattes and walk Freddie.

After the walk, Freddie dozes and I attach the To Do List on the refrigerator with one of the souvenir magnets I gave my aunt and review it. If I really want to help Rachael, I have to find out who called Hatzalah and what they told them.

And even if Rachael evaporates—I need to know what happened when she died. Isaac Kahn is not a generous source of information. Finding the dispatcher is all I have.

93.

I revise my plan slightly and write a short message on a narrow, vertically lined page of my aunt's now dwindling shopping list pad—

"To Whom It May Concern, Sunny Morning Elder Care Living, FYI One of yr. employees smokes weed in the parking lot ALL THE TIME *and dropped this. He also harassed/ assaulted a female resident. Do something."*

I fold the note inside the baggie with the roach, fold the baggie in half and place it in one of the butter yellow Sunny Morning Elder Care envelopes my aunt kept in the secretary, address it, stick one of my aunt's Forever stamps on it, kiss Freddie, turn on CNN, put on my mask and take the envelope with me.

94.

I can't move my aunt's car out of the lot. I don't want to be seen getting into a Lyft near the building. I walk to my aunt's Lexus, then keep moving until I reach the garbage can near the chain link fence that borders the lot and a street of beheaded palm trees and two- and three-story apartment buildings. The fence is too high for me to climb and drop safely to the other side, and a Day-Glo purple bougainvillea with huge, curved thorns has claimed this section of the fence.

I jog around the lot as if I am exercising, slowing my pace when I reach the fence. It's attached to the cinderblock wall on this side of the lot with heavy wires wrapped around metal screws and plates. I trot to the other end, carefully lift a bougainvillea branch out of the way and see that the fence appears to be attached in the same way as the other side, except that here the wires have been cut. I push the fence outward, the wires slide out of the fasteners, and the fence moves about a foot.

Is this how the blunt guy disappeared from the driveway after he knocked me down? If he could exit this way, he can enter this way, too—any time he feels like it.

I run around the perimeter of the parking lot one more time, look over my shoulder, kneel, push the branch out of the way, crawl through the opening, push the fence closed, and—the melted ice-cream colored apartment buildings and murdered trees twirling round me—and consider the implications of my discovery.

95.

I slouch in the driver's seat of a blue Prius I rented from a place in Glendale where I had the Lyft driver drop me. The windows are open because the interior stinks of a psychotically-minty disinfectant. I'm smelling up the No Parking zone and trying to imagine exactly what underlying odor the car rental place is trying and failing to mask or eradicate while parked on Fairfax across from Partridge Place, Isaac Kahn's ambulance and his brown door.

As long as I'm in the car, I'm not breaking the no parking law because I'm not technically parking. I'm waiting.

I'm wearing a fresh blue surgical mask, new black wraparound shades, and a new black hoodie I bought with some truly bad coffee and terrible doughnuts in a 7/11 in North Hollywood. With my hair pulled back I hope I've achieved an unremarkable, androgynous look that doesn't resemble the woman who told Isaac Kahn she was Rachael's niece.

I considered calling the Hatzalah ambulance service and reporting a fake medical emergency at an address close to Isaac Kahn's, but I didn't. Kahn was the opposite of friendly and a hoax call to the ambulance service that could divert him from a real call could get me in serious trouble, could hurt someone and might make a visit to the dispatcher's office impossible.

A platinum-haired mail carrier wearing a hot pink rhinestone bedazzled mask pushes a canvas cart to the mailbox on the corner and unlocks it with a key on a chain despite her five-inch, curving, white glitterized, and ice pick-pointy acrylic nails and reminds me I forgot to mail the envelope with the blunt in it before I got here.

Maybe it's good that I've become forgetful. If the blunt guy is fired and blames me for it, and can still get in and out of Sunny Morning Elder Care through the fence—am I safe?

Was I ever safe?

And if I report the opening in the fence, I forfeit my own private exit and entrance.

A bus that has been transformed into an exhaust-spewing, three-dimensional ad for Family Feud blocks my view of Partridge Place and gridlocks the intersection. I imagine going on the show with my family—my zombified, torched and mangled parents, my dead aunt in her hospital gown with the ventilator still attached—and my dead, bruised, naked Chevra Kadisha acquaintance, Rachael.

96.

The bus groans forward and Isaac Kahn materializes. He's running.

The long chef's apron and the clogs are gone. He's wearing black boots, black jeans, an N95 under a surgical mask, and a reflective yellow safety vest over his black t-shirt. Black must be the uniform. His black baseball cap has the shield logo on the front. "HATZALAH EMT" is printed across the back of his vest in red on a white strip. I could only see the front of the vest for second and it looks like there is something in Hebrew—also in red.

Isaac Kahn unlocks the heavy door to the ambulance and scrambles inside the cab. The red and white emergency lights on the roof spin as he backs out of the parking space and exits the lot to Fairfax and the siren screams.

I tailgate the ambulance through the intersection at Third as the light turns red. Since this is L.A., I'm not the only driver using an emergency vehicle as an excuse to get ahead in traffic. Can Isaac Kahn see me? I'm sure his eyes are on the road or if he does glance into his mirror, he sees a nondescript blue Prius with a nobody driving.

I tail the ambulance through two more red lights, then east on Melrose and as it rumbles onto a street with a Chinese restaurant on the corner. Kahn double parks the ambulance opposite a saffron yellow duplex where a crowd of people—all in masks—has assembled around a prone figure on the plastic lawn.

I pass the ambulance and park in front of a fire hydrant two buildings ahead. I slide down in the drivers' seat and keep my eyes on my rear-view mirror. Kahn—now wearing a shield over his mask—drops from the cab, opens the back doors and pulls out a safety-orange backpack, then speaks into a hand-held radio as he strides to the motionless figure.

Isaac Kahn kneels beside the man on the grass, then waves a masked woman with an auburn wig toward him. Kahn must be speaking to her because she raises and lowers her free hand in response. Her other hand is curled around the hand of a toddler with payot—long, curled sideburns worn by some observant Jewish men and boys. An old, bearded man in a long-sleeved white shirt, a kippah and tzizit kneels next to Isaac Kahn, nods, then joins the woman and boy and speaks into a cell phone.

Isaac Kahn leans over the man, then his wide shoulders and the safety vest bob up and down—he's started CPR.

97.

Isaac Kahn pumps the man's chest. I stop counting pushes when he reaches six hundred and an LAFD paramedics ambulance arrives and the paramedics take over.

Did Isaac Kahn perform cardiopulmonary resuscitation on Rachael? Did it fail? If he did, it would explain some of the bruising on her breastbone and her chest.

Isaac Kahn watches a paramedic attach AED paddles to the man's chest. Black circles darken the armpits of his shirt.

I must have been holding my breath. Why else would I feel like my lungs are full of lead? I swallow the Valium I slid in my pocket and take a sip of bottled water as two LAFD paramedics and Isaac Kahn tilts the man on his side and slides him on a yellow back board, then onto the LAFD gurney. Kahn holds the bag to the I.V. someone has started as the gurney is rolled to the red LAFD ambulance. Then Isaac Kahn steadies the woman in the wig—the old man holds the boy's hand now—as she climbs into the back of the LAFD ambulance to join the stricken man.

98.

Is Isaac Kahn speaking Yiddish or Hebrew to the old man as the LAFD ambulance wails down the street? He pats the boy's head and walks to his ambulance.

The little boy points, the old man speaks and Isaac Kahn turns back, lifts the boy in his arms, places him inside the cab and climbs in the ambulance with him.

The lights spin. The siren squeals. Behind the windshield, the boy's small face is awash with light and wonder.

99.

I follow Isaac Kahn's ambulance to a mikvah—a Jewish ritual bath—on Pico Boulevard. A sign posted on the door says, "Closed During Covid." Kahn knocks, is admitted by a person I can't see, and after a few minutes exits the building. Then he drives the ambulance—lights and siren on—with me two car-lengths behind—to a convalescent home next to a kosher Ethiopian restaurant. He returns to the ambulance with his orange backpack and Styrofoam take-out container.

Isaac Kahn is backing the ambulance into a parking space in a lot behind a two-story brick office building on La Brea.

When Isaac Kahn's boots meet the pavement, he's not wearing the bright yellow safety Hatzalah vest or baseball cap—I see the edge of his black kippah when he pushes a bell or buzzer at the unmarked door at the back of building, then pulls it open and enters.

I'm not quick to get out of the Prius—I parked behind a Dumpster across the street—and can't reach the door before it closes—so I don't try. I pull the hoodie lower on my forehead and get out of the rental car holding my cell phone in front of my face. I walk cross the street and around the corner to the front entrance.

The glass windows on both sides of the entrance have been boarded up as have all the windows on the first floor. A red and white For Rent sign like the ones hardware stores sell is duct taped to one of the boards—with "SM. OFFICE" added in black marker. There is a sudden cessation of movement and sound—no foot traffic—just the wheeze of a bus and hiss of traffic a few streets over. This place feels like a movie set—realistic—not real.

I touch one of the bricks in the wall expecting to feel cardboard, but the surface surprises me by being brick. I push one side of the boarded door and it creaks inward.

The small lobby is dim because of the boarded windows. It's empty and the over-conditioned air is freezing. The floor is some sort of shiny—and this time actually fake—brick. There's a door with STAIRS stenciled on it and one with "PARKING" —in a brownish-green shiny paint. A framed faded Chagall poster for an exhibition in nineteen-ninety hangs askew on one pale green wall. On the other wall there's a laminated list of the building's occupants typed under the word "DIRECTORY" —

R. Klein, CPA, Schwartz Laser Center Hair Removal, Joseph Feller, CPA, R. Cohen, Ph.D.—a psychologist, probably. M. Frankel, Esq.—a lawyer. P. Robbins, Estate Planning——P. Robbins is just another CPA. More Esquires and CPAs. A by-appointment-only wedding dress tailor. A Tay-Sachs disease awareness group. Something called Israel Life and something called HOLA.

I feel at home in the lobby of this dead, soundless hive. My parents' accounting office was in a building like this one—so bland and featureless you could walk past it daily and never notice it between the tropical fish store with its illuminated tanks in the front window and Charlie's shoe repair with the neon spike heels sign. Whenever I entered the lobby of the building my parents' office was in, the air conditioning's pulsations consumed every other sound. I couldn't hear myself breathe or think.

The psychologist my aunt made me see after my parents' deaths had an office in the same kind of place. Nondescript is too flamboyant a word for the somber number-pushing, contract-drafting and strangled and tearful interrogations that go on behind the closed doors of asphyxiating buildings like this.

During tax season I'd spend after school hours and weekends in my parents' office and in their building's hallways. Once my homework was completed or I lied that I'd finished it, I could do what I wanted as long as I was quiet. I photocopied my hands, my face, my hair, my ass. I punched holes in discarded sheets of paper until I had piles of confetti. I made microwave brownies and blender smoothies in the tiny office kitchenette. I tried to skateboard across the carpeted hallway. I triggered the building's sprinkler and alarm systems when—despite the legible warning not to painted on it—I opened the fire door to the gravel-covered roof where I hoped to feed the pigeons.

I try to remember the disappointment on my parents' faces after the roof thing—the sprinklers destroyed a number of tax statements they'd prepared and some of their office equipment——but although I can conjure the smell and feel of their office—a mix of instant coffee, fluorescence, the orange and rose of Coco by Chanel my mother always dabbed behind her ears—the gray chairs, the laminate desks, the gray file cabinets, the packages of paper stacked on a shelf, the stack of gray folders they'd put the completed taxes in—I cannot see them. Two fateful, surreal and annihilating erasures have established themselves in the frigid office air and float exactly where my parents' faces, shoulders and necks should be.

100.

Unless Isaac Kahn is here to file a lawsuit, get fitted for a wedding dress, have hair removed, raise awareness of Tay Sachs disease, do something or other for Israel or file his taxes, I think he's visiting HOLA—not "hello" in Spanish—but an acronym for Hatzalah of Los Angeles. And if I'm lucky—and I'm usually not—this is where the dispatcher works.

Boots thump down the stairs. My choices are the door to the parking lot or an unmarked door on my left.

I run to the unmarked door and turn the knob. It's a dusty closet for janitorial supplies. I squeeze in next to a bucket-and-wringer combo on wheels, and pull the door almost-closed.

A narrow slice of the lobby is visible through the opening and then a sliver of Isaac Kahn moving.

I pull off my hoodie and my cap and stuff them behind the industrial vacuum cleaner, smooth my long-sleeved white shirt, and open the closet door. The lobby is dead empty. I check the directory for HOLA's office number—eighteen—I should have guessed. I climb the stairs to the second floor.

Brown-flecked, sound-absorbent industrial carpeting greets me. The only decoration in the anemic green hallway is a fire extinguisher in a glass case and a plastic sign next to it with a stick figure running down a ziggurat. I find eighteen. There is no HOLA sign—there's nothing except a peephole. I run my fingers through my hair and turn the knob. Like every door I try to open lately, it's locked.

101.

I smile behind my mask at the peephole and knock. I hear the non-sound of air moving in a closed room, a metallic rattle, a crackle, and then a female voice.

"Can I help you?"

"Yes," I say. "May I please come in? I need to speak with you."

The peephole goes black. I smile harder so my eyes look friendly and my eyebrows are in an unthreatening alignment with my invisible mouth.

The door opens a few inches. My face hurts from smiling, but I keep at it.

A short, round, middle-aged woman wearing a wireless, one-ear headset and a pair of reading glasses suspended on a fake gold chain looks me up and down. Her mask matches the floral snood that covers her hair.

"Is this the Hatzalah of Los Angeles office?"

"And if it is?" Her words carry the trace of a Russian accent.

"I've tried to call. To locate you." I try to sound desperate, but harmless. "I live out of town. My aunt died and I wasn't with her. The last person to see her alive was a Hatzalah volunteer. I just have a few questions I hope you or that volunteer can answer. I really need your help."

The woman's shoulders do not relax inside her long-sleeved white turtleneck and the black vest she wears that matches her almost-ankle length skirt.

"What is your name?"

I falter—unable to remember for a moment which false name I gave Isaac Kahn. Then it comes to me— "Ida," I say. "Ida. I'm Rachael Weskinski's niece."

The woman doesn't react to Rachael's name. She doesn't blink. She makes sure to block my view inside the office. She does not open the door. She touches her earphone with one finger and holds the forefinger of her other hand over her mask to indicate silence.

"I'm very sorry for your loss," she says after a moment. "But all our work is confidential. And I'm getting a call. May your aunt's memory be a blessing."

The woman pushes the door closed. As she does, I hear her say, "Hatzalah of Los Angeles, what is your emergency?" And I hear the lock turn.

102.

I travel the narrow, carpeted hallway past the the fire alarm and suppress the impulse to break the glass and press where indicated, then descend the stairs two at a time, and enter the lobby empty of souls except for the ones belonging to the dark-eyed figures frozen in the faded sky of the Chagall poster. I am halfway out the entrance door when I remember that I left my hoodie and my hat in the utility closet.

The building is a mausoleum. I don't bother looking over my shoulder as I backtrack to the closet or before I open the closet door–—there's no one here to see me. I could do cartwheels if I felt like it. I could clatter around the place on my old skateboard and hardly dent the stupefied silence.

I open the door to the utility closet, step inside and bend down to retrieve the balled-up hoodie and the cap on the floor behind the upright vacuum. My hand locates my cap when the pressure of a hand on my back shocks me forward and I lose my balance.

103.

I don't tumble against the coiled black cord wound around the side of the industrial vacuum cleaner because the hand that pushed me decides to pull me upright.

"I'm sorry for scaring you." The voice that belongs to the hand has a trace of an accent. It's Isaac Kahn.

I don't speak—I reach for my hoodie and my cap, and pull the hoodie over my head. My pulse pounds beneath my scalp.

Isaac Khan backs away from the closet until he's in front of the Chagall poster, the figures flying right above his kippah. Despite the lobby's chill, his forehead is flushed and his body language is a big fuck you.

I don't know what to say and I don't want to inflame his anger—so I stand still.

"The way it's supposed to work is that I apologize for startling you, then you apologize for stalking me. And lying."

I shake my head. But that's all I do.

Isaac Kahn steps a few paces toward me. "Who the hell are you, anyway? What's your scam? Or are you just crazy?" His accent isn't Russian like the woman's upstairs—I still can't figure it out.

I have to respond. "I'm sorry. I really am." I step out of the closet, pivot toward the door marked "Parking," push it open and run.

104.

I guess I should tell you that I'm not a graceful runner—I'm not a graceful anything. So when I say I "ran," don't imagine a lithe, lean, muscular blur. Picture a brown-haired young woman whose head is too small and whose ass is too big clunking across the parking lot past the Hatzalah ambulance, onto the sidewalk and across the street to the Dumpster and her rental car.

I make it the driver's seat without Isaac Kahn's hand finding me and pulling me down. I lock the doors, start the engine, pull down my mask, eat the Valium I stuck in my pocket just in case—gulp the air despite the sickly slow-motion mint explosion that is the car's interior, slide on my new shades and drive north on La Brea.

There isn't enough oxygen. My heart gallops. But I promise myself I won't pass out—I can't. Not here. The green light sallows to yellow, then red. I take another long breath, exhale slowly and remind myself that Isaac Kahn can never find me. He will never figure out who I am or know how Rachael led me to him.

I saw what Isaac Kahn does. He's a man who through his own exertion and with his own breath heaves the dead from the underworld's abyss—from wherever death is taking them—and returns them to life. He retrieved a man from nothingness right there on the fake grass. I saw him do it. And if he could have done that for Rachael, I would not be here now, I would not have known her battered and in-need-of-purification body or her troubled soul.

What would have happened if someone like Isaac Kahn had saved my parents?

I'd know what their faces look like—that's what.

I have nothing to worry about.

Isaac Kahn will never enter the locked-down premises of Sunny Morning Elder Care Living and find my green door and kick it open. Well maybe he could—if someone in the Red Zone calls Hatzalah—but that's unlikely. The website was clear—his group works in Los

Angeles and North Hollywood—not where Burbank bleeds into Glendale, not where every goddamned, day is sunny.

A bus advertising a personal injury lawyer whose phone number is "WIPLASH" cuts in front of me. I take this as an admonition to slow down, to breathe, to focus on the road.

What if the blunt man is there when I go in?

I erase the image of him crouching by the hallway door and smoking a joint and try to locate the siren that's loud enough to penetrate the closed windows and getting louder.

105.

I turn left on Santa Monica and south on Highland, consider stopping at Trejo's Coffee and Donuts, but keep going. I have to get back to Freddie, to take him for a walk, give him his meds, feed him and think.

Four mask-less, shirtless teenaged boys on Bird scooters roll silently between cars as the siren's' wail bounces from one unforgiving surface to another—high-rise glass to metal to concrete to pavement—disorienting and impossible to locate.

I follow the slowing traffic up Highland toward Hollywood Boulevard and the siren—alternating with the buzz of an electronic horn—moves with me. Where's the accident? The fire? The ambulance transporting a Covid patient gasping for breath? The water main break? The colorless, odorless gas leak? The suspicious package or malevolent, abandoned backpack? Who was robbed? Carjacked? Murdered in daylight for no good reason?

I turn on the all-news all radio station, listen to the freeway reports and wait for the news update the announcer promises to deliver on the hour. And I wonder why I'm interested in what happens to people from whom I'm so separate and so severed—I am light-years—or maybe darkness-years—away from them.

I mean if light travels, then darkness must travel, too. I can feel it.

The siren is close. I check the rear-view mirror and see flashing red and white lights approaching about five cars back, weaving between lanes, and swerving until the emergency vehicle is right behind me.

It's white.

And Isaac Kahn is driving.

106.

The Hatzalah ambulance——lights flaring, siren screaming—but without the horn——pursues me up Highland. I cross Fountain as the light changes but Isaac Kahn roars through the intersection right behind me.

I see the Fat Sal's sign in the small, L-shaped strip mall, swing the Prius in and then out of the lot and back onto Highland and cut off a UPS truck.

I'm three cars ahead of Isaac Kahn's ambulance.

The UPS driver gives me the finger. I shrug into my rear-view mirror, grateful that his truck obscures Kahn's view. I turn right at DeLongpre, left at Seward and am looking for a break in traffic before turning onto Sunset when I hear the siren yowl again.

I slide the Prius between a black SUV and a white pick-up, hoping the SUV is tall enough to be all that Isaac Kahn sees if he followed me onto Sunset.

Shit. There he is.

Drivers pull over and stop for the ambulance. One of them is the white pick-up which swerves in front of me as it moves toward the curb. I drive straight into it with a hard thud.

Isaac Kahn's ambulance roars up next to my car.

The truck and the ambulance have me trapped.

The pick-up driver—mask-less and sunburned under his red MAGA hat—throws his door open, removes something from under his seat, inspects the gash my car's bumper made in the side of pick-up, takes a cell phone photo of the damage, then marches toward me. His pink nostrils flare as he raises a black-handled machete above his head.

107.

I lock my car and hunch down in the drivers' seat.

Isaac Kahn's black shirt and his reflective yellow emergency vest fill my window "Drop your weapon," Isaac Kahn shouts to the man. "Stay where you are," he tells me. "The police are on the way."

Isaac Kahn steps toward the man with the machete. The man looks Kahn up and down. He doesn't lower his weapon but he stays where he is.

Isaac Kahn retreats and raps on my window with a gloved knuckle. I cover my face with my hands.

"Are you experiencing pain?" He asks. "You're lucky the air bag didn't deploy. But you'll still need a cervical collar. But right now keep doing what you're doing—stay inside your vehicle until the police arrive."

Is he fucking kidding? Does he think I'd let him collar me? This accident is all his fault.

Was he trying to get me maimed? Killed?

The truck guy moves machete to his other hand and flushes as if he is under a sun lamp.

Siren whooping, an LAPD black and white rolls beside the white truck. The door opens and a female officer in a surgical mask—her dishwater blond hair gathered in a scrunchy—crouches behind it and points her gun at the truck driver.

"Drop your weapon!"

The truck driver hate-stares at me, his beet-colored nostrils widening into perfect O's, then surrenders the machete to the pavement.

"That bitch right there? She ran into me! I was just defending myself. I still have the right to self-defense, don't I, Ma'am?" His "Ma'am" is sarcastic. "You are violating my civil and federal rights. I want to make a citizen's arrest."

"On your knees. Hands in the air where I can see them! Now!"

The driver shrugs, then complies with the officer's demands as if this isn't the first time he's received these instructions. The officer sidesteps around her car door, kicks the machete out of the man's reach with one jab of a shiny black shoe, then yanks truck driver's raised hands downward and cuffs his wrists behind his back.

Traffic is backing up. I hear honking and can make out some of the profanities being shouted in my direction. A helicopter's blades churn in the vertical distance and more sirens wail.

Will the police-woman believe me if I tell her Isaac Kahn was chasing me and that he caused the accident?

Isaac Kahn taps on my drivers' window, a plastic blue and white neck brace under one arm.

108.

The officer slides her gun into its holster, then Mirandizes the truck driver as she —hustles him to the back of the police car. She does not shield his head as he slides inside and the skull inside his red hat thunks against the roof. She pulls a surgical mask from her pocket with gloved hands, pulls the mask over his face, fits the loops around his pink ears and shuts the door.

The officer returns to the machete, picks it up daintily by the handle, places it in the trunk of the car, then strides to Isaac Kahn.

I lower the window an inch.

"Hatzalah of L.A." Isaac Kahn points to the I.D. badge on his lanyard. "I was in the area and saw the accident so I stopped."

You didn't see the accident, you caused it.

The police officer presses closer to my window than the Covid six-foot limit. "Are you injured, Miss?"

Isaac Kahn is looking at me and stroking his beard. The policewoman will never believe me if I tell her what he did. I just need to get out of here.

"I'm fine. Just shaken up. That truck guy cut right in front of me. And he was speeding. Then he started road-raging with the knife."

"He won't be doing that again for a while," the officer says. "You're incredibly lucky the EMS happened to be here and can check you out. Make sure to contact your insurer within the next twenty-four hours. Are you able to move your car or do you need help?"

A tow truck arrives behind Isaac Kahn's ambulance. Kahn climbs into the cab, stares at me, then rumbles around the corner and stops––red lights still flashing as if to signal his anger.

The tow truck moves close to the white truck.

The police officer halts traffic. I back up, then maneuver past the white truck and the tow truck. I turn where Kahn did and park ahead of his ambulance despite the urge to keep going.

I can't make the police officer suspicious. And what lie would Kahn tell the police-woman if I told her what he did?

I stay in the car. Isaac Kahn appears at my window again. I lower it just enough for him to hear me clearly. "Just pretend to do what you have to do and let me go." I'm sweating and some sort of electric current vibrates through me. But I can't take another Valium until I find one and Isaac Kahn and his fucking ambulance have gone away.

109.

Isaac Kahn insists that I get out of the car.

His gloved hands circle my neck, then palpate the soft tissue under my jaw. He presses my trachea, lifts my hair and feels behind my ears. His fingers feel reptilian—neither hot nor cold and with a patterned texture.

For months I've longed for a human touch—but this creep-fest is not what I had in mind.

Isaac Kahn presses the base of my skull. "Does that hurt?"

"No. I told you—nothing hurts. Now will you let me leave?" I lean against the front of his ambulance. It's warm.

"Did you lose consciousness at any time during or after the accident?"

"No."

"Do you have a headache? Have you suffered any visual disturbances?"

"No and no."

"Any neck stiffness? A dull pain in your head?"

Isaac Kahn says it is necessary to check my ears with an otoscope. "I'm looking for discharge," he explains.

He slides a penlight from his vest pocket and aims it into my eyes. "I'm assessing pupillary size, reactivity to light and movement. Now, close your eyes as tightly as you can."

I close my eyes and a wave of dizziness hits me, but the ambulance keeps me from swaying.

"Raise and lower your eyebrows, then pull down your mask and give me a big smile."

"Stop," I say. "If you don't stop, I'm going to scream." Can I outrun him? Not now—probably not ever.

"I'm checking for facial asymmetry, a symptom of damage to a cranial nerve," Isaac Kahn says. "Please. Take off your mask and smile."

I pull my surgical mask below my chin, show Isaac Kahn my teeth, then mask myself again. This is getting scary.

"Beautiful," Isaac Kahn says. "You're normocephalic and atraumatic."

Nothing about me is beautiful and he knows it. Isaac Kahn is not content with invading my person. Now he's mocking me.

"Any medications that you take regularly?"

"Well, the pill. And Valium sometimes for anxiety, but that's it." Why did I answer his question? Why did I sort of tell him the truth?

"Now tell me your name, what day of the week it is and who is president of the United States."

"Tuesday. Hillary Clinton."

"You forgot to tell me your name."

"No, I didn't. You already know my name." How long is this weird as fuck exam going to take? And what does he plan to do to me after he's finished?

"Tell me your name?" Isaac Kahn runs his gloved fingers through his beard.

I look past him up the street. A gardener operating a gas leaf blower channels a pile of leaves and swirls of gray dust into the gutter. He won't hear me if I call to him. He won't hear me if I scream. So how do I end this? Maybe cooperating and humoring Isaac Kahn will accomplish that. "My name is the same as before. Ida. Ida Weskinski."

"Your real name." Isaac Kahn strokes his beard again. His black pupils get shiny. "I know that's not your name. That can't be your name."

"Sorry. That's my name."

"Rachael Weskinski lost her whole family in Poland during the Holocaust. Her sister and her brothers." Isaac Kahn puts a gloved hand on my shoulder. "She didn't have a niece." Anger sparks in his eyes. "We will circle back to that later."

"Later." Jesus Christ. And what does he mean by "circle back?" Who talks like that?

Isaac Kahn takes a small foil packet from a one of his vest pockets, tears it open and unfolds the alcohol wipe that was inside. He rubs the wipe against the chest-piece of the stethoscope his neck, then inserts the ear tips into his ears. "I'm going to listen your heart."

110.

Isaac Kahn pulls the neck of my hoodie down about an inch and slides the cool chest-piece to a spot above the place I always thought my heart occupied—then slides the chest-piece out.

Isaac Kahn tilts his head. "How are you feeling?"

One of Magritte's boulders has just dropped from the sky and landed on my chest. Flattened—that's how I'm feeling.

"Fine," I say. "I really need to go. I'm late for something." The boulder doesn't roll away. It has placed itself exactly where Isaac Kahn lightly placed the chest-piece of his stethoscope. I can't believe how much I'm sweating, or that all this sweat doesn't dislodge the suffocating rock. "Please. I have to go."

"Not before I check your pulse." Isaac Kahn takes my right hand, turns it over and presses two snake-skinned fingers against my wrist.

"Your heartbeat's a little fast." Isaac Kahn studies my face. "Well, very fast. A normal rate is sixty to a hundred beats a minute. Your heart is beating two hundred beats a minute. You're in Afib. Atrial fibrillation—your atrial chambers are beating in an abnormal rhythm. You said you take Valium. Too much diazepam can affect cardiac rhythm. How much do you take? Did you take any today?"

"Very little. None today."

"I am going to transport you to the ER. You'll be lying down in my ambulance, and that will help lower your heart rate until you receive IV meds that will restore normal rhythm. Tell them about the diazepam. And you need to make a follow-up appointment with a cardiologist. You may require blood thinners and arrythmia medications. Afib can lead to stroke."

I know that Isaac Kahn is lying. I'm anxious and I'm scared—that's all that's wrong. And the Afib thing is just a scam to get me inside his ambulance. How stupid does he think I am? I've seen hundreds of commercials for Afib medications on CNN, and all they show are ancient, white-haired people with walkers. No way is my heart too fast. No way is there a blood clot swimming toward my brain to paralyze me. Isaac Kahn is a psycho. All I need is a Valium and to get out of here.

"I do not have Afib," I say quietly. "I have anxiety. Panic attacks. And I'm not getting in your ambulance. If you try to force me to, I'm going to fucking scream."

"What are you anxious about, Ida?" Isaac Khan is deeply concerned. "If you are in an abusive relationship, tell me. I'm a mandated reporter."

Complying with his demands is just stretching this out, so I switch to resistance. "Yeah. I'm in an abusive relationship—with you. Did you forget tailgating me in your ambulance? Causing an accident? No wonder my heart rate is high. Go report that, why don't you? Report yourself."

"I'm deeply sorry that I lost my temper. That was completely wrong. But I had to speak with you and the only way to do that was to follow your car."

Isaac Kahn's eyes lose their angry glitter. "Ida, if there's something or someone you're afraid of, you really should tell me."

"I'm afraid of car accidents. I'm afraid of Covid. I'm afraid of lots of things." Maybe because I feel like I'm in a high-speed blender and my heart feels like it might burst that I include some truth-nuggets. "I'm afraid of you and afraid of whatever happened to Rachael Weskinski. Since you're so big on taking turns, what are you afraid of?"

Isaac Kahn strokes his beard with his Blue Man Group-blue fingers. I realize it's a tell—Isaac Kahn reaches for his beard when he's wound-up. "I'm afraid of having my business shut down and losing everything I've worked for." He pats the pristine surface of the ambulance. "All because of you and the sick game you're playing."

111.

Darkness presses on my shoulders like a weighted blanket. My knees are elastic. Isaac Kahn cannot see that I'm breathing the too-thin air open-mouthed inside my mask. Or that his ambulance props me up as he receives a call on his portable radio.

I step beyond the ambulance and push my way through gray Jell-o to my car—which seems to be a mile or two from where I left it. A powdery, moon-colored haze distorts distances. The now whitish-blue Prius is smaller than I remember it, too. I feel blood rushing and retreating inside me. I hear my heart rumble the way you hear an ocean in a shell.

Maybe this is what dying is—the world cocoons around you and dissolves.

I do not die. I reach my rental car and Isaac Kahn's ambulance growls toward me, siren and lights activated, but he doesn't pull over.

As his ambulance passes my car, Isaac Kahn's eyes meet mine. And then he looks away.

The Prius' hood is scratched and flecked with the MAGA truck's white paint. I find the keys, open the door, sink into the driver's seat, lock the car, search my purse for an emergency Valium, can't find one, pull my mask down to breathe and sip water from the bottle the rental guy gave me.

I open the window and wait until the wail of Isaac Kahn's ambulance diminishes to silence.

I close the window, slide the driver's seat forward, climb into the back, pull my hoodie over my head and stretch out on my back across the seat.

112.

I open my eyes to the minty stink, yellow light and mostly mask-less faces—none of which belong to Isaac Kahn.

The faces are pushed against the car's side windows¬. The windshield is how the yellow glow gets in.

One of the faces is gaunt and shadowed with a blue-black beard and has a bandage across the left eyebrow. Another belongs to a woman in a white on black VOTE mask that has slipped beneath the nostrils of her ringed nose. Her short hair must be white because it is the same color as the light. There's a blue teardrop tattooed under one wide, greenish eye. She pulls her mask below her chin and shouts, "Should we call 911? Are you all right?"

No. They should not call 911.

I push myself up into a seated position, wait to see if the boulder is planning to crush me again, remember that I rented this car, that I had a fender bender, that Isaac Kahn tried to run me off the road, gave me a freaky "exam," and that he said my heart beats too fast. I shake my head no and yell, "I'm fine! I was sleeping!" Then I rest my cheek on my hands to pantomime napping. The woman nods and relinquishes her spot at the window and see the source of the yellow-ness is an LED street light.

"Honey, you don't look good." A grandmotherly African American face with a floral cloth mask taps the window and speaks loudly. "Just unlock the car and we can help you out."

"I'm okay," I mouth. "Thank you, though."

"Everybody thought you were dead," a brown-haired, acne-blotched, grinning teen-aged boy face hollers, "You looked like you croaked for sure. Just like a corpse." The boy's face disappears then reappears floating above the sidewalk above an electric, one-wheeled skateboard.

"I appreciate your concern, but I'm fine," I yell this time, my face hot as I slide close to the window and open it a crack. "I'm okay. Really. I worked a double shift and was too tired to drive. But I'm rested now. So, thank you and I'll be on my way." I push the button and close the window as a signal to my would-be rescuers that the party's over. And I remember to smile behind my mask.

Two holdouts stare doubtfully into the car's interior, then—disappointed that I'm not a corpse—turn away from the car and scatter.

I pull my cellphone from my pocket—6:24 P.M. Shit.

How many hours has Freddie been locked in the apartment waiting for me to return?

How will I make it back for the 7 P.M. check?

113.

I collapse into the driver's seat and place my palm on chest. It feels like something is bubbling in there—which doesn't mean anything that Isaac Kahn said is true. I was anxious about something real—him—and as always, I freaked out about freaking out.

I can't leave the rental car parked here—. I can't call a Lyft or an Uber.

What I have to do to reach Freddie is make it to Sunset, then over Laurel Canyon—then onto the 134 Freeway and exit a few blocks from Sunny Morning Elder Care Living—a drive I know by heart.

Forget my heart. Though I'm sure Isaac Kahn was just trying to intimidate me—I've always suspected that I am defective in a structural way.

I sip more water, make sure the headlights are on even though it's not yet twilight, activate the turn signal, look over my shoulder for Isaac Kahn's ambulance and oncoming cars, and pull away from the curb. The kid who said I looked like a corpse sails past me on his skateboard going south this time and waves.

114.

I white-knuckle my way to the street of headless palms. I find a prime parking spot a few spaces from the Sunny Morning Elder Care Living parking lot fence. The plunging sun is too-bright, menacing and hideous—an igneous migraine-trigger and degenerator of the macula.

I pull my mask up, put on the black cap, lock the Prius and walk as fast as I can—not fast—to the fence, then push it hard. I'm spent. Hollowed out. But I have to get into the lot, cross it, enter the building and inside the apartment/condo in the next three minutes—and I need the wellness checker to have not shown up early.

The fence opens when I push it. I crawl through. Bougainvillea thorns scratch my hands as I pull it closed. I keep my head down as I crisscross between parked cars to the unmarked door where the blunt guy is not threateningly crouching or smoking or loitering. The sunset has orange-d the building and heated the doorknob and the surface of the metal door.

Another moment and I'm inside the hallway's rosy coolness. No wellness checker is lying in wait. No PPE-d paramedics are removing another resident from the premises. No masked and gloved janitor is affixing yellow caution tape to the victim's apartment/condo door. It is so quiet I wonder if the residents have been sedated. I locate my key, unlock the door, and open it to a twirling, leaping, joyfully drooling Freddie.

115.

My temperature is ninety-nine—technically normal but barely acceptable to this evening's wellness spy—I hate the word, "wellness." Why not just say "health"? The interrogator this time was a new, weary-looking, tall, large-jointed man with mutton chop sideburns and inked forearms much longer than the sleeves of his peach scrubs. I fed him the reliable lie I was warm because I'd been out running. He looked me over. Though not in running clothes, I was sweaty and disheveled. He made a note on his chart, then presented my paper bag––a reconstituted ham and Velveeta sandwich on wet Hawaiian bread, a toddler-sized container of butterscotch pudding and a bruised peach—and told me to call the night supervisor immediately if my temperature climbed higher or I if I developed myalgia, a headache, loss of my sense of smell or taste, or difficulty breathing.

I want to turn off all the lights, ignore Rachael if she's present, get in bed with Freddie and stay there for a week. Instead I swallow a diazepam, give Freddie a corner of the sandwich, medicate and feed him and give him a treat, then hold my end of the leash as he trots ahead of me along the sidewalk in front of the shuttered Sunny Morning Elder Care Living lobby and around the block.

If someone in a supervisorial position inside the building sees me walking my dog, good. I'm doing what I am permitted—under the extraordinary circumstances—to do. I'm where I'm supposed to be. There's nothing weird or structurally flawed about dutiful and compliant Sunny Morning Elder Care resident and occasional jogger, Ascher Lieb.

Nothing weird at all.

116.

Freddie inhales his post-walk treat and dozes on his back in his dog bed. He's exhausted, which makes me wonder if he stared at the door and worried during the too many hours that I was gone.

I strike a match from the Smoke House matchbook and light the wick of the glass Yahrzeit memorial candle—the one I ordered on Amazon with the pepper spray. I know that I am not using the candle in the traditional way—on the anniversary of a death—but place the candle in a dish and carry it to the secretary. I'm also violating the strict no-candle Sunny Morning Elder Care Living rule. I don't remember the memorial prayer I'm supposed to recite—and I'm too tired to look it up, so I just close my eyes, feel dizzy, open them again after a second and silently wish Rachael well.

Then I look through the mail that I've let pile up on the floor near the door and search for my aunt's death certificate. It has not arrived. Then I turn off the lights and sit in the yellow chair.

I hope the candle will encourage Rachael to appear. I have now-or-never stuff to tell her and questions that require full and clarifying answers.

What the fuck is up with Isaac Kahn? Did he help Rachael? Did he harm her?

And the moment has come to remind Rachael that if I fail to accomplish whatever she's selected me to do—and it's pretty obvious that I will fail—especially since the void between death and life seems too huge for me to reach her or for her to reach me.

I need to remind Rachael that she is safe and sheltered.

That whatever hurt her has been washed away.

That she is forever untouchable and untouched.

Pure.

117.

Rachael does not stir. She's gone full Bartleby the Scrivener and has chosen not to

respond to my telepathic pleas.

I heat up my last, very flat latte in the microwave, put my laptop on the unmade bed, lift Freddie and the yellow blanket next to me, tell myself again that Isaac Kahn can't ever find me and will never know my real name, then get to work on item one on my to-do list.

I find a free online template to download, create my own document and begin to fill in the blanks:

California Last Will and Testament of Ascher Lieb. Pursuant to the California Probate Code. I, Ascher Lieb, resident in the city of Burbank, County of Los Angeles, State of California, being of sound mind, not acting under duress or undue influence, and fully understanding the nature and extent of all my property and the disposition thereof, do hereby make, publish and declare this document to be my Last Will and Testament, and hereby revoke any and all other wills and codicils heretofore made by me.

Expenses and Taxes

I direct that all my debts, and expenses for my last illness, funeral and burial be paid as soon after my death as may be reasonably convenient, and I hereby authorize my Personal Representative, hereinafter appointed, to settle and discharge, in his or her absolute discretion, any claims made against my estate.

I further direct that my Personal Representative shall pay out of my estate any and all inheritance taxes payable by reason of my death in respect of all items included in the computation of such taxes, whether passing under this Will or otherwise. Said taxes shall be paid by my Personal Representative as if such taxes were my debts without recovery of any part of such tax payments from anyone who receives any item included in such computation.

But there are no headings under which I can include the things that are the whole point of the document—at least for me. A request for tahara—but not through Valley Haverim Chevra Kadisha—a shomeret, and a traditional Jewish funeral before I'm planted beside my aunt.

There is also no place in which I can describe Freddie's physical, psychological and medical requirements, outline his daily schedule and food/treat preferences or where I can explain why I am bequeathing my estate to him—which means that he will continue to live in his current residence in the Sunny Morning Elder Care Living apartment/condo which he will inherit. I haven't worked out the caretaker part yet.

I also need room to explain that when Freddie dies—I will specify that he must not be permitted to suffer or to die alone—the proceeds of the sale of the condo and any money in what will be his estate left after funding his cremation, funeral and burial—in that really nice pet cemetery on a hill in Calabasas and with some of some of his ashes reserved for scattering over my aunt's grave and mine—will go the dog rescue group that saved him.

Am I the only person in California who has no "Personal Representative"?

My parents' accountant would probably agree to represent me for a fee—but he doesn't feel like the right choice. I also don't have a trio of beneficiaries. I only have one—Mr. Freddie Mendel, Canine. I don't have witnesses—nowhere on the EasyWill website or in the will template does it suggest that a confused soul or a dog who is also a beneficiary is permitted to witness a legal document in the state of California.

The trip to Goleta—the eviction Hans didn't bother to tell me about and his rushing me off the premises—couldn't have been more educational. The blank spaces in the document signify the holes in my life—are proof that I, Ascher Lieb——did you know that Lieb means love? What a joke—has zero fucking friends or lovers.

There's not one person I'd invite to hang out at my deathbed other than Freddie if Isaac Kahn isn't lying about my goddamned heart.

I had friends and boyfriends before my parents died, in boarding school and in college—but once I met Hans and after I fell in Lieb with him—Hans was the turbulent center around which I—clingy orphan—circulated in a too-tight orbit.

My family died with my aunt. Without my aunt's memories

colorizing and completing my impressions—all is fog. And my parents' absences just get bigger and emptier.

My mother has or had—they are probably dead by now, too—twin older cousins in Detroit I only met once when they visited us on their way to Sea World—two bald men in identical brown suits and black bow ties who finished each other's sentences. My father was estranged from his family for reasons he refused to share but which I got the feeling had to do with his brother, his mother and money.

I have no human beneficiaries upon whom I can bestow anything. Not love. Not money. Not even a pretty good impersonated paper or application essay for free.

I have no witness-possibles except Rachael's mute glow and a few of the wellness checkers who might remember me clearly enough to verify that I existed before my unfortunate and untimely demise blah blah blah.

I have no colleagues, no co-workers, no associates, or as my aunt told me the Disney Company describes their employees, no fellow "cast members." I no longer have my fake paper gig or my journalism "job." My address is not my own. What I have are a bunch of satisfied dishonest, lazy former papers-for-money clients and a padded, out-of-date, heavy on spin LinkedIn profile with a heavily Photoshopped photo.

Freddie observes me as if he comprehends my anguish. His expression is so direct and so intensely knowing that I would not be surprised if he understood its source.

Freddie pushes his damp nose against my hand, a signal for me to resume stroking his head.

Why wouldn't Freddie understand how I feel or why? He's been alone and afraid. He's loved my aunt and lost her. And he knows what it feels like when your body betrays you.

118.

I copy what I've written and paste it into a new document—The Last Will and Testament of Ascher Lieb1—and date it.

I list what I own—my aunt's Lexus, her apartment/condo, a half-used up trust fund, my aunt's possessions, her investments, her insurance policies and the burial plot she bought me. I add "Miscellaneous" to cover my computer, books and clothes and conclude with the accountant's name and phone number.

Then I write about what I want when I die—tahara, shomeret, traditional Jewish burial, an eternity in the cemetery overlooking Burbank with my aunt—and everything Freddie requires to stay happy here in the apartment/condo. I include a list of his medications and the name, address and regular and emergency phone number of his vet.

But who will be Freddie's guardian if—like a pearl in an oyster—the blood in a chamber of my heart coagulates and travels like a bullet to my brain?

I couldn't resist doing a little research and found out about atrial fibrillation and stroke.

Who will walk Freddie, talk to him, turn on the T.V. for him and hold him when he seizes? I leave the part about Freddie's guardian and the percentage of my estate that will go to her or him blank and tell myself that I'll circle back to that later.

Why did I just use that phrase?

"Circle back" is what Isaac Kahn said.

119.

What the fuck is up with Isaac Kahn?

Is he a monster?

Did he harm Rachael? Or did he help her?

Why did Rachael choose me?

What if there's no time to circle back? To accomplish what Rachael needs? To receive my aunt's death certificate and discover the cause of her departure?

What if it's too late for friends?

Well, Isaac Kahn is only half-wrong and my problem is not my heart—it's my soul.

There is no circular approach. There is no "later." There's no direct or indirect anything that will transport me where I must go.

My family is all ghosts. All I dream about are the dead.

I don't need an approach—I need an improvised incendiary time machine. And if I can't get that, it would be helpful if I had a third eye in my forehead and a couple of past-gazing eyes in the back of my skull.

I need a way into the underworld—to the place the psalm in the tahara booklet calls Sheol, pit, destruction, abyss. Not Hell exactly—I looked it up. But not heaven, either. It's the "place of darkness to which the dead go," a "Land of Forgetfulness" —a hang out—where, "under some circumstances [the dead] are thought to be able to be contacted by the living."

I want to apologize to my parents and ask them some questions. I need to memorize their profiles and the contours of their faces—no matter how much death has changed them.

It is necessary also that I ask my aunt to forgive me and tell her I love her and that we say our goodbyes.

I have to find out if dogs are welcome in the afterworld—and if not, where they go.

I need to speak with Rachael—having a translator would be

optimal—but I'm pretty sure that's not possible.

And if there's time, I'd like a chat with Ethel Rosenberg.

I'll require an out, too—a foolproof map or trail of radioactive crumbs that returns me to Freddie and Sunny Morning Elder Care Living—at least until I have my will and a personal representative and everything set up for him if and/or when my heart or soul or some other part of me shatters.

I slide off the bed careful not to wake Freddie and stand in front of my aunt's refrigerator. I use her pen to partially cross out the first item on the To Do List, open the door, take out the plastic gallon bottle of ayahuasca I stole from the Goleta house, unscrew the plastic top and take long swig of the vile, bitter, slightly skunky and waxy brownish liquid.

120.

I explain to the seven A.M. wellness checker—a bougainvillea-colored octopus in peach colored eight-armed short sleeved scrubs—that I am wearing sunglasses indoors because I have a migraine that is making my eyes—he/she/they doesn't know that I have a dozen—hurt.

She/he/they waves a sympathetic suckered arm in my direction before undulating down the purple hallway.

The mollusk believed my story. And I hope you do, too—though I refuse to provide detailed and mind-numbingly boring descriptions of my vomiting jags or my hallucinations.

All I'll tell you is that my profundity-lite, relentlessly unspooling, glow-in-the-dark, Lisa Frank visions were clichés. Brain shit. The standard visual cortex fluff. Meaningless, brightly-colored involuntarily-and-accidentally-chemically-generated helixes, lattices, and grids, circles, fractals and starbursts.

I'm going to skip what I felt, too—except to report prolonged tediums during which I contemplated the fur on Freddie's back, my ankles, and the thousands of mini-stalactites on the ceiling my aunt's ghost crisscrossed after she died. And there were nightmares, too–charred lumps for parents, singed Ethel Rosenberg, my angry aunt shoeless, toeless and worm-eaten in the pantsuit she was buried in, and a naked, battered, unhappy, not very nice Rachael—all of them strapped snugly into electric chairs whose master switch it was my job to pull.

I pulled.

Smoke-mandalas rose from my smoldering victims' heads, comingled and contracted into a blood-cloud.

I mean, how stupid and desperate could I be? I don't know what I expected, but after the rhapsodic sales pitch from Hans about ayahuasca rebirth and communion with ancestors, The Great Unburdening Of My Falsehoods and vibrant Oneness Experience with the Then and the Now, the Living and the Dead, etcetera and a melting of the barrier between death and life, I thought it might be more than this stomach-turning, randomized crap.

So, yeah despite repeatedly refilling my cup throughout the night, my ego did not dissolve like the puke I repeatedly deposited in my aunt's toilet.

I didn't fuck the universe and it didn't fuck me.

Whatever the opposite of reborn is—I'm it.

And I did not receive even a speck of information from the shadows of the suffering, stubborn, venerable and soundless dead.

121.

I sit masked, leaden and squinting through my black shades in the rented Prius with my two companions—Freddie and the worst headache I've ever had—a post-ayahuasca monster that must be a karmic punishment for the lies I've told the wellness checkers about having a migraine. I'm parked in a No Parking zone across from Rachael's apartment building on Silver Street and squishing a bag of frozen peas that I found in my aunt's freezer behind the Marie Callender's frozen meals against my forehead.

Score one point for the Ayahuasca Snake, Hans and Bree and a big fat zero for me.

A Black Lives Matter sign has replaced the one advertising Rachael's studio apartment. The bent and faded aluminum chair is no longer visible on Rachael's balcony. A wooden drying rack garlanded with mostly purple and turquoise tank tops has been erected on one side and the black dome of a Weber grill rises above the wall over which Rachael tumbled or threw herself.

The sliding door is shut and vertical blinds block my view into the apartment. But I'm not here to watch Rachael's former place or to try to detect and commune with the residue of her former presence or her spirit. I'm looking for Rachael's next-door neighbors—the ones that Carlos said had a baby.

Freddie observes a gurgling flock of pigeons feasting on birdseed someone has scattered at the base of a palm tree. I sip a lukewarm, too sweet, drive-thru Cinnamon Dolce latte slowly hoping the sugar will make me feel less numb and weaken the headache which has contorted itself into a pain-knot in my freezing right temple.

I have not seen Carlos, the manager. Bakers' hours begin at three or four A.M.—so I don't expect to. Two Amazon delivery van drivers double park their vans in front of the building and ferry packages into the lobby—one of them a tall box with a drawing of a high chair on it. So, the baby still lives here.

I've seen a man in an orange Haile Selassie t-shirt carry a bicycle out of the lobby and ride it toward Wilshire. A woman with a half-shade haircut and a green, rolled-up yoga mat under one arm got into a Hyundai that had a parking ticket tucked under its windshield. Just seeing that yoga mat returned me to Hans and Bree and their candle-lit, retching victims and triggered some nasty Bree-Hans-ayahuasca queasiness.

Now a homeless woman in a puffer jacket despite the warm morning drags a pink suitcase that a cat has used for sharpening its claws. An obese man in a green Hawaiian shirt has a slim lovebird on his shoulder and exits the building at high speed in an electric wheelchair. An old couple with humped backs jaywalk toward Fairfax while holding hands. A boy skips behind an unleashed Irish wolfhound who seems to be galloping in slow-motion.

I need to lie down and murder the brain-pain with a long, black sleep. But until I do, I'd appreciate it if the world would shut the fuck up and kill the sirens, the lawn mower, the car alarms and the heavy metal oozing like lava from an open apartment window. And maybe the stabbingly too-bright sun could tone it down about a million notches. I feel like I've been Roto-Rooter-ed. The only good thing is that all the puking and unpleasant hallucinating made me forget about my allegedly abnormal heart which is thumping exactly as it should—I just counted—at fifty-six beats a minute.

122.

I lead Freddie a few paces behind the woman pushing the navy-blue baby stroller along Silver Street, then follow as she turns on Third. Tailing her is easy—it's like following a fire engine. She left the apartment building with the baby in full, mid-scream and since then, the harrowing cries have gotten louder.

Passersby stare at the baby, and lob disapproving glances at the mother. The woman—thin and with her brown hair gathered in a braid—keeps her eyes fixed on the stroller handle as she crosses Fairfax, then pushes stroller up Third and enters The Grove.

The baby is miserable. Is it sick? Scared? Hungry? I know nothing about children and I'm too far away from the stroller to peek inside. But anyone could tell that this baby is distressed. These hoarse cries travel from the baby's throat directly into the pit of the stomach.

I pick up Freddie and carry him across Third and enter the Grove. Dean Martin warbles "Amore" with a big band back-up from speakers buried at the base of trees and in planters along the walkway. "When the world seems to shine like you've had too much wine, that's amore...." The woman pushing the stroller does not stop to gaze in the store windows. Maybe she is meeting someone and running late. Or maybe she plans to push the stroller until she reaches the computer-programmed fountain in the fake pond, then scale the fence or jump off the miniature bridge and drown herself.

"Hearts will play tippy-tippy-tay, tippy-tippy-tay, like a gay tarantella..." I decide to keep Freddie in my arms. There are other people strolling and distancing their way through this sound-tracked, fake 1930's city center and many of them have big dogs. I pass a cart selling blinged-out wife-beater dog t-shirts with the L.A. Dodgers' logo in blue and a rhinestoned I Love L.A. with a red, sparkly heart.

"Forgive me, Freddie," I say as I give the man cash for a Dodgers shirt. I unleash Freddie, slip the t-shirt over his harness, clip the leash to his collar and look for the woman with the stroller.

I was right. She's pushed the stroller close to the edge of the fountain. Choreographed geysers writhe in time to the piped-in, booming music ricocheting off Nordstrom's, Barney's, Crate and Barrel and The Gap. "When the stars make you drool just like a pasta fazool, that's amore."

The woman pushes the brake lever at the bottom the stroller with her foot, then reaches in and lifts up a round, red-faced baby in pale yellow footed pajamas and white cap, and presses the baby to her breast. "When you dance down the street with a cloud at your feet, you're in love. When you walk in a dream, but you know you're not dreaming, signore…"

There are other women with children gathered to watch the fountain. Perhaps this woman hopes the brassy soundtrack, the splashing and the froth and glitter of the moving water will calm her baby.

I put Freddie on the grass—and he immediately commences to a detailed nasal inspection—shorten his leash and step toward the stroller and the woman whose hair unbraids itself strand by strand.

She whispers something to the baby and kisses its cheek through her mask and I wonder how to start casual but probing conversation with a person whose eyes are as defeated and exhausted as hers.

I'll have to do what I always do, I guess.

Lie.

123.

Duke Ellington's *"Take The A Train"* explodes from speakers in the foliage. A little boy who can barely walk bobs delightedly in rhythm—but the baby in the tired woman's arms protests more desperately than before.

"Don't worry," I say—the counterfeit smile behind my mask warming my voice. "My mother said I didn't stop screaming until I was two. And I'm just fine now."

The woman is momentarily startled, then notices Freddie and nods at me. "So, you had colic, too?"

"The worst case my pediatrician ever saw," I say. "And I don't think he or my parents ever forgave me for it. Especially my mom. She told me I was the reason her hair turned prematurely gray."

"Your dog is completely adorable," the woman says.

"That's Freddie. He's a diehard Dodger fan."

The baby clenches its fists, inhales, reddens, and lets out a hoarse scream. I understand why your mother's hair turned gray," the woman says. "When she's like this, nothing calms her down. I've tried everything. I thought a walk and the music might help today, but—" The woman shrugs.

"I'm sure you're doing everything you can."

"I hope so," the woman says. "I know in my head that this is something some babies go through. But it's hard when everyone thinks it's my fault. We had a neighbor who hated us and the baby because of the crying. She made me feel that everything I do is wrong. That I'm a horrible mother."

"I can't imagine anyone hating this sweet, beautiful child."

The baby throws her head back and releases a choking cry.

"Luckily our current neighbor is wonderful," the woman dabs a string of spit from the baby's chin. "She's even offered to babysit to give me a break. It was our former neighbor who was the problem. A mean, old woman who wouldn't stop complaining to the manager about the noise—even though she knew we couldn't stop it."

"Well it sounds like it's a good thing that the crying ran her off. I think your baby did you a huge favor."

The baby arches its back and screams—the sound zaps me right between the eyes.

The mother locates a pink pacifier in her pocket, and offers it to the baby. When the baby refuses, the woman looks as though she's going to cry, too. "I shouldn't have said what I said. The manager told me the woman had problems and the crying really upset her. But whenever the baby cried, she'd pound on the wall and yell at us in German. She was a nightmare."

124.

On the drive back I wondered if the mother of the colicky baby could have had an argument with Rachael that escalated into a deadly shoving match on the balcony. I've watched enough "Snapped" episodes to know that being female or a mother does not immunize against rage or cruelty. If Susan Smith could strap her two boys into their car seats, then make her car slid into a lake and Andrea Yates could drown her five kids at bath time—the woman with the braid could have pushed Rachael over the edge of her balcony.

A tree-trimming company has commandeered all the parking spaces on the street behind the Sunny Morning Elder Care Living parking lot. Workers with bandanas over their faces feed chunks of a dead palm tree into the screaming chipper and the noise hammers my forehead.

Freddie doesn't like the noise. His eyes widen and he begins to tremble.

I circle the block again and realize that I'm going to have to take the only available parking space—the one right in front of the Sunny Morning Elder Care lobby which is exactly where I don't want to be.

I park the Prius, keep my sunglasses on, step around the car and lift Freddie from the passenger seat. Shudders ripple through his taut, tiny body and his mouth hangs open.

"Hang in, Freddie," I say as I carry him past the entrance to the driveway and around the corner I've avoided since blunt guy grabbed me. I have just reached the door when an officious female voice reaches me "Miss? Miss Mendel? I need to speak to you immediately.

125.

The voice has a the-principal-has-just-caught-you-smoking-weed-in-the-lavatory tone.

"Sorry, but not now," I say as I enter the hallway. "My dog is having a seizure."

I hear the exit door click shut and click again. The ketchup-colored hallway brightens as the door is opened again and sunlight floods in. "I need to speak with you now, Miss Mendel," the voice insists. "You are in violation of the Los Angeles County of Public Health Mandate to remain on the premises."

"I'm not," I say. "And my dog is ill." I unlock the door and step over the mail—which includes an envelope from the Los Angeles County Department of Health and a small, puffy Amazon mailer——step inside, pull the door closed with one hand and lock it—sure that I have just lost the apartment/condo and ruined everything.

126.

I remove the pad from beneath Freddie, bathe him, dry him in one of my aunt's yellow towels, feed him his pate, give him his medications and his treat, skip the walk and put him in his dog bed under my aunt's sweater and watch him fall asleep.

I do not order fresh lattes or a barbecued chicken pizza, but wait in my aunt's chair for the insolent knock on the door signifying the arrival of someone unconcerned with my body temperature, my toilet paper supply, my supper and snack, my wellness or the opposite—the residential supervisor.

I stare at the door—not the way Freddie gazes at it longing for my aunt's joyous return—but willing the unpleasant thing about to happen and I notice the mail and the package still on the floor and take everything to the tiny kitchen table. AARP Magazine, Entertainment Weekly, People, a catalogue for the Vermont Country Store, and a medium-large rectangular envelope from the health department. I open the puffy mailer and put the cannister of pepper spray inside it in my purse, take a Valium, open the freezer, close my eyes and Pin The Tail On The Dinner style, pull out the first Marie Callender's meal I touch—Kansas City Style Barbecue Sauce and Chicken Cornbread Pie. I open the box, pierce the cellophane as directed and stick it in the microwave. I haven't eaten anything since yesterday and I am playing a punishing game against myself.

127.

While the cornbread sauce pie cooks and I look at ads for walkers, tubs with doors and easy cell phones in AARP magazine and avoid the envelope from the L.A. County Health Department. Maybe the supervisor wasn't pursuing me because she'd reported to the sad-eyed, white-haired woman in charge of the Los Angeles County Health Department who becomes thinner by the day, is always on T.V. reading death statistics, asking people to wear masks, and explaining what "outdoors" means. I'm sure this envelope contains the official document certifying my banishment and Freddie's from Sunny Morning Elder Care Living.

I open the microwave and a pungent, colorless barbecue-sauce-mist drifts into the apartment. The top of the "pie" is a slab of pre-digested cornbread which has browned at the edges of the black, cardboard container. The innards that peek through the crust reveal chicken chunks and carrots in sauce the color of the hallway. I scrape away the cornbread, spear a cube of chicken with my fork, open my mouth and shove it in.

It burns my tongue—but total shockeroo—it's delicious. Tender. Moist. Saucy—as if the bits of chicken I love on the CPK pizza had become more chicken-y, more real. I eat the chicken cubes first, savoring each one, then the carrot cubes and I realize that this past-its-sell-date frozen dinner is more worthy of a foot tattoo than a thirteen-hour ayahuasca colon cleanse could ever be.

When there's nothing left except the deconstructed cornbread—I'm just not into cornbread—I push the container away, rip open the Health Department envelope and start to read my aunt's death certificate.

128.

CITY OF LOS ANGELES – REGISTRAR/RECORDER-COUNTY CLERK

CERTIFICATE OF DEATH

State File Number STATE OF CALIFORNIA–DEPARTMENT OF PUBLIC HEALTH

RegistrationNumber/CertificateNo.

.Name of Deceased.	Middle Name.	Last Name.	Date Of Death	
Evelyn	Paulie	Mendel	March. 23. 2020	11:13. A.M

My mother would address my aunt with Paulie, a diminutive of her middle name—but only when they were alone and she didn't know I was eavesdropping. How did Paulie find its way to the death certificate?

NAME & BIRTHPLACE OF FATHER—Unk.

Well, it's not unknown to me—Joseph Mendel, Rochester, New York.

MAIDEN NAME & BIRTHPLACE OF MOTHER—Unk.

I know that, too—Anna Schwartz, Buffalo, New York.

CITIZEN OF WHAT COUNTRY—USA.

MARRIED/NEVERMARRIED/DIVORCED/SPECIFY—Never married.

NAME OF SURVIVING SPOUSE—blank.

LAST OCCUPATION—Secretary.

Wrong. My aunt's last occupation was Script Supervisor.

NUMBER OF YEARS IN THIS OCCUPATION: Unk.

Nope. 40.

KIND OF INDUSTRY OR BUSINESS—Mot. Picture, TV, Stage.

Bingo.

PLACE OF DEATH-Name of Hospital or Inpatient facility—Sunny Morning Elder Care Living Hospice.

Shouldn't that be Elder Care Dying?

STREET ADDRESS, INSIDE USUAL CITY CORPORATE LIMITS YES/NO, CITY OR TOWN, COUNTY.

All this is correct, of course.

LENGTH OF STAY IN COUNTY OF DEATH–3 yrs.

Wrong.

LENGTH OF STAY IN CALIFORNIA—Unk.

USUAL RESIDENCE. INSIDE CITY CORPORATE LIMITS YES/NO.

NAME AND MAILING ADDRESS OF INFORMANT—

I have never heard of this Heidi L. Grigorian who lives on Alameda in Burbank—but assume she works in Sunny Morning Elder Care Living—the hospice or the administrative office.

Then comes the stuff I want—

PHYSICIAN'S OR CORONER'S CERTIFICATION, FUNERAL DIRECTOR and CAUSE OF DEATH.

The physician is Dr. Christiansen and includes his California medical license number. The funeral director specifies ENTOMBMENT—I like the reverberating sound of that much more than BURIAL or CREMATION. I skip the stuff about the funeral director and jump to CAUSE OF DEATH.

IMMEDIATE CAUSE—Cardiac arrest.

APPROXIMATE INTERVERAL BETWEEN ONSET AND DEATH—three days.

CONDITIONS WHICH GAVE RISE TO THE IMMEDIATE CAUSE STATING THE UNDERLYING CAUSE LAST—Pneumonia. Sepsis. Dementia. Lung cancer.

129.

My aunt was not forgetful. Not confused. Her short-term memory was as robust as her undiminished capacity for long-term recollection. She completed the Jumble puzzle each day in a few seconds. She was the mistress of obscure Hollywood trivia. She knew the names of lighting directors, costume designers——of the obscure novels that movies were based on, the full lyrics to popular songs and actors' real names. She knew most of the questions that matched the entertainment answers on Jeopardy. She knew which film stars were closeted. She knew who was Jewish but pretended they weren't. She knew who was a drunk or an addict, a "womanizer"—to use her terminology—and which men beat their partners. She could list the names of stars and celebrities who'd had abortions before it was legal and the doctors who provided them. She had an elaborate and credible theory about Natalie Wood's death.

Evelyn Paula Mendel was not demented.

And what is this crap about lung cancer? Where did that come from? My aunt's heart stopped because of hypoxia—that's what the nurse said. Before the catastrophe she was healthy. Clear-headed. Fun. Always beautiful. Not dying and not barely-here—she was fully cognizant and completely present to the world—alive.

130.

I brush my hair, put on a clean sweatshirt, slip on my flip-flops, pull a fresh mask from the paper bag, adjust the mask loops over my ears, grab my keys and tiptoe out of the apartment/condo so I don't wake Freddie.

One of the lighting fixtures has gone out and the walls are the color of the A-1 Steak Sauce Hans smothered his scrambled eggs with before he decided to eat clean. But instead of walking to the exit door, I head for a heavy glass door that leads to the lobby—a door with a push bar with a big fat sign that says—DO NOT ENTER, QUARANTINE IN EFFECT and with a red Covid virion cartoon before "QUARANTINE." My mission is to find Heidi L. Grigorian.

I expect an alarm to sound but the glass door opens, then obligingly closes itself with a whisper. I stomp through a narrow corridor until I reach another glass door, then step into the Sunny Morning Elder Care Lobby.

The muted television displays a local news broadcast—the ancient weatherman whose hair stands on end is pointing to a glowing map across which sperm or arrows are flying to signify wind currents. No elder-residents doze in the easy chairs or read newspapers. Stacks of cardboard Costco cartons obscure the yellow carpeted space between the television and the chairs.

I walk past the reception desk on my way to confront Heidi L. about the errors in my aunt's death certificate. The desk is without a receptionist. A yellow posterboard on a wooden easel with SUNNY MORNING ELDER CARE LIVING—THOSE LOST TO COVID—THEY WILL NEVER BE FORGOTTEN written in thick black marker at the top sits where the receptionist is supposed to be.

Photographs are taped to the poster board with brief tributes to the departed. Here's Golfing Gary. There's a man from down the hall and a few women with stiff white clouds of lacquered hair with whom my aunt was friendly.

The photograph of my aunt must have been taken in the dining room on New Year's Eve. Blurry red and blue balloons bob behind the silver party hat on her head. She's wearing her white sweater over a black top and pearls. Her red lipstick is uber-crimson. She holds a noisemaker and smiles into the camera. I look closely and see specks of white confetti in her white hair. Below the image someone has written in black Sharpie, "We will all miss your fun spirit, dear Paulie! R.I.P."

What the fuck else didn't I know? And how much that I thought I knew is wrong? Maybe everyone except me called her Paulie. Maybe I'm not her only niece. Maybe she has triplets living in Sacramento. And a secret family. Maybe she had dementia and lung cancer but didn't tell me just as she decided not to inform me that she was having trouble breathing and was entering hospice.

It doesn't matter what the death certificate says. Why did I think it was so important? Does it matter if her pneumonia was caused by Covid or Ebola? The dénouement would have been the same.

Now that I think of it, she hadn't done the Jumble puzzle and hadn't mentioned Natalie Wood for about a year. And instead of talking, she'd taken to listening to me lie or asking me questions.

I wasn't with her enough to see it—and when I was with her, I refused to see that my careful, sharp-but-become-duller aunt must have been preparing for her exit for a long time and navigating her fear and diminishment without any assistance from me.

131.

I pull a yellow tissue from the box next to the posterboard and use it dab my eyes, then help myself to a glob of hand sanitizer from the industrial sized dispenser when

a smiling face in the photo at the bottom of the memorial poster catches my eye and the writing beneath it— "What will we do without you, Rudy AKA Teddy Bear? You were the kindest, sweetest man we ever knew. R.I.P."

The picture shows a heavyset man with wavy black hair.

Below the hair is the blunt guy's face—clean shaven and without his surgical cap. Instead of an apron, he's dressed in a powder blue tuxedo and black bow tie. He stands close to willowy teenaged girl with a pile of curls arranged in an up-do and who wears a massively-ruffled, sequined violet gown—perhaps a Quinceañera dress. The man and girl stand close to one another and the man has his hand on her shoulder. The beautiful girl's eye shadow matches the violet of her gown. Her black eyeliner is heavy and is the same velvet black as her pupils. The man gazes at the girl elated, proud.

132.

I put down the heavy box of Depends that I took from the lobby and used to block my face when the receptionist returned, open the glass door and enter the hallway which is the color of a human spleen. Success—I make it back into the apartment/condo without alerting the Morning Elder Care Living powers that be to my newest violation public health mandate.

Why hasn't the woman who absolutely had to speak with me not sent her peach-scrubbed posse to hunt me down?

Freddie opens an eye then closes it when he sees it's me and my aunt has not returned.

I take a Valium and with shaky fingers slip the death certificate into the envelope with the others, put it in the top drawer of my aunt's secretary, open my computer and write an email to the accountant explaining that the certificates have finally arrived, that I will be sending them to the bank, etc. and asking him why he didn't inform me that my aunt had cancer and dementia.

Then I delete the email, close my computer and turn off the lights.

133.

I'm only sure something is about to happen. The Big One. Rachael. A stroke or heart attack. The arrival of the police to evict the dog and me. Alien invasion. World War Three. And the blunt guy's—Rudy's–
–shaky voice saying "Your aunt. She was a very nice lady" is the

looping soundtrack to this elastic moment.

Did he call her Paulie, too?

Were he and my Aunt friends? Did he know she was sick?

Did he know about me?

134.

Rachael arrived two minutes before the seven P.M. wellness harassment session and ten minutes after Freddie and I returned from his walk.

He saw her shining weakly next to his dog bed and growled while I sliced his sickening pate into tiny cubes.

It was the same long-armed man as before. He distractedly aimed the scanner at my nose, then said, "Ninety-eight point five. Excellent, Miss."

"Did you know Rudy?" I ask. "The kitchen guy who died of Covid? Teddy Bear?"

"Yeah, I did," the man says. "Terrible tragedy. Such a sweet guy. And he had four kids. The oldest just turned fifteen."

"Yes," I say. "Really terrible."

The man hands me the paper bag—it's heavier than usual—and without the usual toilet paper roll as chaser. "The staff and administrators started a GoFundMe for his family. If you want to contribute, the link is on the Sunny Morning website. Have a sunny evening, Miss."

"You, too," I say.

135.

I tear off a piece of the cheese sandwich for Freddie. He carries it to his dog bed as Rachael flickers—patiently or impatiently, I can't tell—nearby.

Maybe I'm being passive-aggressive, but I make Rachael wait while I check the website for Rudy's GoFundMe link. There's are two photos above a brief obituary. One is of Rudy with his wife and daughter in identical Gagne t-shirts at a Dodger game, the other a close-up of Rudy forcing a smile, his kitchen hair net low across his forehead.

"Rudy Garcia was a long-time Sunny Morning Elder Care Living team member who always went above and beyond. Rudy always went the extra mile with a smile whether that meant cutting up food for residents with eating difficulties or preparing special shakes for residents on restricted diets. Help us honor Rudy's memory with a donation to help his family cover funeral and other expenses during this difficult time of loss."

I send some emails with attachments, return to the GoFundMe page and–still not sure about Rudy—donate fifteen hundred dollars for his funeral and his family, close my computer and let my eyes to adjust to the dark.

136.

I glance at Rachael's feeble, not-very-nice brightness and wish she were a scented candle, then I check my purse twice for the pepper spray, my mask and the diazepam.

I take Freddie out for a quick pee along the parking lot fence, I lead him inside, give him a treat and get him settled on the bed. Then I take out my cell phone and call Hans.

"Hans." Hans says. There are voices in the background. Also coughing and/or retching. I remember from my glimpse of the Goleta house living room that the psychedelic explorers that Sherpas Hans and Bree were guiding to the ayahuasca summit hadn't distanced their yoga mats the required six feet and that their faces were bare.

"I'm sorry to bother you but you're the only person I can call."

"Do you ever wonder why that is?" Hans asks.

"Please, Hans."

"Okay, but make it fast. Bree and I are leading a culmination circle."

"If I don't call or text you by tomorrow morning, please get in touch with Sunny Morning Elder Care and my accountant. I emailed you his contact information. Tell them I'm in trouble and that Freddie is alone in the apartment and needs his medications. The accountant can arrange for someone at the vet to take care of him. If I don't come back, I need you to do this for me, Hans. Will you?"

"What is this, Ascher? What lie is this about?"

"This is real, I swear. Will you just please say you'll call Sunny Morning if you don't hear from me tomorrow?"

"Okay. Yes," Hans says. "But this is it, Ascher. This is our last conversation."

"Did you hear any of that, Rachael?" I address the feeble grayish glow and I pat Freddie's small, sleeping head. "This is my last shot. I could be missing something—and knowing me, probably I am—but I don't see any more options after tonight."

137.

I put on jeans and the black sweater I wore with my Aunt's pearls to her Zoom funeral, slip on my flip-flops, extinguish Rachael by switching on the crystal lamp, turn on the television, kiss Freddie and step into hallway. Someone has replaced the busted light fixture with one whose bluish light turns the walls a Max Factor Ruby Red.

I open the door to the parking lot, walk to the fence, push the bougainvillea aside, and emerge on the other side where the tree-trimmers have transformed beheaded palms into stumps. I walk around the block to Sunny Morning Elder Care Living where this mandate-violating escape from the Red Zone will be visible to all the Ascher Lieb watchers inside.

I'm tired. Maybe it's better if the supervisor sees me. I haven't felt right and I've been dragging my ass for weeks. Punish me now for whatever crimes I've committed, I silently say to the Sunny Morning Elder Care Living supervisors supervising behind the windows.

Evict me. Purge me and Freddie. Go ahead and put me out of the misery of not knowing.

And if Sunny Morning Elder Care living cannot evict me from a Red Zone during a pandemic because of the eviction moratorium—that's their problem.

My problem is Rachael Weskinski.

138.

The Partridge Place parking lot attendant is in his chair asleep. The chain that blocked the entrance is piled on the ground. I park the Prius in an empty space next to one of the filthy Kias. Someone has written BURN ME in the dust filming the rear window. There are no clusters of lavender blossoms beautifying the jacaranda tree.

I eat a Valium, remove the pepper spray canister from my purse, lock the car and walk past the silent Hatzalah ambulance to Isaac Kahn's door.

There are screw-holes where the mezuzah was. I knock twice below the Hatzalah decal, click open the top of my pepper spray canister and place my thumb on the actuator just the way the woman in the video on the manufacturer's website did before disabling her attackers—and aim it at the door. The spray-stream is supposed to reach twelve feet, so this is the sweet spot.

It's quiet except for my pulse and the distant thud of pre-July fourth fireworks. When the door opens, Isaac Kahn—wet and hairy in a not bad way—is wrapped in a bath towel and holds a mask.

139.

Isaac Kahn pulls on his mask. "Ida? What do you want?"

"My name is Ascher. Ascher Lieb. I'm not Rachael Weskinksy's niece. I'm someone else's niece—or I was. And I need to talk with you about official Hatzalah business."

Isaac Kahn tilts his head. The building's security light shines on the bottom of his long beard where droplets form lengthen and fall to the blacktop like fat raindrops.

"What kind of business?"

"You told me you were a mandated reporter, right?"

"Yes. I am."

"I have something to report. Maybe elder abuse. Maybe murder."

140.

Isaac Kahn invites me in, but I refuse. I stand six feet away from his closed door while he dresses, then place myself just outside his open doorway—my pepper spray cannister pointed at his head—while he stands in the entryway.

"Who was abused? Who was murdered, Andrea?"

"Ascher."

"I'm sorry. Just tell me what you know. What you saw and when."

"I didn't see anything. I don't know what happened. But I'm pretty sure something bad happened to Rachael Weskinksy."

"Something bad did happen. She had a terrible fall and then she died."

"I think she didn't fall. I think she might have been helped over the balcony."

"And why do you say that, Ascher?"

"Because I saw her body and it looked wrong. And because her body was trying to tell me something."

Isaac Kahn stands straighter and strokes his beard. "What are you? A nurse?"

"No. I'm a volunteer."

"A volunteer what?"

"I'm on leave right now, but I'm a member of a burial society, a Chevra Kadisha."

"You?"

"Yes. And by talking to you I'm violating my obligation to protect the privacy of those I serve, but I have to find how Rachael Weskinski died."

"Is it necessary to aim that thing at me?"

"Yep," I say. "It has a long range and each canister contains twenty sprays. You tried to run me off the road. You subjected me to an invasive physical exam. I don't trust you. I'm only here because you're my only hope of figuring this out. And because it's possible that you were involved in Rachael's death."

"That's absurd—I wasn't." Isaac Kahn's forehead reddens and his jaw muscles work on the side of his neck.

"Okay, then. I'm going to tell you what I know. Then you'll tell me what you know. That way I can fill in the blanks."

141.

I tell Isaac Kahn—without lying, but with omissions so I don't sound completely batshit—what I know about Rachael and what her body–I leave out her soul—communicated to me. Rachael lived alone, was unmarried, the apartment manager said she wasn't nice and she was a problem, her family died in Polish death camps, her neighbors had a colicky baby that upset her, made her angry. I explain that Rachael not only looked bruised from a fall that a bruise I saw on her wrist might have resulted from being restrained before she was in the ER or after.

I describe the neighbor with the screaming baby and how desperate she seemed. I tell Isaac Kahn that the building manager made it clear that Rachael's neighbors were relieved that she was gone—so she must have been troublesome before the baby arrived.

Isaac Kahn nods. "That all chimes with what she told me," he says. "I don't remember seeing bruising on her wrist after her fall, but I wasn't looking. It takes time for bruises to form and darken, so I wouldn't expect to have seen anything right from the fall."

"Okay," I say.

"But I knew her," Isaac Kahn says. "Miss Weskinski called Hatzalah about five times in the last two months for panic attacks. After the first call, Dispatch would send me because I speak Polish."

"The neighbor said she spoke German."

"No," Isaac Kahn says. "She was Polish. She spoke English, but was most comfortable speaking Polish or Yiddish."

The pepper spray shakes because my hand is trembling—I switch it to my other hand. "Do you know what caused her panic attacks?"

"The panic attacks started with the birth of the baby next door. The incessant crying triggered horrific memories. I'd help her breathe into a paper bag, I tried to teach her some relaxation methods. And I'd let her talk about her family and the war. Having someone understood Polish helped, I think."

"That's so sad."

"It was," Isaac Kahn says. "I urged her to move, but she said she was too old and that the neighborhood was home. She'd been a seamstress and still did alterations for people in the area. And she walked to Fairfax and Farmers' Market to shop. She insisted that couple with the baby were the ones who should move and kept demanding that management kick them out."

142.

Without realizing it, I've stepped closer to Isaac Kahn's door and he's moved closer to me.

"Why don't you come in and sit down? I'll leave the door wide open if that makes you feel more comfortable."

I look at the futon behind Isaac Kahn and it feels like I'm seeing it through the wrong end of a telescope. "No thanks," I say, feeling dizzy. "You didn't transport her to the hospital. So how did your name get on her disposition of remains form?"

"I followed the LAFD paramedics to the E.R. I thought I should be there to translate if necessary. But she died on the way."

"Did something happen that might have made her want to kill herself?"

"The only thing I can think of is the meeting," Isaac Kahn says. "The last time I saw her she told me the manager had set up a meeting with her and the couple with the baby. She told me they frightened her, but said she had no choice and that they were going to meet in her apartment."

"Did she give you a date?"

"I don't remember a date. But it was going to be soon." Isaac Kahn tilts his head. "Why don't you sit down? You don't look great."

"I never look great," I say. "Would you come with me to talk with Rachael's neighbors and the apartment manager? I'd like to go now."

143.

Isaac Khan drives the ambulance. He's put on his kippah and wears his yellow reflective vest over the black pants and black, long-sleeved. I sit on the passenger side close to the window, my hand still holding the pepper spray cannister. We do not speak.

It only takes a minute or two to reach Silver Street. Isaac Kahn parks in the rear Rachael's building, hops out of the cab, trots around to my side to open the door, and leans inside. "There's something I have to say to you."

I flick open the top of the pepper spray with my thumb. "Please," I say. "Not now."

144.

The wind chimes are silent but muffled television voices rumble through the air. Isaac Kahn knocks on the manager's door.

Carlos slips on a mask before speaking through the screen. He looks at Isaac Kahn's vest—not at me. "What's going on? Is one of the occupants having an emergency?"

"No, everything's fine," Isaac Kahn says. "We're here because we have some questions about a former resident, Miss Rachael Weskinksy. We're doing a fatality follow-up." Isaac Kahn holds up a business card with Hatzalah shield on it and Carlos opens the screen door to take it.

"The old lady who fell? If this is about the balcony, the owner has had it inspected and everything is up to code." Carlos's forehead creases with concern.

"I'd like to look at the balcony, yes, but I'd also like to talk to you and her neighbors."

"I don't know," Carlos said. "There's a new occupant in that apartment."

"We just need to do a brief inspection and short interview with the neighbors." I'm impressed—Isaac Kahn is an excellent bullshitter—officious, confident and just a little superior. "And please tell them that we regret any inconvenience."

Carlos closes the door. We hear him speaking to someone on his phone, then a short silence. He emerges holding a heavy key ring jangling with keys. "I'll take you up." An infant's screams boomerang in the stairwell and become more piercing as we ascend. The baby sounds worse than she did at the Grove.

It's not until Carlos has led us to the second floor and knocked on the doors of apartments five and six that he recognizes me. "Wait a minute," he says. "What's going on?"

"I wasn't interested in renting the apartment," I tell him. "I needed to get a look at the layout and the balcony and that was the easiest way. I apologize for not telling you the truth."

"So, you're a paramedic, too?"
"No," I say. "I guess I'm a death worker in training."

145.

The woman I saw leaving the building with a yoga mat lets us into apartment five. It seems cramped now that it holds a queen-sized bed, a big-screen TV on a stand, a rocking chair, small table and chair and a treadmill. The vertical blinds have been pushed to one side and the sky above the barbecue and the drying rack on the balcony is a flat black rectangle.

"Excuse us for the intrusion." Isaac Kahn says.

The woman nods. "Do you need me? Because I have a class. I'm sorry it's so warm in here but I was doing hot yoga."

"That's fine," Isaac Kahn says.

It's not fine. Being here is like being stuck under a broiler.

"I'll lock up with the master key when we're done, Robin," Carlos says. "We all really appreciate your flexibility."

The woman opens the apartment door as she leaves and the baby's cries assault us from two directions—from the hallway and through the wall behind the bed. The woman I spoke with at the Grove enters holding the struggling, red-faced baby dressed in pink polka-dot pajamas. A short, square-chested, solemn-eyed man in gray dress pants and a white button-down shirt holds a half-full baby bottle in one hand and a cloth diaper in the other. He steps inside and shuts the door, but stays close to it.

"What is this about?" the man asks, outrage in his voice. His glasses have clear plastic frames and thick lenses.

"We're following-up on the death of your neighbor, Miss Rachael Weskinski," Isaac Kahn explains. "We need to clarify a few things so we can close her file, and then we'll be on our way."

The woman gives her husband a questioning look, then paces back and forth in front of her husband, rocking the baby. She doesn't recognize me yet.

"We understand there was a meeting here on the day Ms. Weskinski died." Isaac Kahn says, "And that there was some sort of conflict between you and the deceased."

I frown at Isaac Kahn. I never said the meeting happened on the day that Rachael died.

"Yes," the father says. "We had a meeting, but we had no conflict with her. She had a conflict with us. You should include that in your report and also that Miss Weskinski was a nasty, malevolent pest—an entitled Karen who decided that few cries from a baby gave her the right to harass my family get us evicted. I'm sure you know her type."

"Scott, stop," his wife chides. "I'm sorry for what my husband said." The baby is so agitated and her cries so desperate that I fear she will choke. The woman takes the bottle of milk from her husband and pushes the nipple in the baby's mouth, but the baby spits it away. "Maui has colic. Her pediatrician assures us everything is normal and it won't last much longer. But every time Maui cried, Miss Weskinski got angry. Carlos set up the meeting to help us de-escalate."

"Who called Hatzalah?" Isaac Kahn asks.

"I did," the woman lifts her gaze from her baby's face, recognizes me and her arms stiffen around her daughter. "You? What the hell is this?" She paces toward her husband. "Scott, I think we should leave. Now."

"Please don't," Isaac Kahn says. "When my associate spoke with you, she was working for me and doing necessary follow-up. Could you explain why you called Hatzalah?"

The woman stares at me. "The business card was next to the phone. And I'd seen the ambulance in front of the building a few times. Will that do? Or are you going to send a spy to my Mommy And Me to interrogate me further?" She stands so close to me that I can feel the heat rising from the baby's body and hers. "So, did you really have the worst case of colic your doctor had ever seen?"

Sweat trickles from inside my bra to the waistband of my jeans. "I don't know," I say. "My parents and my doctor are deceased."

146.

"Marianne, chill." Carlos ushers the woman away from me. "Can we please just get this over with?" Then Carlos turns faces Isaac Kahn. "What exactly do you need? The building management is more than happy to cooperate."

"We just need a step by step of Miss Weskinski's fall and what led up to it. And contact information for everyone present."

Everyone is silent except Maui. She takes a long breath and holds it, then exhales into a massive scream.

"How did Miss Weskinski get from inside the apartment to the balcony and then over the edge? Why did she go to the balcony? How did she fall? Did she trip on something?" I ask.

"It was hot," Carlos explains. "These really old buildings don't have A.C. so it was almost as hot as it is right now. The slider was open and we were all standing and talking close to the window.

"How was the meeting going before she fell? Did you resolve anything? Arrive at some sort of understanding?" I ask.

The baby's father shifts his weight from one shiny dress-shoe to the other. "No. The old woman lived to complain and to cause trouble. She was impossible. She actually said the crying reminded her of being in a concentration camp. A baby! How insane and self-centered can a person be? She just had to drag the Nazis into this. They always do."

"'They.' Who are 'they'?" Isaac Kahn says.

"Look," the man says. "I know what you are and I'm not going to apologize. Ask anyone in the building. The woman was a bitch. A controlling Jew bitch who thought she was better than everyone else. And if you don't like hearing that, too bad."

"I don't like hearing that." Isaac Kahn seems to get taller.

"Tough shit," the man says. "The truth is that she provoked what happened to her the way you people provoked—."

"Provoked what?" Isaac Kahn steps close to the man, his hands balled into fists.

"Hey, come on, guys," Carlos says. "Cool it, will you?"

"The old bag's fall was her fault. Just like the camps and the ovens." The man's face is red and shiny like a polished apple. "And it was a few thousand—not six million. I'm sick of that bullshit, too."

"Shut up, Scott." Marianne touches her husband's arm, then turns toward Isaac Kahn. "It was an accident." The baby squirms as if she is trying to escape her mother's grip, this stifling room and whatever relentless thing is making her cry. "Yes. My husband lost his temper. So what? The old woman did, too. If you think she was an angel or something, she wasn't. She was yelling and threatening us and then started shaking and gasping like she was having an asthma attack. Scott ran toward her to help her, but when reached for her arm, she backed up onto the balcony and then didn't stop. She just kept going until she wasn't there. It was horrible. We were all just frozen."

Scott looks at his wife, then he stares at me, the pupils behind his lenses magnified pinholes, "And you're just like her. Lying. Causing trouble. Harassing people."

I slide the pepper spray out of my purse.

Scott lunges, then swipes the cannister from my sweaty fingers.

147.

"Let your tears flow." Isaac Kahn holds my hair away from the spray rising from eye wash station next to his industrial sink. "Keep your eyes open, or hold them open with your fingers if you have to."

Isaac Kahn has a darkening purplish bruise around his left eye.

My face burns and my eyes are killing me. I hold my eyelids open with my fingers and stare into blurry froth streaming from the twin outlets. I think I might be crying, too—from the pain and other things. I hope the streaming water hides it.

"Pepper spray inflames the mucous membranes," Isaac Kahn explains. "The longer you flush the affected areas with water, the better. Just don't rub."

After fifteen minutes, my clothes are wet and the heat and sting begin to diminish. Isaac Kahn gives me a towel for my shoulders. "It usually takes about ninety minutes for the pain to subside completely. Would you like to take a shower? Do you need a change of clothes?"

"No thanks. I'm fine. Or I will be in seventy-five minutes." I sit on the futon, my eyes tearing and the wet parts of my pants and sweater soaking the upholstery. Isaac Kahn observes me from across room—the prescribed six-foot distance— "I'm sorry that happened to you, Ascher."

"I'm sorry for what happened to you."

"It's nothing," Isaac Kahn says. "My patients hit me all the time. But I've never had any of them discharge pepper spray near a baby. That guy is special."

"But I thought you said the baby will be fine."

"She will. But that was dangerous. And what he did to you was felony assault. You should press charges."

"I never want to see that fucking coward again," I swallow a sob. "I don't want to go to court or have to explain anything to anyone or answer questions about Rachael." The sobs are making my chest hurt so, I finally let them out.

"It took a lot for me not to punch him back," Isaac Kahn says. "But after I lost my composure with you, I promised myself it would never happen again."

"I think I should go home."

"You can't drive with your eyes like that," Isaac Kahn says. "Let me drive you."

"Aren't you on call? Don't you have a catering job?" I instantly regret what I've said. I sounded mean. Sarcastic. "I'm sorry," I say, "I didn't mean it that way. I just don't want you to see where I live. It's complicated and I can't explain it now. Can I leave my car in the lot overnight? I'll take a Lyft and come back early in the morning to get it.

Isaac Kahn runs his fingers through his beard. "You're a tough one, Ascher Lieb," he says. "But I won't insist on driving you home or asking where you live. Or who you live with—"

"I live with a dog, An old, sick dog. And a ghost," I say. "They're waiting for me."

"Okay," Isaac Kahn says. "But can we talk tomorrow when you come for your car? We really need to talk."

I stand up and see the perfect soggy outline of my too-wide ass imprinted on the futon and my heart starts doing that fluttery thing inside my chest. My face feels cooked. I'm confused and scared. And hopeful. "Yes," I say, "but not tomorrow. Not until I figure out how I feel. I hope that's okay with you."

148.

I ask the Lyft driver let me off in front of Sunny Morning Elder Care Living. I take the trash bag Isaac Kahn gave me to sit on with me, give the driver five stars and twenty percent tip. The driver is an Ethiopian man, a retired engineer with six children—a lawyer, a neurosurgeon, a soccer player, a nurse, a realtor and a special-needs teacher. When he passed me their pictures and the school pictures of his grandchildren, he did not comment on my red face, my rotten egg smell or that I was wet.

I call Hans as I walk down the driveway.

"Hans," Hans says. Voices bubble in the background.

"It's me," I say. "The high alert has been cancelled. I just wanted to let you know."

Hans doesn't say, "Good." Hans doesn't ask me how I am.

"Of, course it was cancelled," Hans says. "We create our own reality. Our own drama. If you want things to suck, they suck. If you don't, they don't. And today, for some weird reason, Ascher Lieb didn't want things to suck."

I hear the click of the disconnect and remember a stanza from a Wallace Stevens poem I wrote about for a sophomore English paper– – "That strange flower, the sun,/Is just what you say./Have it your way./The world is ugly,/And the people are sad."

"You and your fiancée suck." I say out loud. "And you're a dick. And Hans, you will be a dick forever."

I reach the cement slab where the blunt guy smoked and where I found the roach. Shit. I must have left the roach and the letter in the plastic baggie in the Prius. I tell myself I will throw them away as soon as I retrieve the car. As soon as I open the door to the garnet hallway, I hear Freddie's hysterical barking.

149.

Someone has pushed an envelope under the door. It's correctly addressed to Ms. Ascher Lieb, so it must be the eviction notice.

I busy myself with greeting Freddie, giving him a treat, then watching him watch me change out of my wet clothes into dry leggings and a clean sweatshirt. I take a Valium. I toss the black sweater and jeans into the trash bag Isaac Kahn gave me, tie a knot in the bag and carry it to the parking lot Dumpster.

Freddie waits for me in his dog bed, circles it three times, curls up and sleeps.

I'm not sure of anything except that Rachael's back-first, pavement-dive was an accident. But every accident—like my parents' crash—is the flowering of hidden causes, secret failures and provocations.

Rachael's death was also a suicide. And a murder.

Her malicious, exhausted, overwhelmed neighbors wanted to hurt her, to bully her into silence or to drive her from the only home she knew. Sure, she was a pain in the ass and worse than that. But how could they not see that Rachael Weskinski was already a ghost? You're dead, aren't you, when life is just pain and fear?

And I think Rachael was ready for her exit. She received cruelty's final nudge and decide to go where it pushed her.

But what the fuck did Rachael need me for? She knew who she was. She knew what happened.

I move from the chair to the floor to be closer to her light, which ripples because my eyes are watering.

"I did everything I could," I say. "That piece of shit, Scott, and his wife who scared you? I found them—And I think they felt that it was you who sent me. But knowing that won't change anything. You of all people must know that here there is no justice, no peace—just clarifications, approximations. And repudiations. You have to let them go."

Will she find her way? Rachael's soul—like grief and hope—is changeable and slippery.

I find the psalm I found in the tahara booklet and sent myself in an email, switch on the battery tea light because I used up the Yahrzeit candle and read the English translation on my phone screen—

ב אֲרוֹמִמְךָ יְהוָה, כִּי
דִלִּיתָנִי; וְלֹא-שִׂמַּחְתָּ אֹיְבַי לִי.

ג יְהוָה אֱלֹהָי-- שִׁוַּעְתִּי אֵלֶיךָ,
וַתִּרְפָּאֵנִי.

ד יְהוָה--הֶעֱלִיתָ מִן-שְׁאוֹל
נַפְשִׁי; חִיִּיתַנִי, מיורדי-
(מִיָּרְדִי-) בוֹר.

A Psalm; a Song at the Dedication of the House of David.
I will extol thee, O Lord, for Thou hast raised me up, and hast not suffered mine enemies to rejoice over me.
O Lord my God, I cried unto Thee, and Thou didst heal me.
O Lord, Thou broughtest up my soul from the nether-world; Thou didst keep me alive, that I should not go down to the pit…

150.

I left Sunny Morning Elder Care Living right after the wellness check and Freddie's walk. Isaac Kahn occupies the lot attendant's bent metal chair. Next to him are two buckets, big sponges and rags in one of them. The ambulance is shiny and the pavement beneath it is wet.

I hand Isaac Kahn the brown paper shopping bag. He removes the carboard carrier balancing two Starbucks Venti lattes, and the wax bags holding two plain croissants, two almond and two cranberry scones.

"This is very kind of you," he says, "but you shouldn't have."

"Yes, I should have."

"No really," he says. "I can't eat or drink any of it. I keep Kosher, remember?"

"I didn't. I'm sorry," My thoughtlessness stuns me.

"Don't worry about it," he says and stands up. "I already had my coffee. How are you feeling?"

"Much better," I lie. "Good."

"And your eyes?"

"Perfect," I say.

"They're still inflamed. Do you mind if I take a look?"

But Isaac Kahn can't check my eyes if I'm crying or driving, can he?

I drive around for a while, blowing my nose and wiping my eyes at red lights. I take Wilshire to Westwood then circle back to the ruins of the art museum, pass Levitated Mass—which looks anemic in the full morning light, then find myself on Pico. I park the car, take the envelope with the blunt guy's roach and the ridiculous letter I wrote in it, rip it and throw the pieces into the reeking interior of a leaking trash receptacle.

Well, I destroyed the day and a lot more, but that's one thing I can cross off on my revised list—. The others are much more difficult—probably impossible–to accomplish:

Don't challenge eviction/sell apartment/condo/Move.

Stop Valium.

Stop lying—I think the Valium and the lying are connected.

Chevra Kadisha.

Mortuary science degree.

Talk to Isaac Kahn.

Selling a unit during a pandemic seems unlikely, and I don't know where Freddie and I will go. But the world felt different once I realized that Sunny Morning Elder Care Living is—like colic—temporary.

I looked some stuff up and Isaac Kahn was right—taking too much Valium can fuck up your heart rhythm. But going off Valium cold turkey is dangerous and can cause seizures. I envisioned Freddie and me both seizing at the same time, so have begun to taper off. I have an appointment with a cardiologist the accountant recommended next week.

It's pathetic—but helping to perform tahara was the best thing I've ever done. I want to keep doing it—just with a different group.

Getting a degree in mortuary science is iffy. I'm a total disaster with the living and I talk too much. But when I'm with the dead, I listen. I don't know if I'm smart enough or have the discipline and empathy required, and I can't start in-person classes until after the pandemic is over, so I've enrolled in some online prerequisites I'm sure I will be terrible in—chemistry, anatomy and microbiology. I'll see how it goes.

As I walk back to the car, I pass a windowless beige stucco building with a wooden sign lettered in Hebrew and English—Mikvah Miriam–—with a handwritten note taped on the door that says "Closed for Covid."

I knock on the door.

After I saw Isaac Kahn enter the mikvah, I did some reading. I'd heard my grandmother mention the mikvah, but only knew that a mikvah is a pool of natural water in which observant Jewish women immerse themselves before their weddings, after their monthly cycle ends—the mikvah purifies and prepares them for new life—and also after giving birth. Men visit the mikvah before getting married and often before Shabbat. Immersion is like tahara for the living. One article said that the mikvah is about not about the body but the cleansing of the soul.

I don't really expect anyone to answer, but the door opens. A middle-aged woman wearing a surgical mask, a brown and green scarf on her head, and wearing ankle-length, long-sleeved green dress looks at my chipped black nail polish before she looks at my masked face.

"I'm sorry," she says, "We're closed."

"Can I just come in and look around?" I ask. "Just for a few minutes?" I found some online photographs of beautiful tiled mikvah tubs, ornate steps leading to the deep, clear pools—and I want to see it for myself, to feel the otherworldly quiet and remoteness.

"I can't let you in," she says. "Because of Covid. I'm sorry. After we re-open you can go online and make an appointment."

151.

I stop at Starbucks for a Venti latte—decaf this time—and a Puppuccino for Freddie and drive to Sunset, then go west to Pacific Coast Highway. I pull into the Spanish tile-roofed Shell station, get some gas, and buy cheap one-piece bathing suit, a Malibu beach towel, tissues, nail polish remover, baby wipes and a jelly doughnut in the food mart.

Any stretch of beach will do. I turn into the first parking lot I see with beach access—one with a blue and white USE/PAY STATION sign and only a few cars—take a spot facing the water, pay with a credit card, display my receipt on my dashboard, take off my mask, cover myself with the towel, wriggle out of my clothes and pull on the bathing suit. It's hideous—bright purple with orange hibiscus crawling all over it—and the cups are way too small. But they make a good place to stash my car key, my credit card and my drivers' license.

I take the food mart plastic bag with the nail polish remover, wipes and tissues with me, lock my cellphone in the trunk, lock the car, slide the key in its hiding place, and cross the narrow lot.

The sun is fierce and whitens the recently-bulldozed sand. The tide is out. The pale blue lifeguard tower is empty. The Pacific Ocean I've avoided for so long is a heaving expanse of broken blue glass—a deep, vast natural pool where no reservation is required.

I drop my towel and put my flip flops on top of it. The wind rubs salt and grains of sand against my still-tender face, but it feels good to be without a mask.

Two Bree-clones run through the sibilant foam, their chemically-bleached ponytails swinging in unison. A man sleeps under a heavy black parka. I sit in the sand, saturate some tissue with the remover and rub the black polish off my toes and fingers. I use the baby wipes to clean under my armpits, along my arms and legs, between my toes and fingers, and to gingerly clean my face, then I repeat the process since I can't rinse myself off.

I make sure the car key and my license and credit card are secure, then walk into the water. A receding wave sucks the sand from beneath my feet and throws me off balance. I inhale in the pungent air through clenched teeth until the spinning stops. The sea-bottom gets rougher and rockier the farther out I go. My heart beats faster, too, and the water gets colder. I cross the drop-off, slide sideways through a cresting wave—my eyes on the neon-blue horizon-smear—take a breath and sink.

152.

Two blessings—and one optional one—and three complete immersions—with no hair floating on the surface—are required. I tried to learn the blessing recited post-menstruation since birth and marriage don't apply to me and I killed one bird and two people with my first period. But I ended up riffing on the ceremony and creating my own.

My toes touch bottom and my head hums like a tuning fork. My heart gallops. My blood roars. I open my stinging eyes to wave-swaying murk, then struggle to the surface and gasp.

This is not how I planned it, but I speak the first blessing. "Blessed are You In Whom I Don't Believe, pattern-maker, universe-creator, who sanctifies us through selflessness and has enjoined us concerning immersion."

I descend again and open my eyes. The swirling grit could be my parents' ashes mixed with the cremains of multitudes. Or it could be kitty litter. The crushing feeling returns— the boulder is falling from the calm blue sky that I can't see. I break the surface's mirrored underside, breathe until my breathing slows and recite the second prayer. "Blessed is the force behind all creation that has sustained me, brought me to this moment and bestows the breath of life—the soul."

If the immersion is menstruation-related, the woman can stop now or recite a blessing of her choice. A surprise swell slaps me in the face. I let the current carry me farther out, swallow my fear and recite the thing I chose—

"'And the angel raised his voice and said to those standing before him… "Take the filthy garments off her.' And he said to her, 'See, I have removed your iniquity from you, and I have clad you with clean garments.' I am alive. I am here. I am pure."

153.

I drive past Partridge Place on my way back from the beach to Sunny Morning Elder Care Living. My hair and my ugly, chafing bathing suit are full of sand—especially the bra-part.

The Hatzalah ambulance is in its parking place. Isaac Kahn is in his yellow Hatzalah vest and stands in front of his apartment door holding a screw driver. I drive to Sixth Street, make an impulsive U-turn that upsets a few people, and then pull into the lot. I decide not to look at myself in the rear-view mirror. I put on my mask, open the Prius door, wrap the food mart towel around my waist and walk over to Isaac Kahn barefoot.

He attaches a small, brass mezuzah to the door frame, takes a step back to admire his work, must feel someone is behind him and sees me. "Every few days someone rips down my mezuzah. And every few days I put up a new one. I have a box of them I bought on sale."

I'm shaking and I don't smile behind my mask. I can't. "You said you wanted to talk. I can see you're going to work and I have to get back to my dog, but I just thought that maybe you could talk a little now."

Isaac Kahn holds the screwdriver pointing skyward and looks me up and down. Then he runs the fingers of his free hand through his beard and adjusts his surgical mask. "I could," he says, "but you look partially-drowned. Are you?"

"I just went for a swim," I say. "Underwater."

"I have a shift in ten minutes." Isaac Kahn holds the holds the screwdriver in both hands. "What I wanted to say is that I really, really fucked up with you. I thought you were a health inspector trying to shut down my business and I lost it. I was out of line and wrong. I'm ashamed of the way I behaved. I want you to know that wasn't me."

"You mean the catering business?"

"I'm not a caterer. I have a restaurant. Well, a ghost place."

"I still have no idea what you mean. Why would an inspector care about your restaurant?"

"Do you know what a ghost restaurant is?"

"A take-out place in the underworld?"

"Close. Another chef and I opened a strictly take-out pop up during the shutdown. It's doing well and has generated some buzz, but it's illegal. Our plan is to keep it going—we change locations all the time––until we find an investor, get the permits we need and open a brick and mortar place. There aren't any other Kosher New Mexican-Mexican restaurants in L.A. But if they close us down now, that will never happen."

"Is the food good?"

"It's great," Isaac Kahn says. "Unbefuckinglieveable."

"What's it called?"

"Blue Matzo. You know like a blue corn tortilla but Jewish."

"Not bad," I say.

"Well, it's a work in progress. Maybe sometime you could do a menu-tasting and give me your feedback."

"You should know that I'm a picky eater with the food preferences of a six-year old. But I'd love to."

I look at Isaac Kahn and he looks at me.

I wish I were thin, clean, dry and dressed. I wish we weren't masked and distanced and that Isaac Kahn's radio wasn't making a crackling noise. I wish I had brushed my filthy hair and that whoever needs Isaac Kahn wasn't in trouble.

Isaac Kahn backs the ambulance out of the lot and waves at me after he activates the siren and the lights. Then I hang around for a little while—itchy and cold—and watch as the not-ugly sun flowers and then flames out.

THE END

Acknowledgements

I'm grateful to four fine writers whose work has earned THEM the right to be intimidating, impatient and arrogant, but who choose to be kind and generous instead—Steven Cooper, Derek Farrell, Seth Lynch and Thomas Perry—for seeing things in the book I couldn't see.

About the author

Jo Perry earned a PhD in English, taught college literature and writing, produced and wrote episodic television, and has published articles, book reviews, and poetry. She lives in Los Angeles with her husband, novelist Thomas Perry. They have two adult children. Their two cats and two dogs are rescues.

More books from Fahrenheit Press

The Beloved Children by Tina Jackson

Three young women; Chrysanthemum, Rose & Orage are thrown together on the stage of Fankes' Theatre during the closing days of the Second World War performing as The Three Graces.

It's there they come under the spell of wardrobe mistresses Dolores and Janna – a chance encounter that will guide and change all of their fates forever.

Set in the dying days of vaudeville theatre and laced with mysticism, fortune tellers, ghosts, and evocative descriptions of the closing days of the War - The Beloved Children will literally make you laugh out loud and perhaps even shed the odd tear.

The Beloved Children is wise, funny, heart-breaking, joyous, poignant, and entirely entirely enthralling.

The Transit of Lola Jones by Jackie Swift

Debut author Jackie Swift brings some playfulness to the Fahrenheit list with this first book in a series featuring her eponymous hero Lola Jones.

It's fair to say Lola Jones' life is not turning out the way she expected it to.

As the book opens we find Lola recovering from the breast cancer that threatened to prematurely end her life and languishing in a police cell, the main suspect in the murder of businessman Daniel Blain.

As the truth begins to unfold about the events leading up to the untimely demise of the dashing Daniel, we learn more about the journey that brought the normally infectiously vivacious Lola Jones to such an unsatisfactory pass.

But is she guilty, and even if she is guilty, is she to blame?

This is a funny, smart, sexy, modern romp of a book and Lola Jones is a character that you'll instantly want to be your best friend.

Souljourner by Paul Steven Stone

Where to start with Souljourner? Let's start with the author - Paul Steven Stone is either a madman or a genius – probably both – and he's written one of the most gripping and enjoyable books we've ever come across.

It begins with a quote from Pierre Teilhard de Chardin

"We are not human beings on a spiritual journey, we are spiritual beings on a human journey." – and that my friends sets the stage perfectly for all that follows.

The novel, if it is indeed a novel (the narrator insists it is in fact a warning letter from your soul's previous incarnation and aimed directly at you dear reader) - as we will discover though, this narrator is often unreliable - so frankly warning or novel, you pays your money you takes your choice.

One of the central premises of the novel/letter is that our souls make their eternal journey towards enlightenment in the company of a single unchanging 'karmic pod' of companion souls who take on different roles in each of our incarnations.

In one life a soul may appear as your mother, in the next your best friend, in the next your sworn enemy, in the next your lover and so on for eternity. The identities of the souls in your 'karmic pod' are hidden from you in life – this letter/novel seeks to wise you up to who's who in your karmic pod to help you avoid making the same mistakes that landed the narrator, David Rockwood Worthington in prison serving a life sentence for murder.

www.ingramcontent.com/pod-product-compliance
Lightning Source LLC
Chambersburg PA
CBHW020335310726
48979CB00015B/2379/J
* 9 7 8 1 9 1 4 4 7 5 1 1 5 *